Fumbled LOVE

LILA ROSE

USA BESTSELLING AUTHOR

Fumbled Love Copyright © 2018 by Lila Rose

Editor: Hot Tree Editing
Cover Designer: RBA Designs
Photographer: Wander Aguiar
Interior Designer: RMJ Manuscript Service

Fumbled Love is a work of fiction. All names, characters, events, and places found in this book are either from the author's imagination or used fictitiously. Any similarity to persons live or dead, actual events, locations, or organizations is entirely coincidental and not intended by the author.

*Mum, thank you for being that little bit crazy.
Love you forever!*

CHAPTER ONE

REAGAN

*T*he day was going to be a terrible one. I knew it the moment I woke up late, having slept through my alarm again. I really had to get one that sounded like a freight train going through my house because when I slept, I did so deeply.

To make matters worse, I raced from my room, skipped around the Pomeranian named Fozzie, and then slipped in still warm poop.

Gagging and cursing him black and blue, I quickly used some paper towels to wipe it off my foot and I let him out the dog door, which was already built in the door when I bought the house. Thankfully, Fozzie was my parents' dog, and it was my last night minding the little fella.

The cleanup took longer than I thought, which added extra time on my lateness. But I refused to leave my house stinking like dog doo-doo. It wasn't like I could go to work smelling like poop. I could already imagine the less-than-creative names my students would come up with.

Finally managing to get out the door without another incident, it was then I realized I'd put on the panties I should have thrown away a dress size ago. Yes, those deadly small panties. It meant the whole walk to work, they kept making friends with my butt crack. Mid-step, I glanced down and groaned; I'd also managed to pick out the worst outfit ever. A long red skirt, which had a tear in the middle, and a *rainbow*-colored tee. Not only did I look homeless, but it was like a Skittle had thrown up on me.

Of course, as I ran through the halls of Radley High School, where I taught English, the principal stepped out of nowhere, and I nearly collided with him.

With just one look at me, Tom Gallegan's eyes widened. "What happened, Reagan?"

"A rough morning." I hadn't even had the chance to inhale my much needed three morning coffees.

He cleared his throat, apparently not wanting to touch on the fact a unicorn farted rainbows all over me. His lips twitched. "Right, ah... I need your help. It's school assembly in a few minutes and Khloe is out sick. You'll need to fill in on stage."

And the morning just got worse.

Khloe was Tom's assistant; she regularly stood on the stage in assembly and, well, assisted with whatever she had to do. I didn't take much notice of what she actually did. I liked hiding in my corner with Brooke, my friend from college, who happened to get a job at the same school as me. We stood in the back and... to be honest, we bitched. Mainly about Elena, the witch I'd gone to high school with, and who'd made my experience hell. She also, unfortu-nately, worked at the same school as us as the family and consumer science teacher. I'd spent probably far too many hours considering other meanings for FACS, which seemed fitting for Elena. Though, my favorite was: Facts About Cockup Slags

"Erm, I can't."

Tom crossed his arms over his chest and rested them against his beer belly while he stared me down. We all liked Tom; he was a great guy to work for, like a father figure in a way, but there wasn't a chance I was getting up on that stage and pretending I wanted to be there. Tom tended to drone on and on and on. Once, Brooke had even elbowed me hard in the ribs because I'd dozed off standing up.

I could take him on in the stare down.

I really could.

With my hands on my hips, I leaned in a bit and stared right back.

Neither of us blinked, and my left eye started twitching seconds in.

The man was a master at the stare down. Damn him.

Sighing, I blinked a few times, and said, "Fine." I started stalking off, ignoring his grin of triumph.

"You're going the wrong way," he called.

"I need to see if Brooke has a spare top or I'll never live it down with the kids," I called over my shoulder.

I loved my students, and they loved me, but they could also be little shits. One time, I'd somehow managed to go to class with my slippers on, and a Twix chocolate bar stuck in my hair. I blamed the *Supernatural* marathon I'd had the previous night. However, I'd heard their murmurs of how they'd thought I'd been dumped and was wallowing in depression. Then there was also the day I'd got caught, after a quick visit to the restroom, with my skirt in my panties. They'd thought I'd ducked out for a romp with the phys ed teacher. After I'd swallowed the bile in my mouth—because no one would want to romp with stinky Steve, who I was sure didn't own deodorant, regardless of how many times Brooke and I chatted about how good deodorant was in front of him—I assured them it was an accident. I'd been rushing back so they wouldn't get into too much trouble. Or more specifically me, as I really should not be leaving the classroom unattended. But when I needed to pee, nothing was getting in my way.

I managed to catch Brooke as she was leaving her office. She was the school counselor.

My dear friend took one look at me and started laughing. "Oh God, Ree. Did you not look in the mirror this morning?"

"I was running late. Do you have a shirt I could borrow? I have to take Khloe's place on stage."

"Yeah, sure. It's in the locker." She stepped away from the door and started down the hall. "I'll see you on stage. Apparently, I have to help with something too," she yelled back.

Thank the high heavens I wouldn't be alone up there.

Quickly, I slipped into her office and took out a black shirt, then cursed. Damn Brooke was only a size smaller than my size fourteen, but I was larger in the chest area. My boobs looked like they wanted to burst free from the buttons. At least it was a bit better than my rainbow tee. I squished the girls down, so I didn't look like a tramp, and made my way into the gymnasium.

Bustling along with the other teachers and students, I managed to make it on stage just as the final bell rang. Tom ushered us to the left, near the opened curtain, and placed a huge-ass trophy in my hands. It also covered my chest nicely, thank God. Then he placed a small banner into Brooke's hands before he shuffled off. Brooke and I looked at each other. She then read what was on the banner before I could.

"Oh," she whispered.

"Oh? Oh, what?"

"We forgot."

"Forgot what?" I asked snappishly, because her concerned tone was freaking me out.

"That Carter Anthony was coming today." She winced at my face paling, and I knew it was because I suddenly felt sick.

Carter Anthony.

How could I have forgotten he was showing?

Maybe because I'd put it at the back of my mind, in the *very* back of my mind.

"It'll be okay. You don't even have to talk to him."

Nodding, I replied, "There is that. And anyway, it's not like he'll remember me. I was a nobody back then. We didn't even talk." He'd just been my high school crush, the popular football player, and I'd let my infatuation last for years. My love died once I heard him join in with his jock friends laughing at plus-size girls. It also happened to be just before he left town, accepting the big football scholarship with some college out of town. Apparently, he was still a star player and two years ago, he got transferred to one of our city's NFL teams, whatever they were called. Only he still opted to live away from his home stadium, picking to travel the few hours drive instead. Although, it could be possible he already had a place set up back where he was and didn't want to leave it. I'd also heard some talk he was thinking of moving back to settle down. While I knew next to nothing about the sport or even teams, I wasn't surprised by his success. He'd been a brilliant player even in high school. The most recent news I'd overheard was that Carter was finishing up his final year playing, and that he wanted to coach at a local college.

Not that I stalked him. I didn't. It really was the gossip around town.... Okay, so it was one night—two months ago when we found out he was going to do a talk at our school—Brooke and I were drunk and she'd googled him.

Shifting from one foot to another, since my tight panties had ridden up, again, I took the steps needed to move to the spot Tom gestured us to with an annoyed look on his face; we were off to the side, near the curtain.

"Stupid tight panties," I grumbled under my breath. I hadn't had a chance to pull them out discreetly. I scanned the audience and spotted Elena standing on the floor by the stage at the opposite end to us. She appeared eager, and I knew why. Carter had been her high school sweetheart for two years before he'd moved away.

Snorting, I took notice of her outfit, and I'd been worried about my top. Her breasts were close to popping out to say hello.

"What are we snorting about?" Brooke asked discreetly.

"*Her.*"

Brooke looked at Elena. "Oh, *her,*" she snarled. Elena was the worst. One of the coldest people I'd ever met. It was as if she was stuck back in high school and still thought she shit roses.

As Tom finally took to the microphone, I leaned into Brooke, and said, "Her boobs are so perky they're like a Disney Princess's on crack." Brooke coughed through her laugh. "Actually, I bet she'd want to be Dora the Explorer right about now."

She glanced at me, then back out to the audience of pubescent teens. "Why?"

"She'd want to be the first to explore Carter's whole body with her tongue."

She snorted. "Would she be the only one?"

"Yes." I nodded. I rolled my eyes as Tom went on and on about the great Carter Anthony. I was sure Tom had a guy-crush on him, like a lot of males all around the country. Even some of the male staff were salivating for a peek at Carter. Except for Larry, one of the math teachers, who I wasn't sure had moved out of his mom's yet, despite being thirty-seven.

"Why are you moving like that?" Brooke hissed at me. "Do you need to pee?"

"No, I have a wedgie," I whispered.

"What?"

"My panties are riding up my butt. You need to pull it out."

She swung her gaze my way and looked at me as if I'd lost my mind. "Come on," I pleaded. "I can't continue like this the whole time. It's so uncomfortable. My panties are up there making out with my butthole. This thing is too heavy to hold with just one hand while I fix the problem."

"I am not—"

"Remember the time you had me check your boob for a lump? I fondled it for a good while and only found a pimple under it."

"But—"

"Or the time you broke your arm and had trouble dressing, showering, and going to the toilet?" Looking over to Tom, I pretended to pay attention, and snapped in a low tone, "It's only a piece of fabric, but it's annoying the heck out of me. Can you please...?" I felt fingers on my bottom, and then sweet relief. My panties were adjusted. Only what was strange was when my friend patted my ass after it. Still, I said, "Thank you." Then I glanced back to Brooke who had wide eyes. I added, "See, it wasn't that hard."

"Reagan—" Brooke bit out. However, Tom then boomed through the room, "And here he is. Please welcome, Carter Anthony."

Cheers and claps erupted. I shifted my gaze to the far side and behind the curtain, only Carter didn't step out.

My body tensed as I felt a presence step up beside me. "Anytime you need help, I'll be there," Carter's deep voice said out the corner of his mouth while he waved to the audience. Then, as he walked toward Tom, he glanced back and winked.

I felt the need to vomit, pee, poop, scream, and cry all at the same time.

He couldn't have been the one who'd pulled my panties out of my ass.

Nope.

It wasn't him.

"Reagan—"

"No!" I hissed through my heavy breathing as I tried to calm myself. "It was you," I stated in my do-not-screw-with-me tone.

"Oh, got it. You're playing dumb. Right, yep it was totally me who had my hand on your ass adjusting your panties and then patted your rump." She scoffed. "I also whispered that my helping hand was willing to do it again and then winked at you."

She quickly looked away.

Huh, guess my death glare does work sometimes.

God, how long had he been standing behind the curtain?

Shit, shit, shit. I didn't, *couldn't* think about it, or about what he heard.... Did he hear me talk about Elena? Had I said her name? She was currently sending him sultry "come screw me" eyes while he was on stage talking about how awesome his life was.

Actually, I couldn't hear what he was saying because my ears were ringing while my blood pumped frantically through my body because I was having a breakdown.

"Reagan," Brooke barked lowly.

My body jolted. "What?"

"They're calling you."

I froze. They were? Glancing at the microphone, I saw Tom glaring at me while he waved me over. Carter stood beside him smirking. At least Gerry Understock, a top sports student was smiling.

Leaning in a little toward Tom, I whispered-yelled, "What?" I rose my brows at Tom. He sighed and thumped his forehead.

"The trophy in your arms is for Gerry," Brooke supplied.

"Oh, right."

She laughed. "Get it over there before Tom strangles you."

"Reagan." Tom hurled my name at me as if he were praying it would catch me on fire.

I snorted to Brooke. "He's thought it many times, but he would never do it. He loves me too much." I started toward the microphone. In fact, I was sure Tom thought of me as his adopted kid.

Stopping in front of my adopted dad—who I just claimed, something I would tell him later when he tried to kill me—I smiled. He covered the microphone and clipped, "I'm going to staple information about assemblies to your forehead. Then maybe you'll remember what's going on."

Okay, I was his *annoying* adopted child.

"*I'm* usually down there." I gestured with my head. "Bad move on *your* part to have me up here. I get bored easily." The only way I didn't get bored was when I read or watched movies and TV shows. I'd even taken up walking on those random days nothing else satisfied me. Brooke had checked my temperature when I told her that. However, after the first few times, I realized I enjoyed it.

Gerry snorted out a laugh, until Tom scowled at him, then he quickly shut up. And Carter—the sexy mountain-of-a-man Carter— stood off to the side smirking once more. I narrowed my gaze his way; his smirk changed into a shit-eating wide grin. Did I have something on my face? God, his eyes were mesmerizing. I suddenly felt an urge to paint or draw them. Although, I still hadn't passed the stick-figure pictures, so I knew I'd totally suck at it. While I could explain the difference between a simile and metaphor, my artistic credentials sucked.

"Reagan, pass the trophy over to Carter," Tom snapped.

Shaking my head to clear my mind from stick-figures, I then nodded, "Right. Of course." I nodded again like an idiot, and stepped up to Carter, practically throwing the heavy trophy at him. I did it all without meeting his hypnotizing gaze.

"Reagan," Carter called, in his sensual voice.

Goddammit all to hell. The man was sex on legs. He knew it; heck, *everyone* knew it, and I didn't want to fall into his trap. The one where he'd undoubtedly captivate me, then *BAM*, he'd friend-zone me so fast I wouldn't know what hit me.

It was not happening. So, ignoring his call, I tapped Gerry on the arm, and said, "Congrats on your, um, award, trophy, thingy, Gerry. Top notch, young boy. Brilliant job." Shit. I needed to get out of there. I patted Gerry's arm once again and then made my getaway back to Brooke.

Facing the audience, while they listened to Tom and then Carter talk again, I whispered out the corner of my mouth, "Did I look like a total idiot that whole time?"

"Sure did."

"Thanks. I thought I had. Can you please bury me this afternoon?"

"Can do. I'll even bring wine and say something nice after you're in the ground."

"You're sweet."

"It's what best friends are for."

CHAPTER TWO

REAGAN

*O*f course, things couldn't get better for me. Leaning my butt against my desk while discussing my freshman class's assignment, I then cringed when I heard Wesley blow his nose for the millionth time. He sounded like a damn trumpet. What made matters worse—if him bringing his germs to school wasn't enough —was when he pulled the tissue back and then studied his mucus. Everyone knew how gross Wesley was; he didn't hide it, and more power to him for being who he wanted to be... just not when it churned my stomach.

Slamming my copy of *To Kill A Mockingbird* down, I then pointed to Wesley. "If you look at your snot one more time, I just may vomit all over you."

Students started chuckling; they were used to my outbursts. Wesley, the little shit, lifted the tissue up with a cheeky grin on his pimply face.

"Don't do it," I warned, straightening.

"Miss," someone called.

I was too busy holding my glare on Wesley to answer. He slowly parted the folded tissue.

"I swear, my bile is rising, and it's coming for you, kid."

"Miss," was snapped a bit harsher. It was Jenifer, a grade-A student who sat in the front row closest to the door.

Closing my eyes, I dropped my head and sighed. "Someone's opened the door, right?"

"Yes." She giggled.

God, please do not let it be Tom. He was already upset with me enough. If he caught me threatening to vomit on a student, he'd be more than pissed.

"Is it the principal?" I asked, lifting my head and opening my eyes. Still, I didn't glance at the doorway until I knew if I had to make a run for it or not.

"No," Jenifer said in a swoony voice.

Finally smiling, I relaxed my stance and faced the door... then froze, but not before my smile dropped.

Shit.

Double shit.

It was Carter Anthony.

He was leaning against the doorframe with yet another smirk on his face.

I think I'd rather have Tom there instead.

"Ah... can I help you?"

Had he stumbled into the wrong room? Had he taken too many hits to the head and was lost?

Get out, get out, get out.

And suddenly I felt like yelling, "Get off my train," like the spirit in the movie *Ghost.* I clamped my mouth closed in case I did. My students would know what movie I was referencing since I made them watch it, under the guise of its relevance to understanding one of our previous topics of crafting ghost stories, but I wasn't sure Carter would know. He didn't seem like the movie watching type.

What was he doing in my classroom?

He straightened and stepped further in. His lips twitched when I widened my eyes at his approach. "You may have missed the extra information the principal gave this morning. I've been going to selected classrooms to visit to see if anyone has any questions for me."

I caught sight of Wesley opening his mouth. When I shot him a murderous glare, he snapped his lips shut. *Reminder to self: Next time Wesley makes you want to vomit, pull out the deadly glare.*

"Nope." I shook my head. "We're good in here." Did that sound rude? "Thank you, though," I added quickly. *Do not blush.*

He chuckled, and I wanted to throw something at his head, because his damn chuckle did things to my stomach. Nice things.

Never. I would never fall for his charms, his good looks, or how he's grown into his tall frame and huge body nicely. Even his sparkling eyes and sweet lips.

I was a grown woman. I had control of myself.

"Then if no one has any questions, do you mind if I stay for a while? I'd like to watch. I've never heard of a lesson from a teacher where they threatened vomiting before."

Damn. He'd heard that.

Laughing nervously, I shook my head. "Did I say vomit? I meant...." I had nothing. Why was my brain failing me now? Throwing my hands on my hips, I glared at Carter. "Anyway, we were in the middle of something, and I'd really prefer it if my class isn't interrupted."

"But, Miss, you interrupted class just the other day when your mom called," Bradly yelled.

My eyes widened. "Now isn't the time for lies, Bradly."

"But—"

"Bradly!"

My little defiant minions laughed. Carter chuckled.

Clearing my throat, I mentioned, "I'm sure Mr. Rogers, the phys ed teacher, would love to have you visit his class."

"I have a feeling you're trying to get rid of me." Carter grinned, and his head tilted to the side. "Do I know you from somewhere?"

"No!" I snorted, scoffed, and then burped. "Excuse me." I laughed. "And then there's also the FACS class. Something tasty will be cooking right about now. You should go for a taste."

Elena would also love it.

He shook his head. "Thanks for the suggestion, but I'll be fine here."

Dang it all.

"Fine," I bit out through clenched teeth. Ignoring him, though I sensed his movement to behind my desk to sit in *my* seat, I turned my attention back to the class. Wesley raised his hand. "Yes, Wesley?"

"I'd like to ask Mr. Anthony what it's like being famous."

Guess my death glare wore off on the shithead.

Clenching my jaw, I breathed deeply through my nose. "Does anyone else have questions they'd like to ask Mr. Anthony?" Half my students raised their hands. The other half were just staring at Carter like he was their favorite chew toy.

Rubbing an eye, since it started to twitch, I shifted to the side of my desk and glanced at Carter.

"Well?" I said.

"Oh, you want me to answer them?"

"Yes," I clipped.

"But I thought you didn't like—"

"*Please*, just answer them," I snapped.

Laughing, he stood and looked at Wesley. "Honestly, being famous can be a pain sometimes. No matter where I go, I have to watch what I say or do because it could end up in the media."

"But you get to bang all the chicks you want," Bradly called out.

One hand went to cover my chest—I didn't want to flash my bra —as the other shot out and up. "Bradly, the only banging we'll talk about in this class is me banging your head on your desk." Again, Carter chuckled—*shit*—and my students laughed. I winced, knowing I could be in serious doo-doo if he told anyone how sarcasm and regular threats were part of my teaching practice, but I lived dangerously. Plus, the class knew I was all talk. I would never lay a finger on them. That didn't mean I couldn't joke around. It made the day fun. More importantly, it strengthened our classroom relationship, and they knew when they had to get crack-a-lacking with work. I was lucky to teach such amazing kids.

Before the questioning continued, I added, "If anyone else says or asks something ridiculous like that again, I'll do something really drastic."

They quieted.

Carter pointed at Josiah.

"Do you ever get stressed being the quarterback?" Josiah asked.

"Actually, yes." Carter nodded. "Though, I'm sure it happens for any player really. We're a team. It's not just about me."

"What do you do after a loss?" Stacy called out.

Shifting my gaze to Carter, I caught his small smile. "What I prefer to do is go home, watch a movie with a pizza and beer."

Say what?

That sounded... so not like him. I'd heard he was one hell of a party animal. A real Casanova with women too.

"Do you have a girlfriend?" Ariel asked, and for some reason, all my kids' eyes swiveled to me quickly and then back again.

What was up with that?

Carter chuckled. "No. I don't."

"Miss doesn't have a boyfriend," Wesley called out. That kid was just asking for a nose punch.

"I do!" I yelled.

"What's his name?" Ariel questioned.

Did I say I loved my students?

I was so taking that love back.

"Ah, James?" I said slowly. And dang it for making it sound like a question.

A few of the guys snorted, some of the girls rolled their eyes, and

Carter stood, walked around the desk, and leaned his perfect ass against the edge. A smirk played at his lips. I wanted to pinch his cheeks together so he'd quit doing that.

"What's his last name?" Michael called.

Shit. A last name?

"Blunt?" I drew out.

"So you're saying your boyfriend's name is James Blunt, like that old singer guy?" Jenifer said.

Fuck.

I didn't expect anyone to know him. Evil geniuses.

I threw a hand out aimlessly and shot off a nervous laugh. "Yes. Just a coincidence." Clearing my throat, I added, "But we're getting off track. Mr. Anthony is here to answer questions, not me."

There was a knock at the door, thank God. We all turned toward it as it opened. Elena peeked her head in, scanned for a quick second before her eyes landed on her next victim. *I mean Carter.* Carter Anthony who used to date Elena. They had a history. One that could reignite as soon as she got her claws in him.

Did I care?

Nope, not at all.

I didn't.

Anyway, why would I care when I was just trying to get him to leave my room in the first place?

I narrowed my gaze as she smiled sweetly at Carter. It was a habit of mine whenever she was near. A narrowed gaze, a fisted hand, and a thought to throat punch her. Just the usual. After all, she had made my teen years hell, so of course, I had a vendetta against her.

Her past words rushed through my mind.

"Ooh, look it's fat-ass Reagan.

God, Reagan, you're going to break that poor chair with your weight.

Reagan, you stink. Did you wash between your flab?

Reagan, why don't you eat from the floor like all animals do?

I wish I didn't have to deal with such a pig in class all the time."

Laughing and mocking had always accompanied her cruel words from the people around us.

She stepped into the room, and said, "Here you are. Mr. Gallegan said you were still here." She curled her hands around his arm, leaning into him. "Why don't we head to my class?"

"But he only just got here," Wesley called.

Elena smiled up at Carter before looking at Wesley and glared. "Mr. Anthony has an important schedule, so I'm sure he needs to move on anyway."

"I was only supposed to visit the phys ed, math, and English class. I don't have time for any more," Carter explained.

I wanted to high-five him.

Elena giggled. "Oh, I'm sure you don't mind cutting *this* one short to come talk to *my* class." Her evil gaze landed on me. "Miss Wild, I didn't see you there. You don't mind if I steal him away?"

It was times like this I liked that I'd grown into my lady balls.

"Actually, Miss *Roup*." I smiled. "Mr. Anthony and *my* class were just in the middle of something. Maybe next time he visits you could have him in *your* class."

If looks could kill, I would be buried six-feet under.

The room was so damn silent, I was sure the students were holding their breaths. I also didn't miss the way Carter glanced at me with his lips tilted at the corners.

"Right. Of course. Sorry for interrupting." She was all sunshine because Carter was around. If it were just us and we weren't in the classroom, she'd be slitting my throat. The way her eyes burned told me she was at least picturing it. She laughed, and I saw her hands tighten on his arm. "Hopefully I'll get to see you before you have to leave, *Carter*," she purred his name, and then turned, swaying her hips to the door. Only the person she was doing it for wasn't looking her way. His eyes were on the floor, and he was biting his bottom lip. His reaction could be because I happened to cough out quietly "*Slut*" as she left.

When she glanced back and noticed Carter wasn't watching, she clenched her jaw, then stomped the rest of the way and closed the door quickly.

Only it came back open, and the bitch called out, "Oh, Carter." Carter looked her way. "I'm sure you remember Miss Wild from high school, right?" My body locked tight, even my butt cheeks. "Or maybe not since she is forgettable." She smiled, backed out, and closed the door once more.

I wanted to hide.

Crawl under my desk and hide.

Of course Carter wouldn't remember me because Elena was right about that. I had been forgettable. I'd been the large girl, the one who got picked on, and I was also the one who had no friends.

But I had lady balls, I reminded myself. So even with my whole body flushing, I faced my muttering students who were glaring toward the door, and paused. They were loyal to a fault. I wondered briefly if I could give them extra credit for being able to deduce who the bitch in the room had been. Then, ignoring the man to the side of me, I said, "And that class, is what you call an awkward situation. Also, it goes to show flirting doesn't always get you what you want."

Nobody ever said I was exactly appropriate with my classes, but honestly, I think my students were better off with real, tough, and brutal life situations at times.

I preened a little when I heard some of my students talk about how they didn't like Elena as a teacher. How she bitched and moaned about other teachers in the school. And as much as I'd have loved to join in, I couldn't sink to her level and smack talk her. I never would.

In not responding to her bullshit spectacle, I hoped it showed my class it was okay to stand up for yourself in a situation where you weren't happy with what was going on. Elena wasn't better than me. Besides, it was obvious Carter didn't want to go to a cooking class.

What was also important was to move on from an awkward situation, like the man at my side finding out we used to go to school together and him not remembering me, and move on from it.

My students laughed at my comment. I grinned back and then shifted from one foot to another. Carter was too quiet, and I didn't like it.

I clapped my hands. "All right, class, since Mr. Anthony's time is short, why don't you finish the questions you have, and while you do it, I'll just finish grading these papers?"

Moving around my desk, I took my seat and realized Carter's butt was sitting on the papers I needed to grade. Great.

Instead of asking him to move, and also so I didn't have to speak to him, I quietly slid out my phone and fired a text off to Brooke while the class went back to questioning Carter.

Me: Drinks tonight. Thank God it's Friday.

My phone vibrated.

Brooke: Why, what happened besides the looney act at assembly?

Me: Carter Anthony IS IN MY CLASSROOM.

Brooke: BAHAHAHAHA. Enjoy, and hell yes to drinks. I want to know what else you've done.

CHAPTER THREE

CARTER

*W*hen I'd overheard Reagan's conversation on stage, I'd grinned my ass off. At the time, I hadn't understood why she'd indicated Elena wanted me. It was as if Reagan knew the teen me was a douche and had dated the bitch of the century. But I'd had no idea how she'd known, or even if she had known my history with Elena, the girl who'd happily put out. Needless to say, I'd been confused as hell.

And that all happened before I touched her ass.

I still couldn't believe I'd done it, but when her friend didn't help her out, I saw it as my duty to lend a helping hand.

From the first moment I'd heard her as I stood behind that curtain, I was captivated.

She made me laugh with her wit.

She charmed me with her actions.

She intrigued me with her attitude.

I wanted to know all about Reagan Wild.

While she'd seemed familiar, I sucked at placing the puzzle

pieces together. It wasn't until Elena mentioned Reagan had gone to school with us that it all clicked into place, and hell if I was dumbstruck for a moment.

Back in high school days, I hadn't known her name, but I'd seen her around. When I had, I took notice. I just didn't let anyone know I was ogling her. Why? Because back then, I was the biggest douche out there. Reagan was different to the version of the girl people expected me to be with, and back then, I'd been too concerned with what everyone thought.

Foolishly, I'd ended up with Elena. She'd been picture-perfect in looks, but some of the things that came out of her mouth, I'd wanted to slap her for. Obviously, I didn't hit women. Ever. Instead, I'd pretended my life, the two years with her, were awesome, despite being interested in a girl who I hadn't known much about.

At least I'd grown up since then.

Only Reagan didn't know it and probably thought I was still an arrogant, shallow prick.

The memory of the day still stung, the one when I realized that was exactly what the girl I'd crushed on thought of me.

"What about that one?" Mark pointed to a girl a few desks over in the library. She was short, blonde, and curvy.

Henry snorted. "Yeah, and I'd have to roll her in flour to find the wet spot. No way." My three friends chuckled while I wanted to punch the dick in the face for the comment. Still, my smile stayed firm because I was a fake dickhead who cared what they thought about me.

"That one?" Paul pointed to another bigger girl.

"Jesus. You idiots just want all the pretty ones for yourselves and give me all the heifers. Don't think so. I'll find someone to take to formal yet." Henry complained.

"Oh damn." Mark laughed. "That one's for you, Henry."

I clenched my jaw when Mark pointed out yet another larger girl. I didn't see the problem with any of them. Hell, they were pretty in their own way. Something out the corner of my eye caught my attention. I glanced there.

Fuck.

It was her.

I'd seen her around for a long time, but it was the last few weeks she'd grabbed my attention more and more. She was stunning, with long brown hair, dark brown eyes, and curves I wanted to run my hands over.

She stood on the other side of the bookshelf from where we sat at the table pretending to study, and I knew she'd heard everything that was said so far.

My gut tightened.

"I think I just threw up in my mouth," Henry said, and then pretended to gag. They all laughed, and I caught Paul looking at me, so I added my own chuckle into the fray.

Which made me feel like an even bigger asshole.

Her face darkened in disappointment, at me I guessed. Since I'd started taking notice of her, I'd spotted her on more than one occasion looking my way. As if she liked what she saw. Of course, I'd preened over it. I'd even flexed a few times when I discreetly saw her looking.

And now I'd just fucked up by going along with my friends and their dickish ways. Not that I'd do anything about my attraction to her. Hell, I was moving out of town in a few days. Still, I hated the fact she'd heard them and would think I was just like them. But maybe I was. Laughing along was just as bad as making the comments myself, right?

Even as I answered question after question in her class, I couldn't get my mind around the fact Reagan was the same girl I'd lusted after years ago.

There had to be some way I could win her over.

Make her see I wasn't the douche I had been.

Make her see the curves she still had caused all the blood to rush to my dick since *he* was picturing me running my hands over them.

Jesus, dude. Now isn't the time to think about that shit in a class full of kids.

"Yes?" I asked, taking a few steps forward and pointing to a kid with thick glasses.

"Is it true after football you're looking at coaching?"

"Yeah." I nodded. "I have a bachelor's degree and a teaching certificate from my time in college."

"So you didn't just waste your time partying and hooking up with—"

"Bradly," Reagan warned. Some kids snickered. I glanced behind me to see she'd said it without raising her gaze; instead, her gaze was on a paper she pulled in front of her.

Smiling, I shook my head at the kid. "At first I let loose a bit. I mean, it's college. I wanted to have some fun. But then I realized I also wanted to have something to fall back on when football finished. I wanted to do something that I knew I'd like, so I had to find the tools to make sure I could see it happen when the time came." I paused. "Football isn't forever. It wears on your body a lot. Don't get me wrong. I love the game, but everyone needs a backup plan in case it fails, because playing a sport there's always a risk of injury. One so bad you can't play the sport again, and instead of spiraling down into the dark pits of regret, though you'll still have them, you move on eventually, and by completing a degree in fields that prepare you for the future, it'll mean moving onto something you enjoy doing hopefully."

Behind me, I heard Reagan suck in a surprised gasp of air. I glanced to see a soft smile forming on her lips. She nodded once at me, and it seemed as if she were proud of my explanation. My attention went back to the students. They looked at me like I'd just told them the wisest thing they could learn in life. All their reactions felt good.

Reagan's the most.

God, I wanted to know everything I could about the woman.

But would she let me?

I wasn't sure, but I'd try.

A bell sounded in the room. Reagan stood and came around the desk. "Class, please thank Mr. Anthony for his time."

"Thank you, Mr. Anthony," most called out.

The kids started to pack up their things while Reagan moved

back around the desk to do the same. It was lunchtime. I had one more class I had to visit after lunch, a sophomore math class, but I found myself not wanting to. If I had my way, I'd be back in Reagan's class. I was now annoyed with stupid Steve, the phys ed teacher, who was ripe on the nose, for taking up more of my time and making me late to Reagan's. Her class was fun, her students all seemed to adore Reagan as their teacher, and I wondered if her other English students were as easy as those.

"Lunch," I stated like a caveman at her side. I was surprised I didn't grunt and add, "You go with me," then pound my chest.

"Ah, yes. It usually happens around this time of day." She started for the door. A few kids called a farewell to her. She waved and smiled back.

I had the feeling, with her fast pace, she was trying to get away from me.

"Are you going to the teacher's lounge?" I asked, keeping up with her stride.

She glanced to me and then back in front of her. "Um, yes?" It came out like a question. Did I make Reagan Wild nervous?

"I'll join you then."

She tripped, righted herself, and then stopped altogether.

Before she could say anything, I did. "I remember you from school."

A flash of utter shock crossed her face, and then she frowned. "Okay?" she said, uncertain.

"Let's just have some lunch and we can talk," I offered.

Something close to unease dipped her brows for some reason. "Uh, I just remembered I promised I'd have lunch with Brooke in her office, so we can...." She bit her bottom lip, obviously trying to think of something. I wasn't so bad to have lunch with, right? Shit, she probably still thought I was a dick.

"Look, I'm not the same—"

"Yoga!" she all but shouted, and quickly glanced around us.

Students and some teachers were watching our exchange with interest.

I raised a brow and crossed my arms over my chest. "You and Brooke do yoga through lunch?"

She clutched her bag to her chest and nodded. "Yes?" She shook her head. "I mean *yes* we do."

Smiling, I shrugged. "That's good. I don't mind yoga."

Her gorgeous eyes widened. "You can't." She rubbed at the back of her neck.

"Why?" I questioned slowly.

"Um..." She coughed, and again glanced around quickly. She leaned in a little. God, she smelled edible. Out the corner of her mouth, she said, "We do it naked." She groaned, like she couldn't believe that lie just left her mouth.

"Naked?" I questioned, my lips twitching instead of laughing my ass off like I wanted to.

"Yes," she whispered.

"I could do that."

Hell yes I could do that. Naked yoga with Reagan would be a delight. One where I'd have to try to keep my hands to myself... so maybe it was a nightmare because I wasn't sure she'd be happy with my wandering hands.

At least not yet.

Not until I won her over.

Until I proved to her I wasn't a prick.

"No, sorry, it's, um, women only."

"Just you and Brooke?"

She cleared her throat. "A-and sometimes Heather."

"The librarian?" I'd met her briefly after assembly, and suddenly I was shuddering. Heather was in her late sixties, had a mullet and hairy legs.

"Yes, that's her."

"Right." I chuckled. "I get the feeling you just don't want to have lunch with me."

She laughed, sobered, and then forced a laugh again. Yeah, Reagan was nervous, and I swear if she looked around again, as if she were after someone to save her, I was going to spank her ass. My company wasn't that bad. While I liked her being nervous, I didn't want her to feel like she had to run from me or get someone there to distract my attention so she could escape.

"It's not that," she mumbled, but I still caught it.

"Then what is it?"

She sighed. "Fine. We'll be friends. Okay? Now I really have to get to... um...."

"Yoga?"

"Yes. Yoga."

"Naked yoga." I smirked.

A blush lit her cheeks and she cringed. "That's right."

"But we're parting as friends?" I was happy with that. It was better than nothing. So I pushed a little. "And if we're friends, we can exchange numbers."

Her eyes flashed wide. "Why?" she shrieked, then slammed her lips shut.

"Carter," I heard, and I wanted to groan in pain. "You waited for me. That's so sweet," Elena said, appearing out of nowhere.

"Ah." It was my turn to try and think of something to say.

Elena curled her hands around my bicep and I wanted to push them away. "Are you coming to lunch? We can do some catching up."

"Actually—"

"Great!" Reagan shouted. I narrowed my gaze at her. She'd better not leave me. Then she smiled. "That's a brilliant idea. I have to head off..." She backed up. "Things to do...." She backed up again. "Have a nice lunch." Then she turned and dashed away.

Elena snorted. "She's weirder now than she was back in the day. Come on." She smiled and led me toward the teachers' lounge. I had seen it on the quick tour I had after assembly. "It's been so long." Elena giggled, and I cringed. "Are you in town a while?"

"Yeah." I nodded. I was actually moving back, but she didn't need to know that.

"That's great," she purred.

Christ.

We entered, and right away I noticed Brooke, Reagan's friend and colleague, talking to Tom by the coffee machine. Stepping away, I wiggled my arm free. "I'm just getting a coffee. Do you want one?" I asked Elena, even when I didn't want to. I was polite after all.

"Sure. I'll grab you some food and we'll meet at the table."

"Thanks," I said half-heartedly over my shoulder, already moving toward Brooke.

"Carter, are you enjoying your time here?" Tom asked as I stopped beside them. Brooke eyed me up and down with a smile on her lips.

"I am. Thanks again for having me." I nodded. Looking to Brooke, I said, "I thought you were having lunch with Reagan and doing naked yoga?"

She froze, her wide eyes comical. Tom thumped his forehead and then shook his head, while Brooke stuttered, "Y-yeah, um, naked yoga."

"Don't you do it every lunch? Reagan said you did, which was why she couldn't have lunch in here."

Tom sighed, tipping his head back he gazed at the ceiling and muttered, "I seriously need to get her head checked."

"Yes." Brooke nodded. She put her coffee down. "Can't believe I forgot about... naked yoga?"

"That's what Reagan said."

She laughed. "Right. I'll just, ah, go and grab some food for us both, to uh, keep us sustained for..."

"Naked yoga," I supplied.

"Yeah, that's it. Excuse me then." She went to shift around us.

"Brooke?" I called.

"Yes?"

"Reagan didn't get a chance to give me her number before she had to go. I don't suppose you could give it to me?"

She opened her mouth, closed it, and then said, "You want her number?"

Why was it so hard to believe?

I nodded.

Tom cleared his throat. "Are you sure you know what you're getting yourself into?"

I chuckled. "Yes."

Very sure, I am.

Jesus, I sound like Yoda.

CHAPTER FOUR

REAGAN

*N*aked yoga? What had I been thinking? No, what had Carter been thinking wanting lunch with me in the first place? I could seriously slap myself. *Naked yoga. What the hell?* It was all his fault, putting me on the spot like that. It was his fault my brain fried from shock, so I just said the first thing that popped into my head.

I groaned, hitting my forehead, and then I rested my head on the top of Brooke's desk.

Naked yoga?

Why did that pop in my head in the first place? Maybe I'd been thinking about his body at the time and how flexible football had probably made him.

Yes, it was all Carter's fault.

And he remembered me back in high school?

Who? What? When? How? Why?

My brain either just farted or I'd finally lost it.

Again, all because of Carter Anthony... but seriously, how could he remember me when we never spoke? We never hung out in the same crowd.

He was high, I was low.

He was new, I was old.

He was…? *What in the damnation am I going on about?*

Was it too early to start drinking?

Rattled, I needed a drink to calm my nerves. Carter Anthony had obviously rattled me.

Damn me for not asking how he knew me back then. It should have been my first question, but he'd sent me bonkers.

When the door suddenly opened, I quickly straightened in the chair, pretending I was doing yoga. Only, because I didn't actually know any yoga, my jazz hands appeared.

Brooke paused, took me in, and burst out laughing.

She walked in, still laughing, and placed a tray of food on her desk. I grabbed a chocolate croissant and bit into it, chewing while she gained her composure.

"J-jazz hands?" She cackled. One arm went across her stomach while she placed the other on the desk and leaned into it.

"When you're ready." I waved my goodness around in the air. "Laugh it up while I slowly die of humiliation."

"Oh," she gasped. "God. I can't breathe."

"Good," I harrumphed.

"Okay." She inhaled deeply. "All right. I'm good."

"So…," I drew out. "Can we move up burying me to, say… about now?"

She grinned. "This wouldn't have anything to do with naked yoga, would it?"

I gasped, stood, and banged the table with my hands, squishing the croissant in the process. "Who told you?" I demanded.

She snorted out another quick laugh. "Your Carter came up to me and wondered why I wasn't in here doing naked yoga with you."

I groaned and smacked my forehead with the squished crois-sant. Great, just great. I probably had chocolate all over my forehead and it would look like shit. "Was anyone around when he said this?"

"Only Tom."

"Good." I nodded, and took a bite of the squashed croissant. I mumbled around my mouthful, which wasn't a pretty sight, "At least Tom already knows I'm crazy."

"That he does."

"What did you say to Carter?"

"I told him I was heading here, but I had to grab us some sustenance."

Nodding, I dropped back down into her seat. "Good."

"You do know he realizes you're full of it, right?"

Slumping in the chair, I closed my eyes. "Yes."

"Why would you say it?"

Opening my eyes, I told her, "Because he was freaking me out."

"How?"

So, I started from the time he walked into the classroom, to Elena showing up and mentioning how we all went to school together. "Then he said he remembered me from high school." I nodded to her shocked look. "I know. It wasn't something I was prepared for. I told you how we'd never spoken, hung out or... *anything* during our teen years. Hearing him say that confused me and my brain shut down. He wanted to have lunch to talk. I panicked and said... well, you know."

"Why did you panic and not want to have lunch with him?"

With a sigh, I shrugged. "I don't know. The thought of sitting and eating with him makes me nervous. I probably would have choked on my food or done something else stupid. It was best to run."

"Hmm."

"Hmm? Why hmm?"

"I think he likes you."

I scoffed, snorted, and then laughed like a mad woman. Maybe it wasn't me who was crazy, but Brooke. After calming, I asked, "Are you feeling okay?"

Brooke glared and pulled out the chair opposite her desk, sitting in it. "I'm totally fine. You can't live in your little bubble of insanity forever. Carter Anthony likes you."

"Stop saying that please," I whispered.

"Ree-ree." Brooke sighed. "Why do you like to live in denial land?"

"It's safer that way. I can't get hurt then. Anyway, Carter told me himself that we were friends."

"Good." She nodded. "That's a start. At least now you won't kill me when I tell you I gave him your number."

My precious croissant dropped to the floor.

BY THE TIME I'D MADE IT HOME, MY NERVES WERE EATING AT MY insides. Heck, I was even afraid of my phone. It sat on the kitchen counter while I stared at it like it had some decaying disease.

Why was I so scared Carter would text me? All I could put it down to was his attention wasn't the norm for me. In turn, it unnerved me, a lot.

I'd dated. Only a few times admittedly, but I'd had a man's attention. Only those guys were different to Carter. I wasn't one to stereotype, but to put it in a way my brain understood, the men in my past were nerds. Cute nerds who made me happy, but in the end, things never worked out.

Carter was the hottest man who had ever wanted my number, wanted to talk to me… and Brooke saying he liked me wasn't doing me any good. It got my hopes up, but I had to remain realistic.

Carter Anthony was out of my league.

If I started jumping to conclusions, I would most likely make a fool out of myself. All he could possibly want from spending time with me was to make a friend while he was in town. I'd heard he wasn't sticking around forever, he was here for a year while his team promoted the new gridiron stadium. Then he'd move back home.

Could I handle being friends with Carter and keep my heart in check?

I wasn't sure.

But was I willing to try? To have his company if he asked for it?

I didn't know.

My mind was messed up. Confused. Frazzled.

And when my phone vibrated on my counter, my mind exploded in a frenzy of, *oh shit, oh shit, oh shit.*

I snapped it up, fumbled, and then managed to drop it to the floor in a flurry of curses falling from my mouth like I was a badass biker. After picking it up, I noticed the screen had cracked in the corner. "Jesus," I muttered, and Fozzie let out a yip in reply. Absently, I bent over and scratched behind his ear, then straightened and lit my phone up.

My shoulders drooped in relief, yet I felt a pang of sadness low in my belly when I saw it was only a text from Mom.

Stupid stomach.

Mom: Be there in five to grab our baby. The fur one, not the adult one. XOXOX

Smiling, I looked down to Fozzie. "Mommy's on her way." He let out another yip as if he understood me.

I'd just changed into leggings and a shoulder-less long-sleeved shirt for drinks later with Brooke when my front bell rang. Of course, Fozzie reacted immediately. He turned into a dog possessed, barking and running around stupidly, trying to kill whatever the noise was.

"Door's unlocked," I called, slipping my phone into my handbag. I considered leaving my cell at home so my attention would be off it. Then again, what if there was an accident and Brooke was injured, and I needed my phone to call for help? Yep, that was my story and I was sticking to it.

"Ree, you really shouldn't leave your door unlocked. Anyone could come in and rob you," Mom called. Then I heard her cooing to her baby. "Oh, my sweetgums. Mommy has missed you. Yes, I have." I knew she would have Fozzie in her arms and showering kisses all over him. Once again, I was thankful she never reacted like that when I'd come home from school.

"I never get that attention when I get home from work," Dad complained as he entered the living room from the hall.

Mom snorted behind him. "You get enough."

"Don't need to hear about it," I said, walking up to Dad and kissing him on the cheek. "Glad you're both back safely."

"Thanks, angel. But your mom is right. Lock your front door."

"It's safe—"

Dad scowled. "Reagan, someone could enter while you blast that stupid music and murder or molest you."

"She could enjoy it." We both shot Mom a look. "I meant the action part, not the murder. How long has it been, Ree?"

"I seriously wonder about you sometimes, Elaine. I don't think you're right in the head."

Mom grinned. "I'm not, which is why I married you."

"Oooh, burn," I sang.

"Christ," Dad grumbled. "Both women in my life are insane."

"Hey," I snapped half-heartedly. "I haven't done anything lately to warrant that insane comment."

"Tom called," Mom supplied.

Shit.

Mom giggled while rubbing her chin over Fozzie's head, who was still in her arms. "I want to know who it was that got you tongue-tied enough to say you were doing naked yoga."

Double shit.

Tom was a goddamn snitch. Also, he was my dad's close friend and had been ever since I started working at the school, and Dad warned Tom about my uniqueness. Dad only recently became a substitute teacher at the school. One good thing about Tom was that he didn't mention Carter's name. Though I wondered why he didn't.

Sighing, I rolled my eyes. "It doesn't matter who it was. It won't happen again." Dad scoffed. Mom laughed. "At least I'll try to curb my outburst. Now, I have to get going. I'm meeting Brooke." I gave them both a cheek kiss and walked past them. "After you grab Fozzie's stuff, lock up for me, please. Oh, and tell Tom, I'm no longer adopting him as my second father. That man just can't keep his mouth shut."

CHAPTER FIVE

REAGAN

*S*ince Brooke refused to kill me, I made sure she was still up for drinks. We'd arrived at our local corner bar not far from my house and quickly grabbed a spare booth.

"Hey, girls." Merriam, our usual waitress, bounced up. "The usual?" God, it sounded like we got drunk and ate hot wings a lot. Okay, so it was nearly every Friday night. *Nearly.*

"Yes, please." Brooke smiled sweetly; she'd been hot for Merriam for a long time. Only as far as we knew, Merriam didn't swing that way. Her copious flirting with the men around the place, plus the fact she took a lot of them home, was a bit of a giveaway.

"Actually, I think I'll go for a change tonight," I said.

Merriam giggled. "Add a cherry to your beer and cheese to your fries?"

I winked. "It's like you read my mind."

She snorted. "Or anytime you say you want a change it's always that."

"That's true." I nodded. She skipped off while Brooke watched her booty shake. "You should just find out for sure if she's interested or not."

"She's not." Brooke sighed and pointed. I glanced over to see Merriam lip locked to a guy I hadn't seen before.

"Damn," I muttered.

"Yep. Oh well, I'll have to go back to fantasizing about Pink."

"Now, I would even switch sides for her."

"Or The Rock." Brooke grinned.

"You're such a hussy. Can't you just stick to women and leave the men for me?"

She laughed. "Hell no. Both sexes are forms of art to be admired." She winked and then asked, "So, what are your plans this weekend?"

"Since Mom picked up Fozzie today, I'm planning to clean my house top to bottom. I'm sure the monster shit in every corner he could, and I'm convinced I still haven't found one because something's still stinking up my place."

"Bastard."

"Exactly. What about you?"

She groaned. "I have to go see Nana."

I winced. Brooke's nana was sweet in her own way, but ruthless too. She liked to get what she wanted, and she didn't care who she mowed over in the process. The last time Nana Bev called for Brooke's time, it was to take her speed dating. Nana Bev made Brooke sit beside her to "watch her work" in gaining a man's attention because, in her eyes, Brooke should already be married off and pumping out great-grandbabies for her to spoil.

When an eager elderly man suggested a threesome between them, Brooke up and bolted out of there. Nana Bev later rang Brooke and said it was rude how she left so abruptly and maybe she could teach Brooke a few things if she watched her in the sack on how to keep a man's attention. Nana Bev had multiple boyfriends, and they all adored the ground she walked on, going as far as knowing about one another and not caring at all.

Brooke and I put it down to Nana Bev being a voodoo goddess and her putting spells on them.

Still, she was the only living relative Brooke had, and Brooke loved her no matter what she put her through. Well, most of the time.

"What's she asking for this time?"

Brooke sighed. "She's giving me cooking lessons."

My eyes widened. "Again?"

Brooke nodded. "She believes she can still help even after setting her stove on fire the last time she tried."

"And even after the few times before that when you somehow managed to burn everything you cooked?"

"Yep."

"Oh well, one day she'll learn."

"Not likely," Brooke replied as Merriam placed our drinks on the table. "Thanks, honey." Brooke smiled.

"Anytime, sugar." She gave air kisses and left.

I took a long drink of my beer and sighed. It was just what I needed after my day.

An abrupt sound of loud voices caught my attention. I glanced at the door, and my eyes widened. "Oh, damn," I whispered.

"What?" Brooke asked, then looked where I was and started laughing. "Ree-ree, what are you doing?"

What did she think I was doing as I slid down in the booth and under the table? Wasn't it obvious? I was hiding. My blood had rushed through my body at the sight of Carter and some of his friends walking through the entrance. I was sure I'd pass out from the way my blood pumped faster and faster.

"Get up," Brooke snapped. "He's coming this way."

"I'm not here," I hissed.

"Reagan."

"Shut up," I barked low, and then pinched her calf.

"Ow," she cried, then coughed. "Ah, hey there, Carter. What are you doing here?"

Before he could answer, I heard Merriam announce, "Dinner."

Brooke cleared her throat. "Thanks."

"Where's—"

"Yum," Brooke yelled, interrupting Merriam's question. "Looks great. Could I get another two beers? I love to drink." She laughed, then kicked me in the stomach.

God dangit, how did I get myself in these predicaments?

Actually, I knew how. Acting before thinking was the main reason. I really had to stop doing that.

But what was I supposed to do now? Pop up from under the table like a jack-in-the-box? Surely I'd look crazier than I already did.

"Okay…," Merriam drew out and I saw her feet move away. I squished myself further into the corner, as far away from the side of the table where three men still stood.

"That's a lot of food just for you," a man commented.

Brooke giggled. "Ah, I like food, and, um, I have a friend coming soon."

"Would that be Reagan?" Carter asked.

Shit again.

"Yes?" Brooke answered, and she made it sound like a question.

I ran a hand over my face. Great, the floor wasn't the cleanest, so I was probably going to catch something, and I had no one to blame but myself. Brooke was so going to kill me for putting her in this position.

For the sake of keeping my friendship, I had to do something.

"I found it," I yelled. Slowly, I placed my hands on the booth, shifted around and slid back up into my seat. My face burned brightly as I glanced at the muscle show at the booth. Carter stood there with his arms crossed, a small smile on his face, but his lips were also twitching. What Carter wasn't showing was surprise, unlike his two friends staring at the weirdo popping up out from under the table.

"Reagan," Carter said. "Can I ask what you found?"

Shit once more.

"Um...."

"My anal beads," Brooke piped up with.

What in the ever-loving hell?

Why? Why dear God would she say that?

"R-right." I nodded, my blush growing down past my neck.

Brooke laughed, waved her hand around and said, "I was embarrassed I dropped them out of my bag. My good old pal there said she'd get them for me." Then she shoved a chip in her mouth.

"Where are they now?" Carter asked. His eyes light with humor, and his friends beside him started chuckling.

"Backinmybag," Brooke mumbled quickly around her mouthful.

Which was good because I was frozen and still stuck on the fact my friend had blurted the words anal beads.

Anal beads?

"I used a napkin to pick them up," I announced quickly, like it actually mattered.

"Hey, I clean my sex toys." Brooke glared across from me, then blanched. "They were also new." She cleared her throat and took a sip of her beer. I didn't know how she said any of it without turning a deep shade of red. The woman was amazing.

"Carter, you gonna introduce us?" the guy to the left of him asked. He was cute, very cute in a cowboy kind of way, with his Stetson, flannel shirt, and jeans that hugged him nicely.

"Reagan," Carter clipped.

Had he been saying my name long? By his dipped, frustrated brows, I could only assume he'd been trying to get my attention. Great, I'd been caught ogling his friend. That was a bit awkward.

Actually, the whole situation was.

"Reagan and Brooke. This is Dustin," he pointed to the cowboy, "and North,"—the man with the delicious dark skin.

"Hey." North grinned, and I swooned. He had an amazing grin.

"You ladies mind if we join you?" Dustin asked.

"Not at all," Brooke answered before I could yell "No!" I shot her a glare. She smiled and shrugged as Dustin slid into her side of the booth. When I saw Carter start to sit on my side, I jarred myself flinging my body to the right and nearly kissed the wall in the process.

As North went to move in beside Carter, he shook his head. "Go grab a chair,"

"We'll fit," North said, and shoved Carter closer to me.

Oh God. It was either my worst nightmare—stuck in a corner with no escape—or my first wet dream since I was surrounded by hotness.

"Dude," North cried. His hand snapped out and smacked Dustin's as Dustin went to grab a chicken wing. "We'll order."

"It's okay," I said, and when all eyes came to me, I wished I never spoke. "Um, we never usually eat it all anyway."

"See, no harm." Dustin smiled before biting into a wing. He waved it around. "How do you two know Carter?"

I clamped my lips closed. I was also trying not to think about the tingle of feeling Carter's heat at my side since he was very close. With him leaning forward, his elbows on the table, I kind of felt hidden by his bigger frame so I didn't feel the need to answer. But then he went and moved. Leaning back in the seat, he brought his arm up high and behind my head on the seat.

My belly fluttered as he grinned down at me. He glanced at Dustin and then gestured with a tip of his head down to me, then Brooke. "I met them today in fact."

"Ah, the last of the high school promos?" North asked.

"Yep." Carter nodded.

"So you both teach?" Dustin asked.

"I teach English and Brooke is the school counselor," I supplied.

All men slowly turned to the woman who said she had anal beads and were probably thinking the same thing: How was she the school counselor when she carried anal beads?

She swallowed her mouthful and glared at them. "What? It's not like I throw sex toys at them… though that could be a good idea. At least then there'd be fewer STDs or pregnancies."

The guys kept looking at her.

"Kidding. I wouldn't actually do it. I do know what I'm doing when I help the kids." When they didn't shift their stare, she cried, "Stop looking at me."

"Here you go. Another two beers. Would you gents like anything?" Merriam asked, placing our drinks on the table.

The men gave her their order, and while they did, I ate some of my food, hoping I didn't choke on it in the process. Then again, one of them would have to give me mouth to mouth.

"So you both play football with Carter?" Brooke asked.

All their gazes went back to her with a surprised look. Dustin was the first to ask, "Do we play football?"

"Baby, tell me you're joking?" North asked, then he glanced at me. "Do you know us at all?"

I nodded and pointed with a wing. "You're North, and that's Dustin."

Carter chuckled.

"Have you ever seen a football game?" North asked.

"Ah, no," I admitted. Carter's head all but swiveled off his body when he turned it so fast my way.

"You've never seen a game?" he asked.

"No. Neither has Brooke." I had to throw her under the bus so their attention would shift; only it didn't. I heard Brooke giggling.

"Not once? Not even when you were young and your dad watched it?"

"Nope." I shook my head. If Dad watched any type of sports, I quickly ran from the room so he didn't try to tell me all about the rules. It happened once for basketball, and I never wanted it to happen again because I was bored out of my brain.

"You should come to a game," came from Dustin. "Both of you should." He nodded like what he said was final.

"Um, thank you, but—"

"Reagan," Carter said. I glanced at him. "You and Brooke *are* coming to a game."

"Ah... you see, I'm not one—"

"Game. Coming."

Of course when he'd said coming like that, deep and growly, I blushed and quickly looked over to Brooke for some type of help. Though, I wasn't sure her help was any good. *I mean, anal beads, come on.*

"We'd love to come to a game," Brooke said with an evil glint in her eyes. I was going to slap her stupid.

"Good." North grunted. "Settled." He shook his head. "Still can't believe you two haven't seen a football game. We're on the team that's winning the most games for the city. Our stadium's not far."

"I have, and I love it," a new voice piped in. When I looked to the side of the booth, I had to hold back my hand from rising and my middle finger from making an appearance.

"Carter, thank you for meeting with me. Sorry I'm late, baby," Elena said, leaning into the table. I was surprised her boobs didn't pop out of her tight top to greet Carter as well.

Wait... she was sorry she was late?

Carter was here to meet Elena?

The food I digested suddenly felt like it wanted to come back up.

CHAPTER SIX

CARTER

*F*ucking hell.

I'd forgotten about meeting Elena. Why I forgot was because of the woman at my side. The woman who was suddenly looking everywhere else but at me. Dammit I wanted her eyes, so I could tell her the meeting with Elena was nothing. She'd pressured me into it in the first place, which was why I had North and Dustin come with me, so Elena would know it wasn't a date.

There was no way in hell I would ever date Elena or someone like her ever again. She was just another reason I hadn't moved back yet. I'd seen her at some games but was lucky there were enough people around to ignore her and I didn't seem like an ass in doing it. It was too bad she worked at the same school Reagan did and I had no choice but to speak with her.

Only no one knew that. More importantly, Reagan wouldn't know that. She probably thought I'd set up a date with Elena to maybe rekindle things with her.

Shit. I gagged at the thought of rekindling anything with a she-devil like Elena.

What was worse was when Dustin and North took Elena in and read her in seconds. They moved their attention to the food and the ladies.

"Carter, how about we find our own table?" Elena asked.

No! I wanted to scream it in her face, but of course, I didn't.

When I'd noticed Reagan and Brooke, the real reason I'd come to the bar dropped from my mind. All I wanted to do was spend time with Reagan. Especially when I saw her drop under the table after she spotted me. I found it funny, and definitely cute. I wanted to mess with her more, to see where she'd take the scene. It was why I approached the table in the first place. As well as the fact that as soon as I saw her, my heart jumped like an excited little puppy.

I'd spent all afternoon unable to keep her off my mind... *and I'm starting to sound like a damn stalker.*

I had to cool it. Get to know all there was about Reagan Wild, and have her know me for the person I was now.

I didn't think I was so bad.

"Carter?" Elena said with a snappish tone.

"How about you pull up a chair here?" I said. "This is North and Dustin." My ball brothers—which suddenly sounded dirty; it wasn't like we played with each other's balls—shot me a dark look for bringing them into it. Still, they were gentlemen, in a way, and turned their attention to Elena. "Guys, this is an old..." Shit, I didn't want to say girlfriend or even a friend, and she would soon not even be an acquaintance once she realized I wasn't interested in starting anything with her since all she saw were dollar signs when looking at me. "... uh, an old pal from high school, Elena."

I saw Elena's cringe. The guys winced, and I heard Brooke snort out a laugh. Then I felt Reagan shift her leg quickly, and when Brooke cursed low, I knew Reagan had kicked her.

Yeah. That moment was awkward for all of us, especially Elena, and Reagan was nice enough to stop Brooke from laughing. Even though I was sure Reagan and Elena weren't on friendly terms with each other.

"Carter, I'd really love to talk to you. Alone." Elena smiled.

Christ. I couldn't say no when I'd agreed to come here in the first place.

"Ah, sure." I nodded. North shifted out of the seat. "I'll be back," I told the rest of the people at the table but kept my eyes on Reagan.

She bit her bottom lip but didn't say anything.

Sighing, I moved out of the booth and North slid back in.

Into my spot.

Next to Reagan.

Would it be bad if I punched him?

"You guys coming?" I asked my team players like a scared little girl. I did not want to be alone with Elena. I was worried she'd try to, as Reagan had put it, Dora The Explorer me.

"We're good," Dustin replied with a smirk.

Dicks.

Elena took my hand. I caught Reagan noticing it, and I wanted to shrug Elena's hold off, but she was already dragging me away. She stopped at a table across the room. I quickly took a seat so I could keep an eye on the table I wished I was still at.

Elena sighed before sitting. Had she been waiting for me to pull out her chair? It was something I usually did for women, but I'd forgot in my haste to grab the chair I wanted. North had just said something to Reagan to make her throw her head back and roar with laughter.

Cocksucker.

That laugh was supposed to be mine.

"Carter?" Elena snapped.

"Sorry?" I asked, glancing at her.

She sighed again. "I'm glad you agreed to meet me. I didn't realize how much I've missed you since seeing you again. I had tried to see you at some of your games, but it must have been too noisy for you to hear me."

What did I say to that?

"Yeah, it's been good to see you too, and games are always crazy loud with the crowds."

She nodded and giggled. "Do you remember how much we couldn't keep our hands off each other back in school?"

I remembered she liked to cling to me like a leech wanting to suck me dry.

"Sure." I nodded. The food and drinks had arrived at the other table. I was just about to open my mouth to tell Elena I had to get back over there when Dustin pointed my way. The prick was sending my items over to me.

I was stuck.

"—I mean can you believe it?"

Crap. What had she said?

"Sorry?"

She rolled her eyes. "I said its uncanny how I have to deal with Reagan where I work. Do you remember her back in the day? Actually, you probably don't. We were pretty busy with each other."

"Here you go. A burger and a beer," the waitress said, placing it down in front of me. She glanced to Elena. "Can I get you anything?"

Elena looked her over. "Some privacy."

Again, I wished I could have changed the past where Elena was never in my life.

My jaw clenched. "Elena, can I ask you something?"

"Of course." She smiled, leaning into the table so her boobs were even more on show.

"Why did you want to meet up tonight?"

She winked. "To talk about old times. It would be better in a more private environment. Maybe another time we could make that happen?"

"I'm pretty busy with practice, games, and other stuff."

"I'm sure you could make time for an old flame." She licked her lips.

Why did I agree to meet with her? That's right; I thought I had buffers to help me get through the time with her, but no, they were having fun talking and laughing and goddamn leaning into one another across the room.

"We could be friends, but I'm not looking for anything—" A foot was rubbing up the inside of my leg.

"Are you sure," she practically purred.

Yes, she was still stunning. But I knew her. She was vindictive, mean and cunning, and that made her ugly as hell. There was no chance she was going to get anything from me. I hadn't even given her my number when she'd asked for it.

"I'm sure. I think it's best if we don't move past what we already are."

Her foot dropped. Her nose scrunched up, and she spat, "What are we, Carter?"

"Ah, friends?" There was zero certainty in my voice.

"Whatever. Can you at least give my number to your friends?"

Jesus. What a class act. Not.

"All right. But it doesn't mean they'll call you."

"I think they will. I think they'll see what you'll be missing out on and want something from me instead."

Thinning my lips, I held back my chuckle.

Before I could leave with pleasantries between us, she stood abruptly and made her way to the dance floor. There she met with some of her friends and started grinding her hips around, while flipping her hair, trying to gain the attention of my team mates. I had to laugh when I noticed they weren't even looking her way. Then I stopped laughing when I realized they were busy talking to Brooke and Reagan. I had to get back over there before Reagan fell for one of them. I already didn't like the way she'd eyed them when I'd made the introductions.

Picking my beer and burger basket up, I made my way back over. I was actually happy I'd taken Elena up on meeting her since it led me to see Reagan again.

"Hey," I said, stopping at the side, and then gave North a pointed look.

He didn't get it of course. "You're back." He grinned. "Didn't take you long." He shuffled closer to Reagan. "Sit down, man."

Bastard.

I should have told them about Reagan before, but I didn't know she was going to be there and I wanted to keep her to myself for a while.

"How'd it go?" Dustin asked as I sat next to North.

"Fine," I muttered, and took a gulp of the cool beer.

"So," Brooke started with a smirk, "you and Elena again, hey?"

"What do you mean again?" North asked.

Shit.

"I heard they used to date back in high school," Brooke said.

"How'd you hear that? We didn't even know it," Dustin commented. "Then again, we never came here until we got transferred to the same team a couple of years ago."

"Reagan went to the same school," Brooke said.

"But we weren't in the same crowd," Reagan quickly supplied.

"You two knew each other before today?" North asked.

Reagan laughed. "No." She shook her head. "We've never spoken to one another before today. I wasn't a cool kid."

I caught North bump into her shoulder with his own. Would it be bad if I dragged my friend by his hair away from her? He grinned at Reagan, and said, "I was never in the cool club either."

Dustin snorted. "Me either."

"Same." Brooke grinned.

Hell, they were bonding, and I hated it. After grinding my teeth together, I took another long drink of my beer. Suddenly the burger, what little I'd eaten of it, wasn't sitting well in my gut.

"I was a douche back then." The words fell from my mouth.

Dustin mock gasped, his hand covering his chest. "You a douche? I could never believe it."

Rolling my eyes, I chuckled. "Smartass. I can honestly say my douche ways are long gone."

"Did you really date that?" Dustin asked. I looked to where he gestured with his head. We all shifted to see Elena dry humping a pole off to the side.

I winced. "Unfortunately."

Reagan had been very quiet. I should have sat on the other side beside Dustin so I could catch her gaze more. Instead, I was stuck on the end.

I was close to becoming obsessed, and it wasn't good. I hadn't been like that with a woman ever. Shit, I'd probably scare her away. Maybe I should cool it. But what was I cooling? We hadn't even shared more than a handful of words and besides, it was the first day back in each other's lives.

I'd just have to make sure I stayed in her life in some way. God, I wanted to thump my head against the table. I wanted to talk to her, ask her things, and find out if she had someone in her life. Then again, if she did, he would have been here, right? Because there was no way I would let her go to a bar without me. There were perverts around. Dicks who would invite themselves to her table and want to monopolize her time while gazing at her boobs and thinking how they were going to take her home.

Was that a cricket I heard chirping?

No. I wasn't one of those dicks. I hadn't even looked at her boobs... and now I'd thought about them I so wanted to look.

Christ.

My rambling thoughts were verging on pathetic.

All I knew was I wanted to see her whenever I could. I wanted to get to know her.

"Come," I suddenly shouted, and before I could finish my sentence, North and Dustin were laughing their asses off. Brooke was giggling and so was Reagan with her hand over her mouth. A blush also coated her cheeks. Clearing my throat, I added, glancing at both women, "I meant come to our game Sunday?"

"I can't. Nana duties." Brooke shrugged.

"Reagan?" I asked, leaning around North a bit to catch her attention.

"Oh, I, ah, have to—"

"She'd love to," Brooke said for her.

"Shit," North bit out.

Brooke winced. "Sorry, my foot has a mind of its own and spasms on occasions."

North snorted, while Dustin and I laughed. "Sure." North nodded, smiling. And I knew what she had really been trying to do —kick Reagan into agreeing.

"Maybe next weekend? Do you play then?" Reagan asked.

We all stared at her. I still couldn't believe she'd never seen a game.

"Yeah, we have a game every weekend since it's the season."

"Speaking of the game," Dustin put in. "We should get going."

He was right. None of us liked late nights before practice. The younger players called us old-timers for it, but we didn't give two hoots. At least we weren't green and on the verge of throwing up in our helmets while playing.

Funny thing was, we weren't that old. Well, not in the head. It was my body from playing so long that was giving up on me and at the ripe age of thirty. I'd taken too many rough hits to my knee, and if I didn't stop soon, I might not be able to repair it in the end.

Still, even though we liked to rest before early practice and games, I was reluctant to leave. "Do you ladies have a way home?" They'd had a few beers, so I was worried Reagan would drive, oh... and Brooke.

"I'm staying at Reagan's tonight," Brooke said.

"You are?" Reagan asked.

Brooke laughed. "Yes."

"Since when?"

"Since we're going to have a couple more drinks and I won't be able to drive home, and you don't live far from here."

Interesting, she lived close by.

Although, walking could be dangerous as well.

"We'll walk you home," I stated, standing from the table. Dustin and North followed.

"We're good and we'll be staying," Brooke said with a grin.

"It's not safe out at night. I'd prefer to know you both got home safely."

"We've done it a lot, and no one has bothered us before," Reagan said.

I caught her gaze. "Still, I'd like to know you're both safe at your place." And away from the drunken idiots around this place. I'd already noticed a few eyeing the women off.

"We're staying for a bit longer." She narrowed her gaze.

I mimicked her hard stare. "Going," I clipped.

"Staying," she snapped. I wanted to shove North out of my way, reach forward, and plant my mouth on hers. I liked the fire shining in her eyes and flushing her cheeks.

"I need to make sure—" A hand landed on my chest. I glared down at it then up at my friend.

North smirked. "All righty, I think the ladies are capable of getting home. They want to stay, and it's not us who should force them to leave."

"Thank you." Reagan grinned up at him.

I'd never wanted to punch my friend in the face so much.

He was right though, I hated that. Sighing, I reached up and rubbed the back of my neck. "We'll talk before the game next weekend," I told her, and caught her eyes flaring a bit before she bit her bottom lip and nodded.

After bills were paid, which the women tried to argue about, but I ignored them and paid for what they'd had so far, we said our goodbyes and I walked out the front with my friends.

"So...," Dustin drew out, "how long have you had a thing for Reagan?"

North laughed. "It's cute how you become a total fool in front of her."

I grumbled under my breath. "Is it that obvious?"

"Yes." Dustin grinned. "Well, to us, and I'm sure Brooke knows, but Reagan... I don't think she has a clue."

"Back in high school, I was a douche-canoe. Too concerned with what people thought of me. I'd admired Reagan from afar, but never did anything about it. I want things to change."

"I'd take it slow, man. She seems skittish," North said, and then climbed into his car. Dustin and I got in with him.

"I'll do what I can to make her more relaxed around me."

"Shit, never seen you like this for a woman. Usually, it's a tag-and-bag scenario."

"Reagan's different," I told them, because she was.

Reagan was important. A woman who deserved time, the chase, and the capture.

Hell, I was looking forward to the capture part.

CHAPTER SEVEN

REAGAN

*I*t was midweek, and I couldn't get Carter off my mind since our double encounter on Friday. He'd snuck his way inside and made a home in my head. I wanted to evict him, but my stupid brain kept throwing thoughts of his smirk, his eyes, and his body at me like my own private porno.

Damn him for talking to me like we were friends. For even wanting to be friends in the first place. I couldn't help but wish I'd taken him up on his offer of having lunch with him that day. Then maybe something he did would have disgusted me... though, even if he ate with his mouth open, I wasn't sure my lust-filled brain would have been put off.

My brain was a hussy.

God. I needed help. A séance on my mind.

Sighing, I crossed my legs on the couch and picked up the remote. I was already in my pajamas, and it was only 6:00 p.m. However, I'd had a rough day at school, and I lost count of the times Elena glared at me, or Tom asked if I should seek professional help…. I mean, he only caught me jumping on my desk and screaming while a mouse ran around the room. I wasn't the only one freaking out either. Wesley's scream had been higher-pitched than mine. If anything, I expected Tom's question on Monday, post my Carter debacle. Not even once did he mention naked yoga. He probably thought Dad would have given me a good talking to about it, but really, he should know better by now. My parents were just as crazy as I was.

My phone chimed, breaking through my thoughts. I assumed it was Brooke or my parents since they were the only ones who rang or text me. God, I sounded pathetic. But when I picked it up, I saw Carter's name flash over the screen.

My heart plummeted into my stomach and caused it to swirl in a tornado of nerves. How his number was in my phone I didn't know, but if I had to guess it would be on Brooke.

Carter Anthony had texted.

Me.

Damn my hands for shaking, but they were, and it was because it was *Carter Anthony*!

Having seen him at the bar the same day of my disaster with him at school had been a surprise. What shocked me even more was how quickly he returned to our table after talking with Elena. I was sure she'd sink her claws in some way, and he'd be with her all night. However, it was as if he didn't like what she offered—and everyone knew she'd offer something; instead, he came back to our table. He didn't even glance at Elena again, with the exception of his friends mocking him for his choice in exes.

Should I open the text? What does he want? Why did he text me? What if he texted the wrong person? He might have been texting a friend called Reginald, and his name would have been right next to mine.

Shit. I may have received Reginald's text by mistake.

Holy crapoly, I needed to calm the hell down.

Sucking in a deep breath, I opened the text.

Carter: Hey, what have you been up to?

How had I been? Was he asking me or someone else by mistake? What did I do? *Should I reply?*

Biting my bottom lip, I texted back. **Not much, you?**

There. It was nice and simple. So in case he'd sent it to me by mistake, he'd see my name pop up, and the mistake could be easily fixed because neither of us texted anything weird.

My whole body jolted when my phone chimed. I fumbled it a bit and then held it against my chest. I glanced around my empty house as if there were someone else here seeing my klutzy moves over a guy texting me.

But come on, it's Carter Anthony.... I really had to stop saying his whole name in my head. It was like his whole name held power. I guess in a way it did; it certainly caused my body to hum to life.

Carter: Just relaxing after practice. How was school today?

Thank God, he knew it was actually me he was texting... unless he knew another school teacher.

Shit. I had to stop doubting myself. Carter Anthony could have texted me on purpose.

After all, he'd said he wanted to be friends.

Me: Good. Well, except for the mouse running around my classroom and Tom finding me screaming and standing on my desk. I sent that off and then another quickly after. **Oh, and tripping *up* the steps falling to my knees where my face nearly came closely acquainted with Steve's crotch. The kids have already started a story I was giving a BJ on the steps.**

Shit, shit, shit. Why did I tell him that?

Even in texts I blurted out too much, and he probably thought I was getting it on with stinky Steve. Should I add I wasn't? My mouth was nowhere near his junk. If it had been, I was sure I'd vomit all over it since I was sure he smelled even worse in that area. I dry heaved at the thought.

He didn't reply.

Why wasn't he replying?

Had I scared him away?

Did he actually think I gave head on school property?

Could I text him again?

Would that seem too clingy?

Then again, how would it seem clingy since he'd texted me in the first place?

Me: Carter?

At least through a text he couldn't see my panic, the sweat forming on my brow, or hear my heavy breathing.

I let out a little yip when my phone chimed. **Carter: Sorry, I was too busy dying from laughter. Only those sorts of things could happen to you. I'm surprised you didn't pass out from being so close to the Steve smell.**

I smiled widely. It was so big that if anyone were around, they could probably see all of my teeth.

Me: Ha ha, laugh it up. If you come to the school ever again, I'll make sure Steve knows you want a hug. Then you can be on the verge of vomiting.

Carter: Shudder. No thank you.

Me: How was practice? I heard you won the game on the weekend. Good job, you.

Carter: Thanks. What do you mean heard? I thought you would have watched. ;)

Me: Well, I would have... maybe, if I hadn't been forced to help my parents paint. Actually, I didn't have to help; they bribed me with a home cooked meal.

Carter: I don't blame you for that. How did you hear we won then?

Me: Dad's a fan. Your team is the Wolves, right? I really knew for certain Carter played for the Wolves. I just didn't want to come across as I knew everything about him. After all, it was Brooke who stalked him online.

At my parents, I'd been surprised when I'd caught Dad talking on the phone to Tom about the kickass—his words, not mine—game the Wolves played. When he got off the phone, I asked him if the Wolves were his favorite team. He looked at me like I'd grown two heads and asked if I'd been living under a rock. I took that as a yes. He then proceeded to fill me in on the game. Of course, I zoned. He gave up when I started humming under my breath and told me to get back to work.

Carter: Yes, woman. Say, what are your plans this weekend?

Rolling my eyes, I bit my bottom lip to stop the ache in my jaw from the continuous grinning. Texting with Carter was easy. Fun even.

Me: Going to a game like I said I would.

Carter: Good! Make sure you go to the information booth and have ID on you. I'll leave a ticket there for you and Brooke.

Wow. That was nice.

Me: Um. Thank you.

Carter: You're welcome. I've got to go, but we'll talk soon.

Me: Okay. Bye.

Carter: Later :)

WHEN CARTER HAD SAID WE'D TALK SOON, I THOUGHT IT WOULD BE maybe the Sunday of his game. Instead, it was the next night; only he decided to call. My belly swirled with nervous butterflies, or it could have been gas, regardless, I pulled up my big girl panties to answer.

"H-hello?" I whispered. Why I said it in a whisper, I didn't know.

"Hey. Am I interrupting something?"

Even though his deep rough voice woke up my lady bits, the question threw me. I was doing my usual channel surfing before *Supernatural* came on, so I had no idea why he thought he'd be interrupting something.

"No. I'm not doing much."

Should I have said that? Maybe I should have made up I was

doing something exciting like... pole dancing. An image of Elena popped into my head, and I shuddered.

"So, what are you doing?" he asked.

Frantically, I went through the search engine of my brain to think of something other than sitting on the couch being lazy. In the end, I come to the conclusion that if Carter cared that I was relaxing with wine and waiting for hot men on TV, then he wasn't meant to be in my life. He had to accept me for me.

That's what friends did, right?

So I told him the truth. "Sitting on the couch with papers I need to grade, but I'm putting them off because my show is coming on soon. Ah, what about you?"

"What show?" he asked.

"*Supernatural.*"

He chuckled. "What's that about?"

I gasped. "You've never seen *Supernatural*?"

"Can't say I have."

"You... what... how can that be so?"

Another deep chuckle followed, one I liked hearing a bit too much. *Just friends.*

"I'm more of an action movie, documentary-watching kind of guy."

My nose scrunched up.

He let out another chuckle. "I just bet you're pulling a face at that. It's all right, we can compromise."

Compromise?

Why would we need to?

That didn't make sense.

He couldn't mean we'd be watching something together, could he?

Why would he want to?

"Reagan?"

"Sorry... I, um, does that mean you'll give *Supernatural* a try one time?"

My eyes widened. Why did I just ask that? Maybe because I thought everyone should at least try to watch *Supernatural* just once. Dean and Sam were worth sixty minutes of everyone's time.

"Sure, I'll give it a go." When he spoke, it sounded like he was smiling.

"Okay," I breathed. Carter wanted to spend time with me. It deserved a breathy moment.

Still, friends watched shows together. They talked like we were currently. They teased. Laughed at one another.

Shit, I shouldn't have gotten breathy on the phone with him.

Could he tell I liked the thought of having time with him by my voice?

I hoped he couldn't read me that well, but if he did, I was screwed.

I needed to change the subject to calm my mind. "You, ah, didn't tell me what you were doing."

"I just got out of the shower." That damn well didn't help my mind settle. It was impossible. Picturing him naked in a shower, toweling his naked body dry, but he'd miss a few drops that I would have to lick up.... *No, no, no, do not go there, Reagan. Think of something else. Him pooping. Sitting on the toilet and straining.... okay, I'm good now. That's a thought my mind should never have ventured.* "And now I'm going to get some sleep."

Damn Carter Anthony and his evilness.

Carter... in *my* bed.

"I have to go," I blurted.

"Everything okay?" He sounded legitimately concerned, and I felt bad as everything was okay, except for my filthy mind.

"Y-yes. I'm good, I ah, just really should grade some papers before Dean—"

"Who's Dean?" he demanded, his tone low and growly.

Oh my.

Smiling to myself, I said, "He's—"

"Do I know him?"

"No, he's—"

"Is he from high school?"

I laughed. "Carter—"

"A friend?"

"If you just let me—"

"A boyfriend?"

Sheesh, why did he sound so tense?

"Carter," I called loudly through the phone.

"Yes?"

"Dean is from the show *Supernatural*."

Silence.

I started giggling.

"Oh," he said.

"But just because we're becoming friends doesn't mean I can't have others," I stated, since he seemed so concerned another could replace him. Which was really weird since we'd only been in each other's lives for less than a week.

I paused, thinking about something Brooke had said. Did Carter fancy me?

Nope. Nuh-uh.

That was laughable.

He was a football god and dated models.

I was an English teacher and hardly dated at all.

"Right, yeah, I know that… but do you have other male friends?"

I bit my bottom lip. My mind wanted to crash into the thought of Carter wanting me, but my heart pulled on the reins and said, "Whoa."

"Reagan?"

"No. I don't. In fact, I don't have many close friends besides Brooke, and, well, my parents. But they have to put up with me since they brought me into the world."

He snorted. "I say the same to my folks." He took a deep breath. "Anyway, I'll let you go. I've got to be up early for training. If I don't talk to you before Sunday, I'll see you then."

"Sounds good." Crap, was that too forward? "Ah, buddy," I quickly added. His burst of laughter followed before I hung up the phone.

God. I really had to stick to just texting the poor guy, or he would end up knowing I was a head case.

CHAPTER EIGHT

REAGAN

*M*y stomach was in a turmoil of emotions. Nerves, excitement, fear... almost every damn emotion possible swirled in my stomach, all because I was at Carter's game. Football wasn't my thing, but it was Carter's, and I kind of did want to see him play and hoped I understood enough to be interested in it for him.

Yes, I wanted to like a sport because of a man.

Where had my smarts gone? Down the drain along with my rational thoughts when it came to Carter, apparently.

"Ree, these are damn good seats," Brooke said as we made our way to the spot Carter gave us tickets for. "Holy crap, we're sitting in the new boxed in area at the front. I've only recently read about these spots, how they're testing them for important people instead of the glass booths way up the back." She continued to rattle on and on about how she thought people would like it better, but I tuned out. Thank God she'd been willing to come with me since I didn't know the first thing about the stadium or reading a map.

Words, grammar, books, and teaching I could handle. Throw a map at me and tell me there was free coffee and chocolate for a year at the end, I'd try my best to find it, but I wouldn't be able to. I'd get lost and lose my mind, and no doubt end up crying in a corner somewhere for missing out on free goodness.

"That's good," I said, but unsure if it was in fact good. If they were *close*, close enough that Carter could see me, I was worried he'd see a bored look upon my face... or even find me asleep.

"It is good, Ree." She grinned. "Come on, down this way."

Nodding, I then followed her into the seating area. She led me way, way down the steps.

"See," Brooke exclaimed, as she opened the door after giving the attendant our tickets to mark off. "They said it was the two left in the front row," Brooke told me. She must have read on my face that I wasn't absorbing anything in my panicked state, so she took my hand in hers. We passed the other two rows, with a few people already sitting in some of them, to the front where three men sat to the far wall of the boxed area. Brooke sat me in the vacant seat next to an older man, and she took the one on the end. Maybe she was scared I'd make a run for it.

I had been thinking it.

Honestly, I was sort of annoyed at myself for thinking how it was important for me to like this game, but I couldn't seem to stop myself from doing it.

Damn Carter Anthony.

"This is awesome. We'll see all the action." Brooke clapped.

"Yes." I nodded. "Awesome." My lack of enthusiasm caught the attention of the man next to me. He glanced down at me and raised his brows. "Sorry," I muttered, and moved my gaze out onto the field.

It was just in time to hear announced, "And here come the Wolves." People everywhere cheered loudly. My heart perked up and skipped a beat. I shifted forward on my seat to see Carter's team jog onto the field.

Oh. My. God.

"Do you want wine? Snacks?" Brooke asked, but I didn't answer because I was too busy.

Around me, people still cheered a variety of chants. Some even cried they wanted to have some players' babies, and I could finally understand why they'd offer it up so easily.

In the background, I heard Brooke say something, and then the man on the other side of me reply. But my attention and eyes were glued to the glorious sight before me.

I should have asked Carter what number he was.

Not that I minded the trouble of looking for him.

Holy… there he was, and he looked so dang fine.

Tight white pants were burned into my eyes.

Tight.

White.

Pants.

Praise the lord for the football uniform. He was already bulky on top, but the padding helped him look tougher and sexier. His jersey read 32 along with a logo of his team. Under one arm he held a helmet.

The whole package was what wet dreams were made of.

"He should have just told me what he wore, and I'd have been at last weekend's game." Yes, I'd seen football briefly on the TV, but I'd never studied their uniform… until then.

"Reagan," Brooke scolded in a snappy tone.

"What?" I asked, glancing at her. "You can't tell me gear like that doesn't make you hot."

She paled and then palmed her forehead.

I heard a manly chuckle at my back and turned to find an older man glancing at us. A blush touched my cheeks. "Oh, sorry again. I'm not into sports really, but I wanted to try."

"And the uniform helps?" he asked, his lips twitching.

"Well, yes." I nodded. I didn't know the man, so I didn't mind being honest in front of him. The younger man beside the other guffawed.

"Reagan—"

"It's all right," the man said.

I frowned at the strange reply. "What's all right?" I asked, glancing away from the man to my friend and back again.

"Nothing," he replied. "Want me to tell you a few things as the game goes on?"

That was so nice.

Grinning, I nodded. "Yes, please. Even though the uniforms will keep my attention, I could waver halfway through so maybe if I have you talk to me about it, it will help." All three men in the row laughed heartily.

Didn't bother me. Besides, I may actually learn something since it wasn't my father trying to teach me. It would be different. With Dad, I got my back up and enjoyed torturing him too much to learn a thing.

"It'd be a pleasure." He smiled, and he had a really nice smile, so I grinned back.

"By the way, I'm Reagan."

"Patty," he said, but he said it in a way he thought I should recognize the name. I didn't. He smirked, his eyes lit with humor. "My boys, Casper and Calvin."

"Hey." I waved. Casper winked, and Calvin smiled, giving me a chin lift.

"Oi, I need a drink or ten," Brooke said from beside me.

"Sorry, this is—"

"We've already met," Brooke said. "When you were in a daze."

"Right." I laughed, my cheeks heating once again. I sank back in the seat and adjusted my tee. Carter and his team started putting on their helmets and walked out into the middle of the field. The game was about to start.

Out the corner of my eye, I saw a man step up to Brooke's side with a tray of items. She passed me a plastic cup. Beer.

"I thought we had to get these things from the concession stand," I commented.

"Not in here, sweetheart," Patty said.

I glanced to him. "Cool."

Casper leaned around him. "Who are you rooting for?"

"The Wolves." I grinned.

"Yeah, but anyone on the team?"

Patty sent him a look I didn't understand. Brooke coughed on something and Calvin was smirking.

"Ah… Carter Anthony, I guess."

"You guess?" Calvin asked.

"Well, no. I mean I am rooting for Carter."

"How do you know him?" Casper asked, causing another irritated scowl from his dad.

"He visited the school I teach at."

"And he asked you to come to the game?"

Why did I suddenly feel like I was in the hot seat?

"Yes."

"He also gave her tickets," Calvin put in.

"Boys, enough," Patty warned for some reason. Did they know Carter?

"Do you all know Carter?" I asked.

Casper and Calvin laughed. Patty shook his head at them. A horn blasted.

"The game's started," Patty said, pointing out. I shifted my attention there.

FOOTBALL WAS AN AMAZING SPORT. THOUGH AT TIMES, IT WAS SCARY with how rough it was. My pulse didn't stop racing until the very end, worried Carter would end up hurt in some way. He would have bruises with a couple of tackles he took, but he would be okay. Patty reassured me each time he caught me gripping my armrests with white knuckles.

Brooke was just as interested in the game as I was and with Patty's help, we understood it a lot more before it finished.

Heck, I even sprang to my feet a few times and yelled things like, "Make them eat dirt." Or "Take them out." At the end of that one, I added, "Not to dinner, just the game." Which had the men laughing around us. Throughout it, I learned the guys in the rows behind us were a part of Patty's friends and family. How they got such a sweet deal with the box area, I didn't know, but Patty told me every game in town the Wolves had they were there in support.

They were die-hard fans, and I was glad I got to meet them.

"Did you like it, Reagan?" Casper asked after we all stood.

"Loved it. I'll have to come to another one."

"So we've converted you into a fan?" Patty smiled.

"Definitely."

"Sure it's not just the uniforms talking to you?" Casper teased.

Laughing, I shook my head. "No. I honestly enjoyed it. Thank you all for putting up with us newbies."

"It was a pleasure," Patty said.

"Yeah, it was fun." Henry, Patty's brother, said from behind me. "Especially when you nearly face-planted falling from the seat after cheering."

I giggled. At that time, the Wolves had just got a touchdown, their final one to win the game, and I was so excited I climbed up and started screaming like so many others. Unfortunately, I slid, and if it wasn't for Patty and Casper, I would have kissed the floor.

Turning to Brooke, I was about to ask if she was ready to go, but I saw she had her mouth dropped open and wide eyes. I glanced where she was looking and spotted Carter, with his helmet off, jogging our way.

Smiling, I waved.

"We should go," Brooke whispered.

"Why?" I asked. "Carter's coming over."

"Exactly," she mumbled, but I caught it. I gave her a puzzled looked.

"Reagan," Carter called. "Did you like the game?"

Nodding, I went to the edge, leaning my hands on it, and said. "I actually did. Congrats on winning."

"Thanks." He grinned. "Did you understand any of it?"

"Actually, I had help." I thumbed behind me. "Patty was amazing at telling me what was going on."

He glanced behind me. His hand came out, and as Patty stepped up, they shook hands.

"Good game," Patty said.

"Thanks, Dad."

Dad.

Dad?

Dad!

Patty was Carter's father?

No, no, no.

"Reagan?" Carter said.

"Give her a moment," Brooke replied.

Dad.

Carter was the son of Patty.

Oh God. Casper and Calvin.

Both started with C, and I should have connected it all since they all went to the same damn high school, but didn't.

They're brothers.

I'm so damn stupid.

But I'd been nervous. Out of sorts.

Wait... Carter's family heard me say how I loved Carter's uniform.

Oh, dear hell on earth.

Kill me now.

I came back from my thoughts to hear Carter bark, "You didn't tell her who you were?"

"You didn't tell us you had someone else coming in the family box," Casper said.

Family box?

The family box.

As in *the Anthonys' family box.*

"We didn't want to scare Reagan off," Patty said, which was nice. But now he knew I liked Carter in his uniform, a lot. Heck, so did his brothers, uncles, and probably cousins.

Great. Just great.

"I didn't have time to tell you Reagan and her friend were joining you all—"

That was it!

That one word could save me.

"Friend! That's right, I'm Carter's *friend.*"

Shit. All eyes turned to me.

Casper snorted. "A friend you like to—"

"Friend," I cut in with a glare. He shut his mouth, but his lips twitched, as did Patty's, Calvin's, and hell, everyone's.

"She likes to what?" Carter asked.

"Nothing!" I shouted. Then laughed and slugged Carter in the arm. "Anyway, good game, bucko. Really ate them out—up. You ate them up." I ignored the chuckles around me and Brooke's groan.

I backed up. "I should get going. Um, great to meet everyone."

"Reagan, you should come by the house. We like to celebrate after a game," Patty offered.

"I really can't, ah, maybe next time."

When I wasn't dying.

"Reagan," Carter shouted, but then we all heard his name being called. Reporters were on their way over to him.

It was definitely my time to bolt.

Reaching out, I grabbed Brooke's hand.

"Wrong person to take on your escape," Henry said from beside me, and then he chuckled.

My eyes widened. I dropped his hand with a "Sorry," and then moved closer to Brooke. The witch was grinning like a fool.

"Thanks for everything." I waved, turned, and shoved Brooke out the gate.

"Reagan," Carter called, but I pretended I didn't hear him and kept going.

It was halfway to the car when a still smiling Brooke said, "Well, I think the family likes you."

CHAPTER NINE

REAGAN

*S*itting in a corner and rocking back and forth was high on my to-do list.

"You should have told me," I said for the millionth time. I glared at Brooke as she sat across from me at the diner we picked to have a late lunch in. It was the afternoon after my humiliating performance with Carter's family.

She shrugged. "It was entertaining."

"Bitch," I coughed.

She laughed. "Seriously, you should open your eyes a little wider. They all look alike. Besides, I think Patty enjoyed you being yourself without the knowledge of who he was to Carter. And let's face it, if you'd have known from the start you would have—"

"Not perved on his son while he was sitting there?"

She grinned. "He didn't mind. You won them over, Ree. I could tell. They enjoyed the time they spent with you."

I shook my head. "I'll never be able to face them again."

Brooke scoffed. "You'll be fine."

"I won't. If I do have to face them, I'll probably do something else stupid and they'll run from me screaming about what an accident I was."

All my life, I'd spoken before I thought. Most of the time it came back to bite me on the butt. I'd tried to curb the defect in me, but I couldn't most of the time. I blamed my mom. She was the same. Though, it was what Dad loved about her the most.

"You're adorable just the way you are," Brooke said.

Rolling my eyes, I muttered, "Thanks for thinking that."

"I'm not the only one, or else Carter would have run after you talked about naked yoga or when you threatened to throw up on your students." She laughed. "I still can't believe you said that. But it also proves a point. You're adored by many. Your students love your class. I've been told by many it's the only class they enjoy attending each week."

It was only because I was more laid-back than most of the other teachers. When I was in high school and even college, there wasn't a single teacher who made class fun. I was a firm believer that if students enjoyed their lessons, they learned a lot more.

"I just have good kids."

She groaned. "You're down on yourself too much, and it's starting to bug me, woman. Repeat after me: I am awesome." She waited. When instead I took a sip of my coffee, she kicked me under the table. "Repeat it."

"I am awesome," I mumbled.

Brooke sighed. "It'll do. One day though, you'll know it's the truth."

"You're my best friend, you have to say stuff like that."

She snorted. "It's because I'm your best friend I believe it or else I wouldn't be friends with you in the first place."

Brooke's phone chimed. She glanced down and then she blushed but didn't pick it up from the table.

"Who was that?" I asked.

She waved her hand down at her phone before picking up her own coffee. "No one."

"Brooke?"

"Reagan?"

Our waitress came up and placed my eggs benedict and Brooke's blueberry pancakes down. While she was distracted ordering another coffee for the both of us, I reached over and grabbed her cell.

I slipped it under the table and pressed it to life.

My eyes widened.

"Dustin said thanks for the other day?" I all but screeched.

Brooke winced and sent an apologetic smile to the waitress. "I just picked her up at the mental hospital. She has outbursts like this."

The waitress glanced from her to me and then back again. She nodded, as if one look from me had her believing Brooke. I didn't look crazy... did I? I checked my clothes. No rainbow was to be seen, but I was wearing my *I give zero fox* tee.

Whatever.

I didn't care what she thought.

"I-I'll get those drinks for you."

"Thanks." Brooke smiled. Then she turned back to me, scowling. "Give me my phone."

"What aren't you telling me, Brooke Baker?" I glared.

"Phone," she demanded with her hand out.

"What's going on with you and Dustin, and why haven't you told me?"

She huffed. "Nothing is going on."

"Bull." I waved her phone around. "Thanks for the other day?"

"It's nothing. I promise."

"Brooke, we tell each other everything."

She sighed, leaning back in her seat. "Fine. But I'm embarrassed, which is why I never said anything."

I gave her a reassuring smile. "Can't be as bad as anything I've done."

She giggled. "Well, no." After another gulp of her coffee, she started, "Wednesday night Dustin and I ran into each other down the street. We got to chatting about random things, and I asked what he was doing the next night, hoping it would lead to him asking me out." She cringed. "He said he was in a bind. He had some event he had to attend with a date, but still, even then he wasn't sure he could go because he had other commitments. I told him I could help out."

"As in be his date?"

"Well, yes. But obviously, we didn't confirm things since he was in a rush. So he told me my help would be fantastic and gave me his address." She picked up her fork and stabbed at her pancakes. "We didn't exchange numbers, so I wasn't sure what type of event it was and since it was during the day—"

"That's why you took a sick day Thursday?"

She nodded. "I chose to wear a simple black dress. I arrived at his house, he ushered me in, and then... in the living room, of his fan-freaking-tastic house, he introduced me to Benjie, his six-year-old son."

I gasped, my hand flew to my mouth to cover it. "No," I mumbled behind it.

"Yes." She nodded, smiling sadly. "The help he needed was to mind Benjie while he went out. His *date* arrived shortly after and she was stunning. I would have even asked her out. They left and I felt gutted."

"Oh, honey."

She shrugged. "Best thing about it was Benjie. He's a cute and fun little guy. We enjoyed each other's company. So much so that when they came back full of smiles and touches, I offered Dustin help in the future if he was in a bind with Benjie."

I winced. "That would have had to hurt."

"It did, but then it didn't." She took a mouthful of her pancakes. I could see the tension in her body and knew she was gutted over the fact Dustin only used her for a babysitter.

"Fuck him," I stated just as the waitress arrived back.

Brooke laughed. "Another outburst."

The waitress gave Brooke a sympathetic smile, set the drinks down and took off quickly.

"Seriously, Brooke. Fuck him for not wanting to take you out."

"Honestly, it's been a few days since then, and I'm over it. I liked meeting Benjie. So it wasn't terrible."

"Good." I nodded, but I still felt bad for her.

Stupid Dustin.

After eating and talking about school, we made our way out of the diner when I heard my name being called.

Turning, I froze. A smiling Carter ran our way.

"Hide me," I whispered to Brooke.

She laughed, but I didn't want her laughing when he arrived or else he could think we were laughing at him, not that I was laughing, but honestly, I didn't know what I was thinking and I blamed that on my actions. My elbow connected to Brooke's stomach, and she coughed, clutching her belly.

"Oh no, are you okay?" I asked, just as Carter stopped beside us. "Hi, Carter. Good to see you, but as you can see, I have to get Brooke home. She's not feeling well." I started to try and pull her with me, but the trollop planted her feet firmly on the ground and didn't move.

"I'm good," Brooke heaved out. "Fine." She nodded, standing straight. "See, it passed. All better now. How you doing, Carter?" she asked.

His grin widened. "Great. What are you two up to?" He planted his hands on his hips. Dang, he looked good in his jeans and a simple tee. My pulse started to race like it did every time I was around him.

"Nothing." Wait, nothing didn't sound good. It left me open to doing something if he suggested something. "Ah, actually I need to grade some papers and then I have dinner with my parents later." Since I didn't want it to be an actual lie, I would have to ring my parents later and invite myself over.

"I could go to dinner," he said.

Did he mean with me?

To my parents'?

No. Hell no. That would be a disaster.

"I'm sure Reagan would love to take you to her parents' house for dinner. In fact, how about I check with them now." She pulled her phone out, and I smacked her hand.

"I can do it," I snapped. Shit. She played me right into that one. Now I said I could do it, I would as I hated going back on anything I said. Facing Carter again, I asked, "But are you sure? I mean, Mom will probably say random embarrassing things and I've told you my dad is a huge fan. He'll probably fawn over you in some way."

He chuckled. "I think I can handle that."

Maybe *he* was the crazy one.

Oh well, he'd soon understand how loco my parents were.

God, I was going to take Carter to dinner at my parents'.

How did I get in that spot?

He'd invited himself.

Why?

Then again, Brooke had been to my parents' for dinner. Friends hung out with one another.

"Well… as long as you're sure you can put up with it."

"I will. Text me later what time and your address. I'll come pick you up and drive us over there. Also, I wanted to say sorry again about my family not saying—"

My hand came up. "Wait for all the apologizing until after you've dined with my family. It'll probably be me begging for your forgiveness later. But really, it's fine."

He smiled.

Bless my heart and his smile.

He winked. "Okay. I'll see you later."

I nodded. "As long as you're sure."

He chuckled. "I get the feeling you don't want me to come."

Once again, him and the word come in one sentence near short-circuited my brain.

"Ah, um, no, uh, it's not that… let's just say your family is like… a cute little Pomeranian and mine are like a big bulldog that's in your face all the time, barking questions every second. There could even be slobber involved. I just want to prewarn you." I wouldn't be surprised if Dad did drool over Carter a little.

He moved around us. "I'll be fine. Are you sure you're okay with me inviting myself?" He smirked.

Was I?

No. Not at all.

But for some weird reason, I was flattered by him wanting to come to dinner, to meet my family and be involved in all the craziness.

He was brave, that was for sure. Though, maybe I just didn't prepare him enough for how strange my family was. I guess he'd find out in a few hours.

"Yes?" I shook my head, then nodded. "Um, yes. I'm sure."

"Great." He winked again, taking a few steps away. "I have to go, but one last thing. Don't worry about the articles in the newspapers. Reporters like to talk out of their asses." He turned and started moving off.

"Articles? Newspaper? What reporters?" I asked.

"See you later," he called over his shoulder.

Meeting Brooke's amused gaze, I said, "What did he mean about the articles in the papers?"

"I'm not sure, but I want to find out."

I wasn't sure if I did.

CHAPTER TEN

REAGAN

$\mathcal{B}$rooke came home with me, our arms filled with newspapers. We sat at the table and immediately Brooke took one, and I opened another, starting to flick through.

"I think it'll be in the sports section," Brooke said. She picked up several pages and opened to the sports area. I saw her eyes widen.

"What?" I asked.

"Um…." She started laughing and pushed her paper in front of me. On the first page in the sports part was a big picture of Carter's back standing before his family boxed seats with *me*, hands on the ledge smiling down at him. The title read, "Who is Carter Anthony's mystery woman?"

Whoa.

I was a mystery woman?

But for all they knew, I could have been part of Carter's family.

"I can't read it." I shook my head and stepped back from the table, then laughed nervously. "Wait until they find out we're just friends. They'll look like fools."

Brooke hummed in the back of her throat. "How about you go and ring your parents to tell them you're bringing your"—she used air quotes with her fingers for the next word out of her mouth—"*friend* for dinner."

"Yeah, I'll do that. Good thinking." I nodded, and then turned to head to my bedroom.

Stupid reporters.

Involving me in Carter's life like that.

Poor guy was probably embarrassed.

Though, it wasn't a very good photo. I doubted anyone could really tell it was me. If no one said anything to me on Monday, I knew I was in the clear and then I'd breathe easy.

Picking up the phone from my bedside table, I dialed in my parents' number.

"Ree-ree, what's my girl up to?" Mom answered.

"Mom, can I come to dinner tonight?"

"Of course you can. Sunday night is roast night, and you know there's always a lot."

"Good because I have a *friend* who'd like to come as well."

"Brooke is always welcome, you know that."

Clearing my throat, I admitted, "It's not Brooke. His name's Carter—"

Silence for a beat and then, "Oh my God. Oh my God. My girl is bringing a boy?"

"A *friend* who happens to be a guy, yes."

"Of course he can come. Is there anything he doesn't like to eat? Oh, I'll have to bring out the good china. This is so exciting. Would six be okay? Wait until I tell your father. He's been worried about you. We both have."

"Mom!" I shouted to get her attention before she rattled off more.

"Yes, dear?"

"Promise me that you and Dad will be on your best behavior? Do not mention in front of him about us dating or that you think we'd

79

look good together. None of that. Let's just have a nice, normal dinner."

"Sure. Totally. Can't wait. See you then," she sang, then hung up.

I hit my forehead with the receiver and groaned. She agreed way too quickly for my liking.

Dinner was going to be hell.

CARTER

I felt like a dick for inviting myself over to her folks' home for dinner, but I didn't see any other way to be able to spend some time with her. She was too skittish that morning after the game, and I blamed my family for not telling her who they were. Also, I couldn't exactly say, "Hey, you mind if I come over to your place to get to know each other so eventually, we can move to the next level and become an item?"

Hell, I sounded like I was back in high school.

I wasn't even sure if she'd be interested in me in that way. Yeah, she got flustered around me, but was it because she was attracted to me?

Then again, from what my brother Casper told me, she sure did like me in my uniform.

A smile tipped up my lips. Then I lost it at my next thought.

Or could it be she liked all my teammates in their uniform?

Do not go there, Carter, or you'll kill the other players.

Why did Reagan Wild make me violent?

While I'd been possessive before, it was never to the extent of wanting to harm my friends to the point of bloodshed. Maybe it was just that the other women weren't important enough to some part of my brain, the part where Reagan was. She had me by my balls, brain, and body.

It near gutted me when she'd told my family we were just

friends, like that was all she saw us as, or perhaps she was worried that friendship was all *I* could ever want from her. I continued to overthink her reaction to me, her responses. Maybe she was scared in some way that, hell, maybe she thought I could hurt her. I hope it wasn't that though. I'd never hurt her intentionally.

My overthinking was driving me insane.

What I did know was that I knew nothing. I was grasping at straws when it came to Reagan. A woman's mind was like the Rubik's cube for people like me. Something I couldn't for the life of me figure out.

However, I was hoping I would get more of an insight into Reagan's life by meeting her parents. Also, I wanted to make a good impression, and by what Reagan said, her dad was already a fan, which would be an advantage.

Pulling my car up to the curb in front of Reagan's house, I took it all in. It seemed like a good neighborhood. At least there weren't any drug dealings or hookers on any corner. I noticed as I climbed out of my Hummer, the street was quiet. Reagan's house was a small brick one, with a cute flower garden out the front. I could totally see her in a tee and shorty shorts kneeling under the warm sun tending to her flower garden. *Hell, do not go there or little Carter will perk up, and Reagan will open the door to me with a stiffy.*

With a few deep breaths, I calmed myself and stepped up onto the front porch. A cute setting was arranged with two wicker chairs and a round wicker table in between.

It was pretty damn sweet. Like Reagan.

As I just raised my hand to knock on the door, it flew open.

Reagan stood there waving a shoe around. "I lost a shoe. Sorry, I should have been waiting out in front. I swear my mom's dog, Fozzie, who I minded for a while, stole the thing and put it under my couch just to peeve me off. He was vindictive like that." She stepped out after placing her shoe on and turned to lock the door.

"I'm kind of early anyway." I'd been hoping to see inside Reagan's domain.

"All good. We should get going. You'll probably want the night over with as quickly as possible anyway." She laughed, but it wasn't her normal one. It seemed forced and nervous. She made her way past me, down the footpath and to my car before I'd even stepped off the porch. Shaking my head and smirking, I quickly jogged down to the car.

Pressing the button to unlock it, I stepped up to Reagan's side and opened her door for her. I had to bite my bottom lip and look down so she didn't see how amused I was at her wide eyes and gaping mouth. Too damn cute.

"Reagan," I called before she got in.

"Y-yes?"

"Relax, okay?"

She sighed and ran a hand through her hair. "I can't. You don't know them like I do."

I smiled. "It'll be fine."

Her eyes became a little frantic. "We need a signal." She grabbed the front of my tee and shook me a little. "Yes!" she cried. "It's a good idea. If you're feeling uncomfortable at any time you can... I don't know... scratch your nose? No, wait. That'll seem too obvious. Dad likes those 007 movies. He might look for a sign like that." She pinched her bottom lip with her free hand while she thought of something. All I wanted to do was laugh my ass off and kiss her soundly.

Regret filled me. I wished I'd have known her in high school. I'd missed out on a lot. I was sure of it.

I swiped the thought away, refusing to live in the past. Instead, I'd concentrate on how we were back in each other's lives. It was meant to happen. I was meant to have a chance with her.

Christ. I hoped I was.

She glanced up, grinning big. "I've got it. Lift your foot up to rest on your knee and then tap your foot three times. That will look normal enough." She released my tee to smack my stomach and then froze. Slowly, she shifted her gaze down to her hand and quickly pulled it back as if it were on fire. "Sorry, ah, I didn't mean that." Another nervous laugh. "We'd better get going." She slid into the seat and pulled her door from my grasp to shut it herself.

I walked around the back of the car so she wouldn't see me laughing.

CHAPTER ELEVEN

REAGAN

*S*top thinking about his hard abs. *If you walk into your parents'
home and they see the look of desire on your face, it'll go down-
hill from there.*

Mom had always read me too well.

In fact, she'd known the night I lost my virginity. I'd made it
home by my curfew, which was good for an eighteen-year-old with
a curfew of 11:00 p.m. At first, I'd thought they were both in bed.
The house had been dark when I unlocked the front door and snuck
in with my heels in my hand.

Then boom.

A light flicked on, and I'd screamed, turning to find Mom sitting
in the corner chair in the living room. She had, at the time, my large
lizard sitting on her lap and she was stroking it while her gaze ran
over me.

Then she'd quickly stood, flung my poor lizard to the chair, and
cried, "You had sex. Oh my God. My baby isn't a baby anymore.
She's been deflowered."

She didn't stop there.

"Herb," she yelled for Dad.

"Mom, I swear to God, if you tell him in front of me, I'll disown you and hook up with a drug dealer."

Her mouth snapped closed. "Fine. And a mother always knows these things. Well, there's also the fact you have your top inside out." She started to walk toward me. "Now, you know your first time is never the best time."

"Mom!" I'd snapped, turning redder by the second.

"Especially with a boy your age. They don't know how to please a woman or that women have many spots—"

"I'm going to bed," I'd announced quickly, and made a run for it.

"We'll talk tomorrow," she'd called. I'd tried my best to dodge her, but the woman had been persistent. It was one of those moments where a therapy session was needed, after a good session of rocking back and forth in a corner.

When we pulled up in front of my parents' place, Carter was already out and on his way to open my door. But I was nervous. I didn't want him to think I thought it was a date. Just the thought of him and my parents in the same place was enough for my hands to start sweating.

So again, once I was out and in front of him, I asked, "Are you really sure?"

He chuckled. "Yes."

With a sigh, I nodded and led the way up the path to the front door. Usually, I'd just walk in, but I'd decided it was best to knock as a warning, hoping they wouldn't be doing anything... I didn't know what exactly, just anything they usually did. Then again, I remembered they knew we were coming and surely, they would be on their best behavior. I checked my phone. It was five minutes past the time we had to be there.

So, with another sigh, I turned the handle and stepped in.

I should have knocked.

Mom was standing on the other side of the couch half crouched down, and Dad was… I didn't want to know honestly, but I couldn't see him.

I was just about to open my mouth when Mom snapped, "Lick it. Just lick it."

"Mom!" I cried when I realized she had a hold of Dad's head in front of her.

She straightened and looked over her shoulder. "Oh, hi."

"Breathe," I heard Carter say from my side with a light voice.

How on earth could he find that scene funny?

"Let Dad up. What are you trying to get him…? No! Actually, I do not want to know." I shook my head again and again.

Carter wheezed a little.

Dad snorted and poked his head up. "Honey, it's not what it looks like—"

"Dad, I don't want to know."

"Ree, don't be silly." Mom rolled her eyes. "Your dad spilled something, and I've just cleaned the house top to bottom. I was making him clean it up. He wasn't going down on me."

I groaned, loudly, and then slapped my forehead.

"Don't," I begged. "Please don't mention that action again in front of me."

"What? Cleaning?" Dad laughed at his own joke and stood. It was then he finally fully took in Carter. "Holy fuck."

"Herb!" Mom scolded. "We don't swear in front of guests." Mom stepped around and walked toward us with her hand held out. Carter stepped just in front of me.

They were about to touch when Dad jumped the couch, wrapped his arm around Mom's waist, and shoved her to the side. He faced Carter, his eyes wide with… something akin to awe, maybe fear, and something else. He seemed a little pale. He placed his hands on Mom's shoulders and shook her a little.

"Do you know who that is?"

"Ree's friend?"

"Do you know who that is?" he asked again.

"Dad," I said gently, easing up to their side.

"Woman, you don't touch greatness without washing your hands first," Dad told Mom.

I groaned. "Dad!" I yelled. "Stop shaking Mom."

He dropped his head in his hands and turned a little green.

"Ah, sir. I'm just Carter Anthony. A friend of your daughter's."

Dad teetered on his feet. I grabbed his arm.

"Herb?"

"Dad?"

He blinked. "He called our daughter his friend," he whispered to Mom, only we all heard. I glanced over my shoulder at Carter, and his lips twitched.

"Herb, I think you need to sit down." We led him over to a chair and sat him down. He looked up and just stared at Carter.

Walking back over to Carter near the door, I started, "I'm so sorry about—"

He grinned. "Don't worry about it."

Mom stepped up. "I'm sorry about my husband, but you must be pretty important for him to lose it like that. I'm Elaine Wild." Her hand came out again. Dad murmured something unintelligible. We all ignored him.

Carter shook Mom's hand. "Carter Anthony. I'm the quarterback to the Wolves football team."

Dad whimpered.

"Ahh, now I understand." Mom nodded. "Herb just watched your game live this morning."

We all glanced at my father; he was still just sitting and staring at Carter. It was even beginning to freak me out.

"So how did you two meet?" Mom asked.

"School," I shot out with. "Carter came into the school I teach at and—"

"That bastard!" Dad cried. "Tom didn't tell me."

And I now understood why Tom never said anything to Dad. Dad was a big fan, one who freaked out upon meeting someone famous apparently.

"You should call him," I suggested, an evil smile lifting my lips. Both Mom and Carter laughed.

"Damn right I will." He stood and quickly stormed off into the kitchen, nearly tripping on his way because his eyes stayed glued to Carter. I figured he thought Carter would disappear on him. He sped around the corner, no doubt to snap up the phone, because in the next second, he appeared again. His eyes went back to Carter while he placed the phone against his ear.

"I think you should be scared," I muttered out the corner of my mouth to Carter. All he did was chuckle.

"No, really. He's even freaking me out the way he's staring at you. He'll probably try to have your baby next."

Dad's eyes narrowed. "That's plain impossible, Reagan." He flicked his eyes to Carter, a blush forming on his cheeks. "My daughter can have babies though."

Mom laughed. Carter grinned, while I cried, "Dad, you can't just offer me up like that."

His hand came up. "Tom. You listen here you little fucker."

"Herb!" Mom snapped harshly.

"Dad!" I cried.

"No. You're on my shit list. Why? You want to know why? I'll tell you why. Guess who's standing in my living room with my daughter after they met at your school."

"Well," I tried to cut in before Dad cut Tom from his life.

"That's right. Carter Anthony."

Dear God. Dad sighed after saying Carter's full name.

"You had him at your school without telling me. Me! Your friend. Your buddy. What? Well, no. I could have. I didn't freak out too bad." Mom and I gave Dad a look. "Shit, maybe I did." He sighed. "Fine. But you owe me big. Next time you bring the beer, even though it's my turn." He quickly hung up the phone.

Carter stepped toward him, and Dad's eyes widened a little. Carter's hand came out. Dad looked down at it, up to him, and then down at it again before gripping it.

"Good to meet you, Mr. Wild."

"Yes. Right. You too, son. You too. Drink? Snack? Chair? A nap?"

Holy hell. Next, he could offer him a blowjob. I had to step in.

"Carter would probably love a beer, Dad. And I'm sure we're having dinner soon. Right?" I asked, turning to Mom.

She snapped out of her dazed look at Dad, probably having never seen him act that way, and nodded. "Yes, dinner. Why don't you and Carter have a seat, and we'll get drinks and check on dinner, which should be ready any second now."

Smiling gratefully, I went over to the couch and sat down. Only I looked back to see Dad still holding Carter's hand.

Groaning, I said, "Dad, let go of Carter so you can get him a beer."

"Right. Yes." He nodded. He dropped Carter's hand and then, to my horror, he placed his arm around Carter's back and led him forcefully over to the couch and helped him sit right next to me. "Stay. Beer. Talk to Reagan." He patted Carter's shoulder. "You know she's single."

"Dad," I hissed.

Carter, with a humorous glint in his eyes, glanced at me. "But I thought she had a boyfriend named James Blunt."

Oh, crap.

I'd forgotten about him.

Dad snorted. "No. She's single and ready to mingle."

"Jesus, Dad."

"What?" he asked in an innocent tone.

"Herb, get in here," Mom called roughly.

"Right." Dad nodded again and glanced from Carter to me. He gave me some type of weird look that apparently I was supposed to know what he meant. When I raised my brows in question, he scowled and then walked off in a huff.

As soon as he was out of sight, I whispered, "It's not too late to leave."

He faced me. "Hell no. I'm having the time of my life."

My head jerked back in shock. I narrowed my eyes. "Are you feeling okay? My dad could come back in here and offer to rub your feet next."

He gave me a sweet smile. "Reagan, it's fine. Once he gets over the shock, he'll be back to normal."

I scoffed. "I doubt that. We're not a normal family."

He winked, and my body shivered. "I like different."

Sweet Mother Mary.

He liked different.

I was different.

"Reagan's always been different," Dad announced as he entered.

Slumping back on the couch, I groaned. "Next you'll try and sell me to Carter."

Dad stopped. He glanced to Carter, his brows rose. "Is that an option?"

"Dad!" I yelled.

"Herb," Mom snapped as she entered. "We talked about this."

"Yeah. Okay." He sighed, and then continued forward with Carter's beer. "Here you go, Carter Anthony."

He was worse than me.

"Just Carter, Mr. Wild."

Dad giggled. Never in my life had I thought Dad would ever giggle, but there it was.

He was going to kill himself after we left.

"You can call me Herb."

"Okay. Thanks, Herb." Carter took the beer from Dad's shaky hand. Mom came forward and handed me a lemonade.

They sat on the couch opposite us.

"Where's Fozzie?" I asked.

Mom rolled her eyes. "He's in a timeout. The monster chewed up a pair of my panties."

I waved my hand around. "Okay, moving on."

Mom snorted, then turned to Carter... uh-oh.

"So, Carter, do you like to play with balls?" Mom asked. It wasn't the question that unnerved me, because Carter did play with balls, it was the way Mom said it, the innuendo in her voice, and her brows rising up and down with it.

Dad gasped. "Elaine."

"Oh my God. Kill me now, please," I begged.

Carter just laughed it off. "I do actually. It's worked out well for me so far."

"I'll say," Dad said with a big proud grin.

I took a sip of my drink to stop myself from laughing, despite my embarrassment. However, the way Carter talked to Mom about football and with the content smile on his face, he didn't seem to mind at all.

It put me at ease, the simple action of taking my parents as they were. Really, who was I to ask them to behave and not be themselves for someone I hardly knew? I shouldn't have, and I was glad they weren't... at least most of the time. But if Dad offered me up again, I was going to trip the idiot up.

A buzzer sounded, and Mom bounced up, and sang, "Dinner's ready."

We all made our way into the dining room. Dad helped Mom dish out the meal and bring it to the table. At first, Carter offered to help, but Dad ushered him into a seat and told him to rest. My eyes widened a fraction before I sat in my chair opposite Carter when I caught Dad leaning into Carter, as if he were either going to smell him or kiss him on the head.

"Dad!" I cried. His body jolted. "Erm, Mom needs help."

"Right," he said and quickly left.

Carter smirked across at me. "Since I've come to dinner at your parents', I think you'll need to come to mine. If my mom found out I was here first, she'd kick me in the ass."

Dinner.

At his parents' place.

Friends did do that… right?

Well, he was here, sitting at my parents' table.

So I supposed I could do that.

I gulped. "Uh, sure?"

His smirk formed into a full grin. "Great."

"What's great?" Mom asked as she entered. Carter stood to help her with the tray of vegetables. She gave him a warm smile.

After he sat back down, and Dad had placed his meat tray on the table, Carter said, "I was saying to Reagan it'd be great if she came to my family's house for dinner one night."

They both looked from him to me. I was sure I saw Dad's eyes tear up.

Mom cleared her throat. "So, um, you two are *just* friends, right?"

"Yes," I said quickly. Then laughed nervously. "Friends. In fact, Carter and I used to go to high school together. Not that we knew each other back then, but we do now, and it's good to have male friends. They're… handy." *Handy? Handy for what?* "For, um, you know, fixing things and, uh, stuff."

"And for protecting," Carter added. My parents' gaze swung his way. A soft pink shaded his cheeks. "Because a woman can never have enough people protecting them from, you know, men and such."

"Right," Dad drew out, then sniffed. "Friends. It's good." He nodded.

"Are you gay?" Mom blurted.

Carter had just taken a drink and then choked, spraying the contents of his mouth to the table in front of him.

"Mom, you can't ask that," I scolded.

"Elaine, he's not gay," Dad growled.

Carter cleared his throat. "No, Mrs. Wild—"

"Elaine."

Carter nodded. "Elaine, I'm not gay."

"Okay then." She smiled, and then looked at me and winked. I ran a hand over my face and groaned. Would I even survive the night? I wasn't so sure.

CHAPTER TWELVE

CARTER

*R*eagan's parents were a damn hoot. Like their daughter, Elaine didn't seem to have a filter. It seemed I wouldn't have to try too hard to win them over, either. In fact, I was sure Herb loved me already. It'd been on the tip of my tongue to take him up on the many offerings of having his daughter, but I refrained.

I had to get Reagan to fall for me as much as her parents were. Actually more.

Throughout dinner, Reagan seemed to relax more. She'd been shocked, embarrassed, and perturbed by her parents and worried on how I would react to them, but it was the best night I'd had in so goddamn long.

It was what I'd wanted all along.

A special someone who would sit around with me and the family, just enjoying each other's company. Someone to share things with. Someone who meant a great deal to me, so much so I'd want to spend the rest of my life with them.

I was already seeing that someone as Reagan.

It was scary as hell, because it was so fast, but I blamed my infatuation back in high school for me wanting to go full-steam ahead.

Reagan was a whole package deal. Funny, sweet, shy, bumbling, hot, and damn amazing. How could I deny what I was already feeling when it was so strong? Even though I was a man's man, I was in touch with my feelings and they were all pointed toward Reagan.

Hell, that sounded cheesy.

Did I care? Not at all.

"—and then I had to go and get a drunk Tom and Dad from the bar after they got kicked out and banned for making a scene," Reagan finished, and I had to laugh. It wasn't about the story, though it was entertaining, or the way Herb cursed her for telling it in the first place. It was because of her giggle. The way her voice tinkled like a little bell, the way her eyes shone with mirth. Her laughter was catching. I wanted to laugh with her because she made people enjoy the story.

"Hmm," Elaine suddenly said. I turned to see she'd been watching me instead of her daughter or husband.

Shit. Could she tell I wanted her daughter?

"Tell me something, Carter," she said. Reagan and Herb's attention went to us.

"Y-yes?" I suddenly felt like my collar on my tee was too tight. Had she seen me look at Reagan in a puppy-dog adoration kind of way? My gut twisted, worried my feelings were out of the bag before I even got to share them with Reagan.

Did I need to move things up?

Should I declare to Reagan right then I wanted to date her before her mom said anything else?

She grinned, and that grin didn't put me at ease.

"Do you have a home in town? I heard you still had a house a few hours away. How does that work? You must get sick of traveling or do you stay someplace in town for when you play? Once your football career is done, since you mentioned coaching before, will you be looking for a job around here?"

What was with the twenty questions?

At least none of them were about my infatuation with her daughter.

So maybe she didn't see anything.

"Mom, Carter doesn't—"

"It's okay, Reagan." I smiled at her. She studied me a moment.

"At least let's head to the living room to get comfy before answering," she suggested.

"Sounds good," Elaine said.

We all stood and started for the living room when I felt my wrist seized. Since Elaine and Herb were in front of me, I knew it wasn't them. I was spun back around, and Reagan got close. She even went up on her tippy-toes to get in my face. "We can go. The back door is just through the kitchen. We can slip out and make a run for it."

I snorted, shaking my head at her, but I did it smiling. Reaching over, I ran my hand up and down the top of her arm, and was pleased to feel her shiver from my touch.

"Honestly, it's a couple of normal questions by concerned parents who know we'll be spending time with each other."

Her eyes widened.

"As friends," I added, and felt like crap for adding it since it was a lie. Perhaps our initial time together would be based on friendship. But I wanted her to know a lot of couples who started out as friends stayed together forever. I just hadn't figured out how to share that yet. And hell, so soon into our "friendship," there was the real fear of moving far too fast for Reagan, possibly enough to send her running. But I was basing the whole friends-to-lovers phenomenon off my parents. They'd started out as friends until Dad wore Mom down to date him—my dad's words—and they were still very much in love.

She licked her lips. I wanted to follow the trail with my own tongue. "Okay." She nodded and dropped my wrist. "But if at any time it gets scary in there, because it could—Mom may bring up your past sexual partners for some reason—then you give me the signal."

I winked. "I will."

When we walked into the living room, Elaine asked, "Anything wrong?"

"Nope," Reagan replied. "All good. Peachy in fact."

"Good." Elaine clapped. "Take a seat you two."

We sat on the couch opposite Elaine and Herb, Reagan close beside me. I noticed Herb quickly glance away. Did the man have tears in his eyes?

What the hell?

Why?

Unless Elaine did see my starry-eyed look at her daughter and she'd told Herb, who no doubt would be overwhelmed with the possibility of Reagan and I being more than friends.

Would they say anything to her?

Push their daughter on me more?

I didn't want that to happen because it could do the opposite and Reagan would probably not want to spend any time with me if her parents were forcing her on me.

"Carter?" Elaine called.

"Ah, yeah. So to answer you're earlier questions, I've been wanting to move back for a while, but until recently, I've been reluctant to leave my beach house."

"But now you want to?"

"Yes, or at the very least keep it to rent out. Then I can have someplace to stay on my holidays."

"So do you enjoy the traveling all the time?" Elaine asked.

"Dad?" Reagan called out to Herb. "Are you okay?"

Elaine scoffed. "He's fine. Allergies are playing up."

Reagan's brows dipped. "But he doesn't have allergies."

Herb sniffed. "I'm good."

Clearing my throat, I answered Elaine's question. "No, I don't actually enjoy it. That's why I've been staying in a hotel on the really long days of meetings, training, and games."

"Why not your parents' home?" Elaine asked.

"Or Dustin's?" Reagan added, with a small frown on her lips.

I shrugged. "Dustin has things going on, North has a one-bedroom apartment, and I didn't want to live with my parents again." Reagan snorted. She understood. No one wanted to ever live with their parents again after moving out. "I'm also waiting to find the perfect place for myself."

"Must be terrible flitting here and there all the time. And hotels aren't always pleasant," Elaine commented.

Running a hand through my hair, I said, "It's not bad."

Elaine slapped her hand down on Herb's leg. He jumped. "I have a perfect idea."

"Oh no," I heard Reagan mutter beside me.

"What's that?" I asked, trying not to laugh.

"You can move in here." Both Herb and Reagan gasped. A big smile soon formed on Herb's and Reagan paled.

"Ah...."

"It's perfect. We have the room, and we're not your parents. You can start renting your place out while you take your time finding the perfect house for yourself. Here would be way better than a hotel." Elaine smiled, her hands rubbing together like an evil genius. I didn't understand it.

Until I saw the panic on Reagan's face.

Could Elaine be playing her daughter? But why?

Reagan stood, then sat back down, only to shift on the seat to the edge while running her hands up and down her thighs.

"He can't," she announced.

"I can't?" I asked.

"Why not?" Herb questioned with a pout.

"Because, he, um, he's moving into my place."

Holy crap.

Holy, holy, crap.

Elaine *was* an evil genius.

"I am?" I questioned slowly and then wanted to slap myself for questioning it in the first place. Hell, if Reagan was offering up her place, I was all for it because it meant more time with her... in her house... in close quarters with the woman I was obsessed with.

Wow.

The day had just gotten better.

"But Carter just said he was living in a hotel," Herb commented.

"I did." I nodded. *Jesus, shut the hell up, man.*

Reagan laughed nervously. "Yes, but, ah, it was just a new idea. I brought it up on the way over here and he, um, he wasn't sure about it, but I think he's, ah, still thinking about it, right?" Reagan asked me. I was starting to get a little worried about how green her face was becoming.

"Yes. That's, uh, right. But I've concluded it's a great idea."

"You did?" Reagan squeaked out.

"Well then, that's fantastic." Elaine beamed. "When are you moving in? In fact, we'll help you move in."

"When?" I asked.

"Yes, when?" she queried.

"Now hang on," Herb said. "I liked the idea of Carter staying here."

Elaine spun her gaze to her husband and glared. Shit, I was even scared of that look.

Herb sat straighter. "Then again, we wouldn't want to cramp your style. Moving in with Reagan would be better than here." He looked at his daughter. "It's nice of you to help out your friend, honey." He paused. "Honey?"

We all glanced at Reagan. She seemed to be in some type of daze, looking down at her lap. Her hands fidgeted with the ends of her summer dress... and what a summer dress it was. It fit her body perfectly.

"Reagan?" Elaine called.

"Present!" she yelled, and then blushed. I stifled my laugh behind my hand with a fake cough. "Sorry." She smiled softly. "I was, um, just thinking of the best day to move Carter in."

"What about next weekend? Saturday, since Carter has a game Sunday?" Herb said.

"S-sure?" she said, and it sounded like its own question. I had to double check Reagan would be okay with it.

"Great." Elaine clapped again, and she seemed so smug with the plan. I didn't blame her; it was pretty brilliant.

Did it mean Elaine and Herb gave me their blessing with their daughter?

I guessed it did.

Hell, I felt myself puff up like a proud peacock.

"Let's have some cake to celebrate. Herb, come and help me in the kitchen." Elaine stood, and when Herb hesitated, she grabbed the neck of his tee and pulled him up.

As soon as they were out of sight, I turned to Reagan, however, before I could say anything she whispered frantically, "You have to move in. If you don't they'll know I lied, I hate lying to my parents. You have to move in—" She gulped. "—with me, into my house, my home… even if it's just for a little while, just so my parents don't catch me in the lie." She shrugged. "I mean, I could tell them you don't want to but I know them, they'll pressure you into moving in with them and that…." She shuddered. "It wouldn't be good. If you did, you'd probably wake in the middle of the night with Dad standing over you just staring down at you. Worse, Mom will follow you around and tell you how important it is to practice safe sex and then you'll find condoms appearing all over the place to make sure you wrap it before you tap it." She turned red after saying that. "You have to move in… with me."

"Okay."

Her eyes widened. "Okay?"

I smiled. "Yeah, okay. I don't mind. We get along great, and you'll be saving me money on a hotel. So really, you're doing me a favor."

She blinked slowly. "Well… okay then."

"Thanks." I smiled.

"Um, no worries?"

"As long as you're sure you don't mind if I move in. I mean, I won't be there much. I have gym in the morning and practice in the afternoon, which makes me tired, so I'll probably just come home and crash after it."

"Oh, sure, it won't be a problem."

CHAPTER THIRTEEN

REAGAN

*I*t won't be a problem?
It was a *big* problem.

The biggest out of anything else that had happened to me.

Carter Anthony was moving in with me, and it was all my parents' fault.

Oh God. Carter was moving into my home, my house, with me.

Insert a huge amount of freak-outs. But I couldn't let him move in with my parents; I wasn't even sure if he would. I just couldn't risk it. He wouldn't survive. Hell, I nearly didn't. Okay, that was a lie. I loved my parents with everything in me, but it would be different for an outsider staying with them all the time. Carter only had a few hours of them; multiply that by all the time, and he would certainly be admitting himself into an insane asylum.

Quite possibly I was overreacting, but I had to justify my outburst for inviting him to live with me somehow.

Brooke sat across from me in the teachers' lounge and just

stared. I'd just told her what had happened since I hadn't spoken to her the night before or that morning.

She blinked, opened her mouth and then closed it.

"Say something," I demanded.

"I...." She sighed. Leaning forward with her elbows on the table, she rubbed at her temples. "Let me get this straight." I nodded. "You and Carter went to dinner at your parents' place, and by the end of it, you have Carter moving in with you this weekend?"

"Yes."

She blinked.

"Well?" I asked, my voice rising, and when people looked our way, I slouched my shoulders.

It was then Brooke leaned back, lifted her face to the ceiling, and burst out laughing.

"Brooke," I hissed.

Her hand came out, waved in front of me, and I knew that meant I had to let her have her episode or she'd never calm down to talk rationally.

Sighing, I leaned back in my chair and glanced around at everyone watching Brooke. Rolling my eyes, I said, "Don't mind her, she's finally lost it." Some nodded in understanding, then all went back to whatever they were doing. Except for Elena. She kept glaring our way. I waved. When she wouldn't look away, I was about to turn my hand around and give her the finger because I wasn't in the mood for her as I was a ball of panic, but Tom suddenly appeared in front of me.

Glancing up, I saw him scowling down at me.

Brooke's laughter waned when she noticed Tom standing next to her.

"You took Carter to dinner at your parents' house," he stated.

"Y-yes?" I hesitated, sure no matter what I said, it would be wrong in that moment.

"Carter Anthony," he confirmed.

I nodded. "He and I are, ah... have become friends."

His jaw clenched. "Where was my invite?"

I blinked slowly like Brooke had only moments before. "Sorry?"

He sighed, his shoulders moved up and down with how big it was. "I didn't get to spend much time with him when he was here. You should have invited me over as well, and now I have your dad ringing me up and bragging how amazing it was to have Carter in his house. How he fed him, laughed with him, and drank with him. Next time I expect an invitation."

"Um, okay... but it's kind of fair since you had Carter here without telling Dad about him visiting."

"And he got that time with George Stutterfield in the shopping center to himself. I wanted one time where I could have bragging rights. One time, Reagan."

"Who's George Stutterfield?" Brooke asked.

Tom's head moved terrifyingly slowly to focus on Brooke. "Never mind," she quickly said.

But it was too late.

"Who's George Stutterfield?" Tom asked in outrage.

Brooke didn't say anything or move. It was too dangerous.

"George Stutterfield is the best wide receiver to the..." He went into detail about who George was, but of course, I tuned it all out because it wasn't information I needed to ever learn. Instead, I went back to eating my sandwich and waited for him to finish.

A moment later had my head snapping up. "Reagan?"

"Sorry?" I asked, swallowing my last bite.

"Tell me if Carter is ever having dinner with your dad again so I can be there."

"Sure." I nodded.

"You know," Brooke said, gaining Tom's attention. From the demonic look in her eyes, I knew she was going to throw me under the bus since I'd left her to deal with Tom's rant over George Stutterfield. "Carter's moving in with Reagan this weekend. You should come help."

For a while, Tom looked like he wasn't breathing. His face

turned bright red. He opened and closed his mouth like an oxygen-deprived fish.

"Tom, are you okay?" I asked.

"Carter," was all he said.

"Yes. That's right, Carter," I said gently.

"He's moving in with you?"

"Yes." I nodded. Why did he look like I just kicked a puppy? "Is that a problem for you?"

"You. Accident prone. You could hurt him."

I scoffed. "He'll be fine."

Suddenly, he pulled out the chair next to Brooke, and slumped down in it while muttering to himself, "Everyone around me is crazy."

"Things will be fine," I reassured him, and he glared. Of course he wouldn't believe me. "I won't harm him. There'll be no house fires, no obstacles, or slippery tiles for him to hurt himself on so he can still play football while he lives with me."

"Promise?"

Rolling my eyes, I nodded.

"Reagan, promise," he growled out.

Damn. I had to live up to my promise. I wasn't the tidiest person, but I'd make sure I left nothing around for Carter to fall over. "Okay, fine. I promise."

"Good." He stood. "I'll be at your place on Saturday. I presume it's Saturday since Carter has a game Sunday."

"Yes."

"Great. I'll be there bright and early." He started to walk away.

"Not too early," I called. He waved me off.

I glanced at Brooke; she had a smug smile. "That wasn't fair."

"Neither was you leaving me to listen to him. Besides, I did it for my entertainment as well. I plan to be there Saturday just to watch them fawn over Carter. Was your dad really that bad?"

I winced. "Worse. He hugged Carter before we left, and I was sure he was about to kiss him on the cheek until I pulled him back."

Brooke started cackling. "I can't wait for Saturday."

"I can," I muttered, and took a sip of my juice.

"Come on, you'll be fine living with Carter."

I gave her an unimpressed look. "Really?"

"Okay." She grinned. "It's a disaster waiting to happen."

Yes. Yes, it was.

"All right, class, let's go over the first line again. Then I want you to tell me what it implies about women. 'It is a truth universally acknowledged, that a single man in possession of a good fortune, must be in want of a wife.'"

Wesley's hand shot up.

"Yes?" I asked, pointing to him.

"It implies that women should get up in the rich guy's grill because they deserve all women's attention because he's rolling in the money."

Dear God.

Sighing, I pointed to Bradly just as his hand lowered. "Sorry, Miss. I was gonna say the same as Wesley."

Clenching my teeth, I moved on. "Forget that one. Next—"

"Miss?" Jenifer called.

"Yes?"

"Is it true that Mr. Anthony is moving in with you?"

I blanched. I even *felt* it.

The students started murmuring among themselves.

"Is it?" Michael called.

"No way," I heard a male student say.

"That'd be so cool. He's hot," a girl said.

"Maybe she could get him to come back in," someone else mentioned.

"Class," I called, coming out of my state of shock. Everyone quieted. "Jenifer, where did you hear that from?"

"I overheard a conversation."

"Who?"

She smirked. "I can't say."

Damn, so I won't find out who I needed to kill.

"So is it true?" Michael asked again.

Did I lie to them? Obviously they hadn't seen the news article and since no one else had picked up on it, thankfully, I was scot-free to voice a little lie.

Would it be safer for me and Carter?

But I didn't like to lie... much. Little ones to my students were okay, like when I told them that quadratic equations were important, and they should behave more in math to learn them. At the time, I'd just felt bad for Harrold, the older math teacher, who'd since left because he didn't want to put up with little punks any longer.

"Um...."

What did I say?

For the first time in my life, I wished Tom would burst in checking up on me or someone would pull the fire alarm. Anything would have been good instead of having each and every eye on me while they waited for my answer.

It felt like their stares were burning into my mind.

Little shits.

"Okay, so the thing is..." To hell with it. "Carter was in a tight spot, and I offered him a room for only a little while." I was sure they would find out sooner or later and it would probably be better to actually hear it from me so nothing would be taken out of context. Then again, they could be just using this time to get out of work.

They started again to talk amongst themselves in giddy voices.

It was then my mind ran over something else. What would happen if Elena found out? I didn't want to find out because I was sure it would lead to me not breathing.

I could be overreacting, but I had to be careful.

"Quiet down," I shouted. When they did, I added, "This information doesn't leave this room." Bradly's hand shot up. "And no, Bradly, none of you can come over for dinner." He lowered his hand.

Who was I kidding? The rumor, or truth really, would be flying all over the school by the end of the day.

My belly dropped.

I hoped Brooke would pick out a nice casket for me.

When the bell rang, I jumped. My nerves were on high alert as I walked out of my classroom at the end of the day. Surely my students didn't have time to spread the rumor before school finished. On Mondays, I was their last class of the day. A triple period of English would usually kill a student, but this class didn't seem to mind.

I'd just rounded the corner, entering the last hallway to freedom when Elena stepped out in front of me. I screamed. She glared.

"Carter's moving in with you."

"What? Really?" I huffed. "I didn't know."

Her glare darkened. "Don't play stupid with me."

My tense shoulders dropped. "Okay. Yes, he is. It's not because there's anything between us, we're just friends." I felt like I had to tell her that because I didn't want her to think I was trying for her ex... and deep down, *way deep down*, I didn't want to hurt her feelings. Okay, so maybe I also said it to remind myself, once again, Carter and I were just friends.

Her face brightened and then she laughed. "You thought I would think there was something going on between you two. Oh, that's hilarious."

Straightening, I scowled. "It's not that funny."

"It is. I just wanted to catch you and get you to tell Carter if he wants to move in with me instead, I'm sure it'd be better than with you."

Was she serious or just stupid? She was laughing at me and yet wanted a favor from me.

I was going to go with stupid.

"Sure, Elena, I'll mention it to him. But why don't you just call him?"

She stiffened. "I didn't grab his number."

"Oh, he didn't give it to you?" I questioned evilly. Then added, "Huh."

"Huh? What does huh mean?"

"Nothing." I paused. "It's just, if Carter wanted you to have his number, he would have given it. So since he didn't give you his number, I don't think he'll move in with you, but still, I'll be sure to pass on your message."

She looked confused. "Whatever," she snipped and then moved around me, walking off.

Honestly, I didn't know who won there or if anyone needed to win. Speaking with Elena confused me as much as my words confused her.

I was just happy she understood Carter wouldn't be moving in with her. At least, I thought she understood.

On the walk home, I couldn't help but go over how Elena considered it funny that Carter would be interested in me.

From what Brooke said, there was a chance Carter and I could be something more than friends, but I couldn't think about it, especially since Carter was moving in with me.

We'd be housemates, and that was it.

I had to think that way, to overrule my overexcited beating heart.

Living with Carter Anthony was either going to be amazing or be the end of me.

My thoughts ground to a halt momentarily just as a new thought popped in there unbidden. What happened if he wanted to bring someone home? I wasn't sure I could handle that. I'd probably have to run out and find some stranger to take home and sleep with so he wouldn't think I was crying into my pillow about him plowing into some woman.

Oh my God. What was I thinking?

Sex with some stranger?

While Carter hip locked with another woman under my roof?

Yep, I was going to go insane living with Carter. Quite possibly more insane than I already was.

CHAPTER FOURTEEN

REAGAN

Saturday came too fast. Way too fast. Carter had invited Brooke and me to some charity game Friday night, but I didn't want to face Carter's family just yet, plus I had to clean out the spare room. In doing that, more fear bombarded me because when I'd offered Carter the room, I'd forgotten how close it was to *my* room. As in, right next door to it. What happened if I needed to masturbate? Would he hear? Or if I blew my nose? Worst of all, what happened if I needed to fart? I couldn't let one go in case Carter heard through the wall. I wasn't sure how thick the walls were, but I wasn't going to risk letting one go.

God, my stomach was going to hate me in the end.

It was already on the way since my nerves were all over the place.

Loud knocking on my front door got me out of bed. My pulse kicked up its pace. It was only six in the morning. Carter couldn't have been here already.

I dragged my exhausted body down the hall and into the living room. Glancing down, I realized I should have probably dressed; I was still wearing my nightie and sleep socks. I peeked through the curtain from the living room window beside the front door and held my breath. It was only Tom.

Tom?

What in the world was he doing here so early?

Not caring what the hell I looked like since it was Tom, I went to the door, unlocked it and swung it open.

"Is he here yet?" was the first thing out of his mouth.

"Good morning to you too." I gestured down at my attire. "Does it look like he's here and moving in when I've only just got out of bed, and it's only six in the damn morning?"

He took in my pj's. "Huh, I'll get the coffee on then." He pushed past and headed for the kitchen, calling over his shoulder, "You'd better get dressed before everyone arrives."

I blanched at "everyone," but I couldn't even deal with Tom. Rather than crawling back into bed, which was what I truly wanted to do, instead, I grumbled to myself about rude early people and headed back into my room to grab leggings and a long top.

Just as I opened the bathroom door, I heard boomed, "What in the hell are you doing here?"

"Herb," Mom warned.

"What? He can't be here. This is *my* day. My Carter and my daughter."

Tom scoffed. "This is *my* employee and *my* Carter, who I met first."

Darn it. I threw my dirty clothes into the laundry room as I ran past on my way into the kitchen. As soon as I entered, Dad turned to me and demanded, "You invited him." He pointed to Tom, who leaned back against my counter and sipped his coffee, smirking.

"Blame Brooke. She mentioned it to him."

"Goddamn it. This moment is mine," Dad said, stamping his foot.

"Herb, how about you start acting your age and get over it," Mom suggested.

"Agreed," I stated. "You two need to stop taunting each other and hug it out or I'll... tell Carter he can't move in and we can't be friends. Then you both won't get to see him."

Both Dad and Tom gasped.

"Fine. I can forgive him for George if he can forgive me for not telling him about Carter coming to the school," Tom said; it would have been better if he wasn't glaring at Dad while saying it. Though Dad was just as bad and scowled back.

"Fine," Dad bit out.

"Now, honey," Mom warned as she fixed herself a coffee and Tom handed me one. "Do you have a plan of action for today? Do you know what he's bringing? Will there be enough room in your house for his things?"

When I stared at her blankly and took gulps of coffee, she sighed.

"Jesus," Tom groaned.

"Reagan, do you know anything about what Carter is bringing?" Dad asked.

"Um... no."

We hadn't actually spoken during the week. There'd been a few texts here and there, but nothing about him moving in. I guessed it was because he probably knew I was unsure of it even after I forced it upon him, so maybe he hadn't brought it up because he was afraid of scaring me off. I was doing a damn good job of that on my own.

We'd been friends for two weeks.

Two. Weeks.

And he was moving in.

One good thing about it was that at least I knew he wasn't a murderer. He was in the public eye too much to go off and kill someone. But other than that, I didn't know much about him. He played football. He dated Elena in high school. He liked action movies and documentaries, and for some strange reason, he wanted to be friends with me. And he took my family and me as we came. Well, so far he did.

Right, I had to get through the day and see if Carter was still okay living here. Especially after having spent more time with me and my family.

The front door opened, and I was sure my heart rolled over in my chest. I glanced through the breakfast window to see Brooke walk in. "Morning," I called, relieved it wasn't Carter yet. I hadn't even finished my first coffee.

"Morning, there's a car pulling up out front. I think it's Carter."

Well damn.

Behind me, I heard a clatter. I turned to see Tom's mug was on the counter and he and Dad were moving. They got stuck in the kitchen doorway, both shoving at each other.

"Let me through," Dad snapped.

"You let me through," Tom barked.

Brooke entered the living room, caught sight of Tom and Dad struggling and started laughing. Dad finally managed to get through first and made a dash for the front door. On the way, he glared at Brooke. "We'll be having words." Before she could reply, he was off outside with Tom on his heels.

Brooke looked at me and Mom. "What was that about?"

I rolled my eyes. "He's upset with you for telling Tom Carter's moving in."

"Oh." She grinned.

Mom sighed. "Come on, we better get out there before they start fighting over either carrying Carter inside or his things."

"Good thinking." I nodded, and quickly finished off my coffee before making my way out the front just behind Brooke. Only Brooke stopped abruptly, so I crashed into her and then Mom into me. We all stumbled forward. A giggle erupted from my previously tense body when I realized what had Brooke slamming on her brakes. Dad and Tom were in front of Carter, trying to talk at the same time. Clearly bewildered, Carter's gaze switched back and forth quickly to each man, like he was at a tennis match. However, I didn't think it was that scene that stopped Brooke. It was the fact Dustin stood beside Carter.

Tom and Dad were also fawning over him. Heck, Dustin was even blushing from something one of them said, which had Carter chuckling.

"We need to save them," I whispered to Mom and Brooke.

"Let's do it." Mom nodded and cracked her fingers, like she thought she was going to be in for a fight. She strode forward first. I followed, only to turn around to see Brooke remained in one spot. I took her hand in mine and dragged her with me.

"His loss, remember?" I mumbled to her as we approached.

"Yes." She nodded.

"Morning," Mom called cheerily. "Herb and Tom, do you think you two can step back and let the fellas through?"

They did, complaining under their breaths.

"Hey," I said with a lame wave. "Ah, my parents made me realize I have no idea what you're bringing. Do you have a truck coming with some more stuff?"

His truck seemed to be loaded full, but I was sure a man like Carter would have more items. Like furniture.

"Nope, this is it. I presumed your house would be furnished, so I didn't bother with anything except a few personal items. When I find a renter, I'll store my furniture and then after I'm in my own place, I'll shift it all then. That was okay, right? You do have furniture?"

Smiling, I rolled my eyes. "Yes, even a spare bed so you don't have to sleep on the floor." Now I wished I didn't have one. Then I could have offered to share mine like the good housemate I was going to be. With a shake of my head, I clapped. "Let's get started then, and it should be done in no time." I wondered if I could keep Brooke and my parents, even Tom, around the whole day after he was settled in so I wouldn't have to be alone with him.

Then again, I did have to get used to it.

I was sure, however, I could find other things to keep me occupied and out of the house like going to the movies, or perhaps I could start a dog walking business. Actually no, Fozzie put me off that idea. I had a few hours to think of something else though.

"Hi, Dustin, did you come to help?" I asked.

"Sure did, but I didn't realize you'd have so much help already. Hey, Brooke."

Out the corner of my eye, I noticed Brooke tense. Her face shaded red and she blurted, "How's Benjie?"

Dustin smiled. "He's good. With his momma this weekend."

Brooke nodded.

Everything went silent.

"Right," I said. "Tom and Dad, since you've met both guys, how about you start unpacking Carter's truck." They got down to work and only fought a couple of times on who was going to unhook the tarp. "Dustin, this is my mom, Elaine. Mom, Dustin. Also a football player."

Dustin stepped up, took hold of Mom's outstretched hand and then brought it up to his lips and kissed the back of it. Mom sighed dreamily.

"Lovely to meet you, Elaine."

Mom giggled. "You too, Dustin."

"Elaine," Dad barked. "Come here." For the first time, Dad glared at Dustin. To my horror, Mom curtsied to Dustin and headed toward Dad. He glared over her head at Dustin.

Carter laughed. "Guess I'm still his favorite."

"Damn," Dustin commented with a smile.

Dad knew Mom was a looker. He'd told me it was his burden to bear since he'd managed to snag her as his; he knew he'd have to put up with every man and his dog drooling over her. But it didn't stop him from turning into the possessive male we saw before us.

Dear God... he just ran a finger across his throat at Dustin.

"Dad," I yelled. "Stop threatening him."

He huffed, grabbed a box and followed Tom and Mom into the house.

"Dustin, whatever you see or hear here today, please don't be scared. My family is a little—"

"Crazy," Brooke said with a grin. "It's why I love them." She then swatted me on the ass and trotted off to the back of Carter's truck.

"All good, babe. As long as that's a thing in the family, slapping butts, I could get used— Fuck." He coughed as Carter elbowed him in the side. "I'll keep my hands to myself." He shook his head, scowling at Carter as he passed him.

We stared at each other.

"Um, are you still okay with staying here?"

Please say no and run for your life.

"Yes." He smiled. My knees wobbled.

"Okay. Then, ah, let's do it."

"As in me move in?" he asked.

I tilted my head to the side in confusion. "Yes, what else would I mean?"

"Nothing." He shook his head and then went to grab his own box.

Following him, I asked, "Where will you store your things when you rent your place out?" His truck was stacked full and high. I took a smaller one and then a pillow from the back seat.

Which was a bad, bad move.

The pillow smelled like him.

I wanted to lift it to my nose and inhale deeply.

Just one sniff.

No, Reagan, you'll look like a weirdo.

However, when Carter started up the path before me, I took the chance to bring it up to my nose and drew in a breath.

My belly swirled.

Carter Anthony's scent was one any woman would masturbate over.

"Dustin was— Did you just smell my pillow?"

Oh, snap.

He must have looked over his shoulder.

In a panic, I laughed nervously, snorted, scoffed, and rolled my eyes. "No," I said, and then threw the pillow to the ground guiltily. Then I remembered it was his pillow and that was rude, so I quickly adjusted the smaller box to my hip and picked it up. Only I held it down at my side.

While heat rose on my face, Carter grinned at me. He then chuckled, before turning and continuing. "What I was saying was Dustin's offered or I might just get a storage unit."

I took the chance to move past my stalker move and quickly offered, "I have a garage with hardly anything in it. You could use that also when the time comes."

"Thanks." He nodded with a warm smile.

We entered the house, and the hostess in me took over. "The house isn't that big. This is the living room. Through to the left are the dining room and kitchen. Then right down the hallway are the bedrooms, bathroom, and laundry. I'll show you your room." I made my way through the living room to the hall and down past the bathroom to the second bedroom of the house.

"—he told me once he doesn't like his testes being restricted, which is why he's a boxer guy. I prefer a tighter type of boxer... just in case anyone was wondering," Dustin said, picking up some boxers from within a box.

"We weren't," Dad replied.

"Jesus Christ, Dustin," Carter cried. He lunged for his boxers and snapped them out of his hands, shoving them back in the box and closing it. "Is nothing sacred with you?"

"What? We're all guys here—"

"Hey!" Brooke snapped.

Dustin winced. "Oops, sorry, forgot you were in the room."

Brooke clenched her jaw, threw the box she was unpacking to the floor, then stormed out. How freaking dare he upset her. After stalking over to Dustin, I placed the box on the bed and then slapped Dustin upside the head.

"What was that for?" he cried.

With a glare, I shook my head at him, then spun to follow Brooke out. Only to quickly return and place Carter's pillow, which I'd been clutching to my chest, on the bed.

"You two don't know what you've got yourself into hanging with them," I heard Tom say.

Dad snorted.

"What did I do?" Dustin asked.

"Is he always stupid?" Dad asked.

I caught Carter's, "Yep," before I stepped into the living room. With no Brooke in sight, I went into the kitchen. She was standing in there with Mom.

"How come you're not unpacking, Mom?"

She scoffed. "Your father didn't want me in the room while Dustin's in there. I got demoted to coffee and snack duty."

"Maybe it's for the best. He's a douche." I glanced to Brooke; her eyes were down on the floor. "You okay?"

She huffed out a breath. "Fine."

"What happened?" Mom asked. I shook my head slightly. She nodded. "The only advice I can give you both, without knowing fully what's going on, is that men can screw up, a lot, and sometimes it's good to just forgive their stupidity. Other times it's better to make them pay while they grovel for forgiveness."

Brooke straightened. "Another thing to do would be to go out tonight, get tanked and sleep with a random to get over everything."

Mom gave me wide eyes. "Ah, maybe. I mean, you're not attached to anyone, but be sure he's not a criminal and will use protection."

Sheesh, Mom sure gave sound advice… sometimes.

CHAPTER FIFTEEN

CARTER

We all stared at Dustin after Reagan left. He glanced from each of us and finally stopped on me. "How am I stupid?"

"If you weren't on the Wolves, I'd hit you myself," Tom stated.

He threw his hands up in the air. "Why?"

Herb opened his mouth to reply when Tom placed his hand on Herb's arm and then shook his head. Herb nodded. "You're right. He needs to learn on his own."

"And if he doesn't, we kick his ass. Just not too much. He'll have to play still."

Chuckling, I placed my box on the bed and straightened. "Where are you going?" Dustin was moving toward the door.

"Obviously I need to figure out what I did. I'm going to ask the women."

Herb laughed.

Tom snorted.

I shook my head at him. He wasn't gone long when I said, "Maybe I should check on him."

"Could be wise." Herb nodded. "He is entering a kitchen full of women, and they have weapons close by."

Shit.

I rushed out of the room but stopped when I spotted Dustin at the end of the hall. I could also hear Herb and Tom following me. I stepped behind Dustin and whispered, "What are you doing?"

"They're talking," he hissed.

"So?"

"Listen," he ordered.

Leaning in—Herb and Tom close to our backs—we heard Elaine say, "The only advice I can give you both, without knowing fully what's going on, is that men can screw up *a lot*. Sometimes it's good to just forgive their stupidity. Other times it's better to make them pay while they grovel for forgiveness."

Brooke replied, "Another thing to do would be to go out tonight, get tanked and sleep with a random to get over everything."

"Ah, maybe. I mean, you're not attached to anyone, but be sure he's not a criminal and will use protection," Elaine said, her voice steady.

Then Reagan said, "While sleeping with someone could be nice —" I didn't hear the rest, my ears started ringing at thoughts of Reagan sleeping with some random. It didn't sit right in my chest or gut.

Hands grabbed my arms. I tried to struggle free, to run into that damn kitchen and order Reagan that she wouldn't be joining Brooke and most definitely wouldn't be sleeping with anyone but me.

"Christ, it's like working with a train. Calm down, son," Herb ordered, backing me down the hall with Tom's help. "Hey," he snapped in my face. My eyes fixed on his. "Sorry for snapping, son, but you can't go in there half-cocked and ready to take charge. I know my girl, and her back will come up. There'll be a fight because she doesn't like anyone telling her what to do."

Hell, I'd just lost it in front of her dad.

He must have read the panic on my face because he laughed. "Elaine's good at reading people and even Tom mentioned you liking my daughter." He sniffed and patted me on the shoulder. "Even though you're a brilliant football player, who's a god on the field, you won't win me over until you've won my daughter. She's our world, and if you hurt her in any way, I'm going to have to make you pay. I won't enjoy doing it, but I will for Reagan."

"And I'd help him," Tom added. "But are you sure you don't want a psychological evaluation first?"

"Hey," Herb barked. "That's my daughter."

Tom raised his brows and waited.

Herb rolled his eyes. "She takes after her mom. She's unique, but has the biggest heart out of anyone I know."

"I know," I said. It was why I wanted to be in her life. She was smart, loving, playful, funny… just amazing.

Loud voices caught our attention. I started back down the hall once again with Herb and Tom at my back. We stepped into the living room.

"Quiet," Reagan yelled. The room fell silent. She put her hands on her hips and gave a stern look to the newcomers. "I thought I told you no one was to come over."

"Sorry, Miss, but we were in the neighborhood, and we were like, 'Hey, Miss Wild lives just there. I bet she'd like a visit from her favorite students.'" I recognized Bradly at the front of three other kids from one of Reagan's English classes.

Reagan groaned, her head dropping back, eyes to the ceiling. Walking to her side, I noticed the guys spotting me.

"Hey, Mr. Anthony." Bradly smiled.

"Hi, Mr. Anthony," Wesley said with a wave.

"S'up, Mr. Anthony." Michael gave me a chin lift.

"Carter, I didn't—"

I placed my hand on her lower back, and she stopped talking. I'd never noticed if she'd done it before or not, but it sure could come in handy for the future. If she ever got pissed at me, all I had to do was touch her, and she'd stop ranting.

"It's okay," I reassured her. "Glad you guys popped in. We could use some help."

"Really?" Wesley asked, excitement in his voice.

"Sure." I nodded. "You can help me and Dustin unload the truck while the others unpack stuff inside, yeah?"

"Dustin?" Michael muttered.

I nodded, just as I heard the bathroom door open. "Whoa, I wouldn't go in there for a while."

"Holy—"

"Bradly," Reagan snapped.

"Ah, holy cubical, that's Dustin Grant."

"Hey," Dustin said.

"I think I'm gonna pee myself," Wesley mumbled.

"Wesley—" Reagan started, but I ran my hand up her back.

"It's all right."

She turned to me. "Are you sure?"

"Yeah." I nodded.

"Okay," she whispered.

Winking, I left her there and walked past the guys. "Come on, let's get me moved in."

By lunch, we had all boxes out of my truck and in the house. Herb and Tom thought it'd be a good idea to grill some meat out back, and I was surprised at the size of the outside space. There was a back patio where the ladies sat and watched, and Dustin and I were down one end of the lawn while we tossed the ball to the other end with Reagan's students.

Dustin was standing next to me when he said, "What do you think of Brooke?"

After tossing the ball to Wesley, I said, "She's nice. Funny."

"Yeah," he agreed.

"Dust, don't fuck around with her."

"I won't. I think I hurt her feelings earlier."

I gave him a dumbfounded look. "You think?"

"Yep. She hasn't spoken to me since. She's good with Benjie." He threw the ball, and it landed in Wesley's arms, but not before smashing into his face. Blood poured out of his nose.

"Wesley!" Reagan cried. She was up and out of her chair running for him. "Let me see," she ordered as he tried to fight her off. But she cupped both cheeks and lifted his head.

Damn. It was a scene I could see her doing with our kids.

Our kids?

I was already jumping into having kids with her when she didn't even know I wanted her.

Jesus.

"You okay?" I asked Wesley, stopping at their side.

"Yeah," he mumbled, and when he did, blood splattered around his mouth.

Reagan paled and swayed.

"Ree?" I questioned.

"I-I'm good," she whispered.

"Sorry about that, kid," Dustin said.

"No worries," he replied, and more blood splattered down onto his tee.

Reagan again swayed.

I closed in to her back and took her hands in mine, a giddy little thrill spreading throughout me at touching her. I pried her hands off Wesley's face and tucked her into me. Jesus, she felt so right in my arms. "Dustin will get Wesley cleaned up. Let's get you sitting down."

All she managed was a nod. With my arm around her shoulders,

I walked her back up to the patio, turned her and sat her between Brooke and Elaine.

"She's never been good with blood," Elaine explained.

I smiled. "It's okay. She doesn't need to see it then."

"Lunch is ready," Herb called. Bradly and Michael came running. Elaine stood and gestured me into the seat next to Reagan. Since I wanted to make sure she was okay, I took it. Reagan stayed quiet for a while as we all sat around and talked while eating. I tried to get her to have a burger, but she refused, breathing deeply through her nose.

We cleaned up after lunch, and I made sure there was a plate for when Reagan was feeling better later. I didn't want to get back to unpacking and leave her, but I also wanted it all done so there wouldn't be anything to do after everyone left and Reagan and I had our first night together. People filtered back inside, but I stayed put until they'd all left, wanting to make sure Reagan was fine.

"Are you going to be okay?" I asked.

She nodded.

"Ree, I need a verbal answer," I said. My lips twitched when her eyes widened after I used her nickname her close friends and family did.

"I will."

"Promise?"

"Yes. Sorry about that, but, um, blood and my stomach don't mix. Is Wesley okay now?"

"If you count the two hamburgers, four chicken sticks, and one hot dog he ate as okay, then yes."

She giggled. "I think he'll be fine."

"Besides, it'll give him something for him to brag about at school."

She grinned. "That's true." Then her grin faded. "Carter, I'm not sure...." I tensed, but she didn't notice as she stared off into the backyard, biting her bottom lip. Then she sucked in a deep breath and turned to me. "Um, having you move in is fine, but... I worry for your sake."

"Why?"

"I don't have a filter. I always say random crazy things. My family and friends are just as loco as I am. I'm sure people will come over more often knowing you're living here. You won't get to relax. You'll be living in a funny farm instead of what you probably need, peace and quiet after training and games."

Wanting, no, needing to touch her, I reached out to take her hand in mine. Hers shook a little. "Reagan, none of anything you just said bothers me. In fact, I look forward to it all. I know I'll also enjoy getting to know you. But I don't want you to feel pressured to have me here. If it stresses you out, then I can stop everything and leave."

She shook her head. "No. I, um, I don't mind. I just wanted you to be sure."

"I am."

She nodded, her gaze ran over my face, and I was sure they lingered on my lips before she brought them up to my eyes. "Okay then, and, ah, I'm looking forward to getting to know you as well, Carter."

"Good." She seemed to relax a bit more, which I was glad about. "I better get back in there." She nodded. I gave her hand a squeeze and stood, walking back inside, but of course I looked back to see if she was watching and caught her gaze on my butt. Smiling to myself, I pretended I didn't see her and went through the door.

CHAPTER SIXTEEN

REAGAN

*E*veryone had gone. I was alone in the house with Carter, and where was I? In my bedroom being a chicken. I'd just had another shower as moving someone in was a dirty job. Admittedly, I couldn't help but wish I was dirty for another reason. *Best not go there, Reagan.*

It had been bad enough when Carter had touched me innocently the few times during the day. My body wanted to melt and drop to the floor from the intense reactions from just one touch.

One touch and I was about to jump him.

Thank God, I'd been rational enough to know it would be bad to do in front of everyone.

Though I still couldn't believe he was living with me.

A knock sounded at my door. I jumped, then bounced up. "Yes?" I called, crossing my arms over my chest and then I thought that would look defensive, like I didn't want him in my room, so I uncrossed them and placed them on my hips.

My door opened, and Carter's handsome face appeared. He took me in, his eyes widened a fraction before they went back to normal. "I was wondering if you'd be okay with pizza for dinner. I could call one through now."

"Oh, um, yes, or I could cook."

He shook his head. "We've had a busy day. Let's just relax in front of the TV with a pizza. Sound good?"

My heart warmed.

"Yes."

"Great, anything you don't like on it?"

"Anchovies."

"Got it." He winked and shut my door again. I then took stock and glanced down, my eyes widening. I was in a damn towel.

Carter had seen *me* in a towel.

Heck, I shrugged. I'd talked about naked yoga with him. This was nothing. I just had to roll with things. Treat Carter like I did Brooke and not care what he saw while living with me.

I got dressed in my flannel pink pajama pants and a loose tee. Sucking in a deep breath, I opened my door and made my way down the hall. Coming into the living room, I saw Carter sitting on the couch thumbing through his phone.

"Pizza's ordered," he announced.

"Great," I said with a smile and sat at the opposite end of the couch. "What do you want to watch? I'm sorry, but unless you want me asleep within seconds, it won't be a documentary."

He laughed. "That's okay. Can't bore you to death. What about just a sitcom?"

"I could do that."

"Or..."

My pulse went crazy with that one word.

Or we could make out?

Or we could grope each other?

Or we could look at his naked body?

Or we could what?

"Or?" I asked, and dang it for coming out all breathy.

"Or we could play twenty questions."

"Oh," slipped out before I could snap my lips together.

Carter smirked. "You don't sound happy with that idea."

"No." I shook my head. "That sounds like fun."

"All right, I'll go first. What day do you like best?"

"Saturday."

"Same. Our morning trainings are usually more relaxed than the rest so we don't injure ourselves before a game. Why for you?"

Because he moved in on a Saturday.

"Um, the same really. Saturday's are just easier." He nodded. "Okay, my turn. What's your favorite food?"

"Pasta."

"What type?"

"Any kind and I'll eat it. What about you?"

"Chocolate croissants." For some reason, I blushed, and for a split second, I wished I'd have said some type of fruit or a salad, something healthy. But screw it. I was glad I told him the truth.

I am who I am, and I'm happy. That's the most important thing in life. Happiness.

"I'll have to pick some up one morning after my run."

And I'd have to marry him if he did that.

"What, um, what time do you run in the morning?"

"Five."

My eyes widened. "As in 5:00 a.m.?"

He chuckled. "Yes."

"Wow, that's early, and then you go to the gym, right?"

He nodded and lifted his leg up so his ankle rested on his knee. "After my run, I come back and have a protein shake, then head to the gym and work out for a few hours, have brunch, then catch up on things before I head to training. On game days, I get in a run before heading to the stadium, it warms me up."

"You never get tired of it?"

"I do. It's another reason why I'm looking at retiring. Still, when I do, I'll work out, just not as much."

"Aren't you young to be retiring?"

He shrugged. "It can happen at any age really. Depends on what injuries we have to deal with. My knee's not as strong as it used to be, so I'd rather get out before I do more damage." He rocked his leg my way, his bare foot knocking into my leg. "Why did you want to become a teacher? And why English?"

It was my turn to shrug. "My dad I guess. He's a teacher too, but a substitute, so casual. When I was younger, I used to love it when he came home from school and told me all these stories about what happened during the day. It always sounded like so much fun. One day I got to go to his high school with him. I think I was about eight and at the time he was teaching a sophomore class. I got to see the way the students listened with rapt attention to him. They respected him and how he taught. I wanted that."

"You've got it. Even in the short time I got to see it, I could tell that class loved you teaching them."

Another blush hit my cheeks. "I'm glad."

"You should be, you help shape young minds... even when threatening them."

My mouth lifted in a big smile. "They enjoy me being my strange self."

"I can understand why. Though you're not strange. You haven't met my family yet."

"I've met your dad and brothers, and they seemed normal to me."

"Just wait and see when they're all together."

"Do you have more siblings?" I couldn't remember more at high school. However, I hadn't stalked him back then. Not that I did now either. I didn't have to; he was living with me.

"I have a sister."

"Wait, let me guess her name. Cameron?"

He chuckled. "No."

"Carmen?"

He shook his head, smiling.

"Clarissa?"

"Nope."

"Does it start with a c?"

"Yes."

"Claire?"

"No."

"Courtney?"

"Yes."

"Yay. What about your mom. Does she start with a *C* also?"

"No, her name is Beth. But as you can tell, she's always liked names starting with it. Even the family cat had one. Clara."

There was a knock at the front door. Carter stood as I did. "I'll just grab my purse," I said.

"I've got it." He walked toward the door.

"But—"

"It's fine. You grab the next one."

"Deal." I nodded, and then went into the kitchen for some plates and soft drinks. I was amazed at how easy it was to talk with Carter. Doing so, made me smile a lot. Getting to know him, know the man he'd grown into was exciting too. Never would I ever have thought the boy I used to crush on would come back into my life and want to be friends. Then be willing to move in with me because of my parents' conniving ways. Carter could have said no, though.

When I entered the living room, Carter was just shutting the front door. "Hope you like passionfruit soft drink."

"I'll drink anything," he replied. We sat back down on the couch. He placed the pizza on the coffee table, and I passed him a plate. He opened the box, put two slices on and then handed it back over to me and grabbed the other plate for himself.

That was sweet, serving me first.

After a bite, and swallowing, since I didn't want to share with him my chewed-up pizza, I mentioned, "We kind of got off track before. Did you still want to do twenty questions?"

"Sounds good."

"Not sure who's turn it is, but I'll go." I grinned, which he returned and nodded. "Okay, favorite movie?"

"*Transformers*. And before you ask, the first one is the best. Can't beat the Autobots."

"True. I love all of those, but mine, at the moment anyway, is *Baywatch*."

He snorted. "Zac Efron or The Rock fan?"

"The Rock, of course."

He rolled his eyes and grinned. "Of course."

While we ate, we talked, and it just got better and better. My nerves were held at bay. It made chatting easy, natural even. I was honest with my answers, and as far as I knew, Carter was too. We got to know one another. While it wasn't intimate, it was friendly and I enjoyed my time with him. Heck, we hadn't even turned on the TV, only shared each other's company with random questions.

By the time eleven rolled around, I picked up my plate and his and stood. "I have to head to bed. Every fourth weekend, I run a study group for the kids who want it at the local library bright and early. If I'm not on my game with them tomorrow, they'll stomp all over me."

"I can't believe that."

I smiled. "All right, if I'm too tired, I tend to blurt out more than I should."

He laughed, standing. "Now that I believe." He grabbed our empty drink cans and followed me into the kitchen. We paused, standing near the sink.

Did I hug him goodnight?

Kiss his cheek?

Slap his butt?

What did I do?

What would I usually do with Brooke? Probably say goodnight and that was it.

Easy enough.

"I better get some sleep too, with the game tomorrow," he said. "But, Ree."

Ree. Sigh. I loved hearing him call me Ree.

"Yes?"

"Thank you."

"You're welcome."

He smirked. "I'm not just talking about having me here. I wanted to thank you for trusting me, for accepting me into your life."

My belly and heart did a shimmy; it was the only way I could describe the way his words affected me.

"Then, you're welcome again."

His eyes softened. Slowly, while my pulse took off, he leaned in. His hand gripped my elbow and he pressed his lips to my cheek... lingering. The whole time I stared ahead wide-eyed.

Friends, friends, friends.

I was sure it was a chant I would have to use every day while Carter lived with me.

"Goodnight," he whispered against my cheek. I made a sound in the back of my throat, but it was all I could manage as a goodnight because the sensation of his warmth against me was overriding my senses.

His breath whooshed across my face as he chuckled. He pulled back, smiled, and then walked out of the kitchen. I stood there for a few moments more, unsure of how long exactly, but eventually, I made my way down to my room. Sneaking past Carter's closed door, I talked myself down from leaning my head against it to listen to his breathing like some creeper.

I wasn't sure if I would find sleep. Carter was just on the other side of the wall. Sleeping in my spare double bed, under some spare sheets of my own.

Man, oh, man.

Carter Anthony was sleeping under my roof.

Would I ever get used to it?

CHAPTER SEVENTEEN

REAGAN

*S*omeone shook my shoulder. I slapped the hand away and curled up on my side. Only I then registered the sound of my alarm blaring. I shot up, only to hit something on the way up, slamming my head against something hard.

"Ouch," I cried, and pried my eyes open to see Carter standing over me holding his chin. His mouth moved to shape words, but I couldn't hear any of it. "What?" I yelled. Reaching over, I then pressed the button to stop my alarm. My ears rang in the silence.

Rubbing my eyes, then my forehead, I blinked a few times before my eyes sprang wide.

Carter was standing beside my bed.

Carter was standing beside my bed in nothing but running shorts.

Had my wet dream come true?

I rubbed at my eyes again.

He was still there.

I popped my mouth closed in case I started drooling over his body. It was like he'd been carved out of stone. A rock-hard chest and stomach of muscles galore.

"You okay?" he asked.

I blinked slowly as I watched his stomach muscles work.

"Reagan?"

"So pretty," I mumbled to myself, and started to reach out for just one touch.

Just one.

His chuckle was what brought me back. I quickly slapped my hands on the bed, and under my thighs so I wouldn't be tempted to grope him.

"Is your head okay?" he asked.

I nodded, my gaze not wavering from his body.

"Is your alarm usually that loud?"

I nodded.

"You're sweaty," I commented, watching a droplet slide down his pec to his stomach and disappear beneath his shorts. I wanted to pull his shorts out so I could see where that droplet stopped.

"Yeah, I've just come back from a run when I heard your alarm. Was worried when it didn't switch off. Had to check."

"Uh-huh."

"Jesus, you're cute."

That had my head snapping up to meet his amused gaze. "What?"

He smiled, small crinkles appearing next to his eyes; then he shook his head. "Nothing. So, you're not a morning person."

I stretched. "Nope, sorry. I should have warned you about the alarm."

"It's all right, now I know. If I hear it still going when I come in from my morning runs, I'll help wake you."

It was on the tip of my tongue to ask how he'd wake me—with his hands, his body, his mouth—but I stopped myself. I was learning.

"Um, okay, ah, thanks."

"Cute."

"Sorry?" I asked again, because I wasn't sure if I'd heard him right. Had he really called me cute?

"Nothing." He smirked. "I'll get coffee on. You want the first shower?"

"Yes?"

His smirk morphed into a full-blown grin, teeth showing and all.

Wow. What a nice way to wake up.

"All right, I'll leave you to it." He started for the door before I called him. He turned.

"Is your chin okay?"

His eyes warmed. "Yeah, I'll be sure to move faster next time." He tapped the doorway twice before leaving.

I could so get used to waking up to sweaty Carter each morning. At least I wouldn't have to fake deep sleeping. Though, even if I didn't have to, I probably still would so I could see that body again and again.

As I walked into the kitchen after my shower and getting ready for study group, I paused in the doorway. I should have looked through the window from the kitchen into the living room to prepare myself. But I didn't. And seeing Carter's half-naked body again did things to my belly and below.

"Shower. You can have one and get dressed. You've got your game to get to." Not that I wanted him to, but I hoped my brain would work more without the distraction.

He lifted his coffee cup to his lips, but I caught his lips twitching before he took a sip.

"Thanks." He picked up another mug and walked my way. My nipples hardened with every step he took. "White with one, right?" He handed me the mug.

"Yes," I whispered. When I grabbed the mug, my eyes had the chance to glance down his body. I locked my legs tight when I noticed some hardness going on in his shorts.

Whoa. He was packing a big... package.

My cheeks heated. I shifted my gaze to my drink. My hands shook as I lifted the mug to my lips and drank.

"You okay?" he asked, and his voice was light, amused.

"Fine," I chirped. "Good." I nodded, and took another gulp. "Ah, morning."

He laughed, and it was both deep and amazing. "Morning. I'm going to hit the shower."

"Good—I mean, okay, enjoy."

Another chuckle followed. "I will." He moved around me. "Oh, I nearly forgot, I might not see you before you go. Needed to let you know we're going to my parents' house for dinner tonight."

I froze.

Carter started whistling as he walked off.

"Carter!" I yelled, ready to tell him I had mono.

"See you later," he called back, and then I heard the bathroom door close.

Oh God.

I was going to die.

AFTER MY DAY AT THE LIBRARY, I WALKED HOME PLANNING MY FAKE illness. I put my hate for lying aside. Like I usually did when I knew nothing good could come of situations I was forced into. Besides, it was a little one to get me out of something that could save Carter and myself from embarrassment. Carter wouldn't be back yet, which would give me time to press a heat pack against my face and mix up a concoction to pour into the toilet—once he got home—so I could pretend I was vomiting. My acting skills were passable, and I was confident I could belt out a few loud heaves and groans.

Unfortunately, as I grew closer to home, I spotted Carter's truck parked in the driveway.

"Shit," I bit out. *Think, Reagan, think.*

There wasn't a chance I was going to his parents' place tonight.

Throughout the day, I'd broken out in sweats at random times when I thought about going and making a fool of myself. His family would think I was a mental case and in turn, would warn Carter to run as far away from me as he could. I was getting used to having Carter in my life. In fact, I liked having him in my life and my house. I didn't want to give him up.

Hopping on one foot, I slipped my shoe off the other and started to limp toward the house, up the pathway, and to the front door.

A sprained ankle was all I could think of in my time of panic. I just prayed it would be enough to get me out of dinner.

The door was already unlocked, so I opened it and limped in. "Oh, ow, that hurt," I said loudly.

"Reagan, are you okay?" Carter called from the kitchen. I limped my way in there, to find him leaning his butt against the kitchen counter. At least he was dressed in jeans and a tee so I wouldn't be distracted.

"Hey, I think I sprained my ankle."

"Really?" he questioned, crossing his arms over his chest.

"Yeah, on the walk home. Hey, um, what are you doing home? I thought you had meetings after your game? How did you go anyway?"

"We won." He grinned, and added, "And I got out of the interviews early. Do you want me to look at your ankle?"

"No! Ah, thanks though, I think I just have to rest it. But I don't think I can go tonight. Should stay off it and all that."

"Hmm."

"So, pass on my apologies." Turning, I moaned and limped my way into the living room and sat on the couch, placing my shoe on the floor.

Carter followed.

"Reagan?" he said, stopping at the end of the couch.

I winced and lifted my foot up onto the coffee table. "Yes?"

His lips twitched. "You're going to dinner."

"But... my foot."

"I'll carry you."

"You can't. I'm too heavy."

His eyes narrowed. "Never say that again," he growled out from the back of his throat.

Oh, wow.

"O-okay."

"Good."

"Still, you can't carry me into your parents' place. It would be just weird."

He huffed out a breath. "Do you know I had an enlightening call just before?"

"Really? From who?"

His fingers played with the arm on the couch as he stared down at me. "Your dad."

Damn.

"So my dad's calling you now."

"Yep." He grinned.

I scowled at him. "And what did he have to say that was so enlightening?"

"I mentioned about dinner, and my concerns about you being too scared to go."

How did he know me so well already?

The ass.

"And?"

"School debate team? School dance? Your cousin's wedding? Dinner with the Morrisons? When work has their swimming carnivals? Any of them ring any bells?"

That asshole father of mine sold me out.

I stood abruptly, with my hands on my hips and leaned toward Carter. "The debate team did so much better when I wasn't there fumbling through things. I couldn't dance to save my life, so there was no way I was going to that school one. My cousin, who's a second cousin really, is a pecker head. He tried to shove his hand down my bra one day. I would have drunk too much to get through

139

the night and then probably would have told his wife exactly what I thought of him. Dinner with the Morrisons, our old neighbors who were nudists… no, just no. And the swimming carnivals, well, it's in the heart of summer, and the teachers don't get to take a dip, only the students, so why would I want to go?"

"And my parents?"

"I'll make a fool out of you and me by saying or doing something." I thinned my lips. The bastard caught me on a roll, and I just blurted that out. "Damn it." I stomped my foot.

He gazed down, and then back up with a smug smile on his face. "Your foot seems to be better. Fancy that."

"You… I…." I threw my hands up in the air and growled under my breath. I picked up my shoe, put it on, and stomped my way to the front door. "Fine, you want me to go, I'll go, but don't blame me when your mom thinks you've lost the plot for having me in your life."

Still wearing a smile that I wanted to smack off his face, he came toward me. Picking up his phone, wallet, and keys from the stand near the door, he swiftly touched his lips to my cheek and said, "You have nothing to worry about. She'll love you."

I didn't know what to say. Actually, I couldn't say anything because I was still focusing on how his lips felt against my skin. How his kiss sent my belly dipping, my skin tingling, and my panties melting.

He walked out the door and started down the path, only to look back and see I was still in the same spot inside the front door. Rolling his eyes, he made his way back, took my hand in his and tugged me out the door, locking it before he led me to the side where his truck was parked.

If the age-old "don't get in cars with strangers" would have worked, I'd have tried it, but I had the feeling nothing I did or said would matter. Carter wanted me to go to his parents' for dinner, so I was. Though, I supposed it was fair. They should meet the person he was living with.

Gasping, I turned to him as he climbed into the driver's side. "Tell me you've told them you're living at my home."

He paused.

And that was all I needed.

Unclicking my seat belt, I nearly made it out of the car when the back of my shirt was snatched.

Laughing, he said, "Relax. They won't care. Actually, they'll like the idea I'm no longer living in a hotel."

With a sigh, I wiggled back in the seat and said, "They'd better or you'll pay."

CHAPTER EIGHTEEN

REAGAN

I gripped my seat belt and stared up at the beautiful home. My body jolted when Carter was suddenly at my side and opening my door.

When had he got out of the car or even turned it off?

"Come on." He smiled warmly at me.

"I think I'm good here."

"Reagan," he scolded. "This is my family. They're like me, and I like you the way you are, so I know they will as well."

He liked me the way I was.

That was nice.

If I wasn't on the verge of freaking out, I would have pondered on those words for a bit longer. Carter reached around me and unclipped my seat belt. I still clung to it like it was my lifeline. He tried to pull it from me, but I didn't let go.

He snorted. "Reagan, let go."

"No. I can't do this to you."

"Reagan," he said with a sigh.

I shook my head.

"Right. You leave me no choice. Just remember that."

"What— Carter no!" I yelled when the belt was yanked from my hand and in the next second, I was out of the car and up and over his shoulder. He slammed my door closed and started for the front of the house. I slapped his back, wiggled around and pushed up to see if he'd let me down. No luck. "Let me down, please. I promise I won't run. I promise I'll be good, just let me down."

"No."

"Carter, I'm not having your mom meet my butt first."

He laughed. "Why not, it's a fine one."

My struggles stopped.

"What did you say?"

"Oh, look there are Dad and my brothers in the front window." One hand dropped from my thigh. He must have waved.

"Carter, I swear to God, if you don't put me down—" He placed me on my feet on the front steps just as the front door started to open. Before it came all the way open, I smacked my palm into his rock-hard stomach hard. He grunted.

"Patty," I cried. "It's good to see you again."

His lips twitched. "You too, Reagan. It seemed you were having trouble walking up here."

"Oh no." I laughed humorlessly while hitting Carter in the gut again. "My feet were just sore from being on them all day... ah, teaching at the study group I run and... um... running, and Carter was concerned. I told him not to worry, but your son doesn't listen." I laughed again and went to hit Carter once more, but he took my hand in his and led me into the house once Patty stepped aside.

"Hey, Reagan," Casper greeted.

"How are you, Reagan?" Calvin grinned, and it was just like Casper's.

"Hi, guys. I'm fine. Great." I nodded and glanced around the foyer. Already it felt homey. There were stairs just inside the door that led to the second story. To the left was a living room, where

Carter's brothers were standing. To the right was a study, where there was a desk up against the front window with papers and such scattered over it.

I didn't get to see much more because Carter, still with his hand in mine, dragged me into the living room. When I noticed his brothers looking down at our hands, I tried to pull mine free. Carter refused to let go. He even shot me a glare.

I harrumphed and scowled right back. I thought I heard some chuckles, but when I glanced at the other three men, they had straight faces. Well, except for the twitching lips.

"Where's Mom and Court?"

"In the kitchen with the monsters," Patty said. I must have reacted to it because Patty added, "Court has two kids. Crispin's six and Caitlyn's four."

"They sound cute." They all gave me a look.

Carter snorted. "You'll see."

"Is Courtney the eldest?"

"Nope, Carter is, then Calvin, then Court and finally me, I'm the sweetest baby brother there is," Casper explained.

"Is that my boy?" was called from down a hall.

"Unka Cart is here. Unka Cart," was screamed just before the one who must have been Caitlyn came running down the hall. Carter dropped my hand, braced, and as Caitlyn jumped, Carter swung her up into his arms.

"How's my favorite niece?"

"She's your only one, Uncle Carter," a boy I assumed was Crispin said as he entered the living room. He was so adorable. Both of them were, with freckles on their noses and cheeks. Both had dark brown hair, only Caitlyn's was curly and long, and she had big caramel-colored eyes.

"And she'll always be my favorite," Carter cooed at Caitlyn, and my heart melted.

Crispin rolled his eyes, and then he noticed me. "You Uncle Carter's girlfriend?"

I waited.

And waited for Carter to deny it.

When he didn't, I shook my head and said, "No, we're just friends."

It was at the same time as Casper muttered, "He wishes." But I brushed it aside, sure I heard him wrong.

"Cool. Wanna be my girlfriend?" Crispin grinned.

"Crispin," Patty warned.

"No way, kid," Carter said with a bite to his tone.

Calvin started laughing.

"What's so funny?" a woman asked as she entered. It was Carter's mom. They had the same eyes. Her graying brown-blonde hair was tied up in a messy bun. She was shorter, like me, and also fuller in her figure.

"Crisp's trying to get Reagan to agree to be his girlfriend," Casper explained.

Her eyes came to me. "Reagan, so good to meet you. I'm Beth." She came forward, and I held my hand out. She looked at it and grinned. Taking hold of it, she used my hand to tug me forward into a hug.

Heck, why not? Dad did hug Carter.

I placed my arms around her and patted her back. "It's nice to meet you, Mrs. Anthony."

She pulled back. "Bah, I'm just Beth here."

"And I'm just Reagan," I said lamely. Everyone chuckled. I shot dagger eyes to Carter. As if to say, "See, I'm already messing up." I quickly added, "Or my family calls me Ree."

"Ree, I like it. Carter tells me you both used to go to the same high school."

"Yes. But we didn't know each other back then."

"Mom," Crispin yelled, causing me to jump.

"I'm coming," was screamed back. I heard footsteps pounding down the hall, and then Beth's lookalike entered the living room. "What's happening?"

145

Crispin moved over to my side, even pushed at his grandma so she didn't stand in front of me. "This is Reagan, my girlfriend."

"Jesus, control your boy, Court," Carter complained.

"Isn't he too young to be looking for a girlfriend?" Calvin commented.

A grinning Courtney shrugged. "When he knows, he knows. Besides, he's his father's son." She stepped over and held out her hand. I shook it. "Hey, I'm those three losers' sister, Courtney."

"Reagan or Ree. I'll answer to anything really." I smiled.

"Nice to meet you." I watched her glance to Carter and wink for some reason.

Maybe his family was as different as mine. That thought eased some tension in my shoulders.

"Anyway," Carter called, "I have some news."

I blanched. He wouldn't just share he lived with me like that, would he?

"I'm no longer living in a hotel."

The bastard would.

"Oh, where are you living?" Beth asked.

"You have a beautiful home," I yelled, blushing.

Beth glanced at me and smiled. "Thank you." She turned back to Carter. "So where?"

"With Ree."

"It's my parents' fault," I blurted. Three manly chuckles were heard around me, and one sweet one. Courtney.

Beth's look of shock snapped to me.

"Really, it is. My dad has a man crush on him, and when we went to dinner at their place—"

"You met them before coming to dinner here?" Beth accused Carter.

Oh no.

"Shit," he bit out.

"Shit," Caitlyn copied.

"Caitlyn sweetheart, you shouldn't copy your uncle with that word," I said, and then glared at Carter. "And really you shouldn't swear in front of her." I threw my hands up in the air, and added, "I mean really, next she'll be saying the *C* word or the *F* word, and it'll all be your fault. Then how would you feel?"

"You're living with Reagan?" Beth said.

"Hold up, let's get back to Carter and his swearing," I suggested. Anything to divert the attention from Carter living with me.

"Later, honey," Beth replied gently.

"Besides, wait until you meet the grandkids father. Carter behaves like an angel compared to him," Patty mentioned.

"Really?" I asked. "Who's their father?" And he swore in front of them?

"When did you move in? Why didn't you ask for help?" Beth questioned Carter. The woman didn't waver. Damn it.

"Just yesterday, and we had a lot of help."

Beth cocked her hip to the side, her hand landed on it. "Who?"

"Ah… maybe we should get back to it being all my parents' fault?" At least they could take any blame since they weren't there. "They put him on the spot and offered Carter to live with them, and I couldn't do it to him. *Friends* help each other out, so I had to suggest Carter was already moving into my place to get him out of it, else if he did move in with them, he could wake up to Dad in bed with him, just staring." I shuddered. "That wouldn't be fun. So I did my friendly duty and saved him. I'm sorry if Carter moving in with me, and not in here, in this wonderful home— Did I mention it's wonderful?" There were more chuckles. I moved on. "—is upsetting in some way. I promise I'm not a stalker and I won't go cooking his bunny on him—"

"Darlin'," Patty called. I snapped my mouth closed and turned to him. "Beth's not upset with Carter living with you. She's annoyed at him for not telling us about it before it happened."

"Oh, well, okay." I faced Beth. "Continue being upset with him."

She giggled. "Thank you."

"Yo, what's goin' on in here?" was boomed from the front door.

"Daddy!" Caitlyn cried. She was out of Carter's arms and running for the man who stepped around the corner.

"Hey, pumpkin." He grinned, swinging her up in his arms and planting a kiss on her cheek. "Boy," he called. Crispin, who had still been standing at my side, sighed and then walked to his father to give him a side hug.

"Hey, Dad."

All others greeted him, but I was still looking at his attire to really listen. He wore black jeans, black boots, a tight white tee, but over the top of it was a leather vest. The patch I could read on his upper chest said Vice President. I ran my gaze up to find a full beard trimmed nicely around plump lips that were smiling, then up again to a straight nose and then eyes crinkled at the corners, lit with humor.

"Hey, babe." He nodded.

"Hey," I breathed, and then blushed for having an instant attraction to Courtney's husband.

"Fucking hell," I heard Carter mutter. Next, he was standing in front of me. "Hey, remember me?"

My head tilted in confusion. Why would he have asked if I remembered him? Of course I remembered him and his handsome face, his glorious hair, his wide shoulders, his built body—

"I'm guessing she does now," Casper said from somewhere, laughing along with others.

But I was still staring at Carter, who was now grinning down at me. He moved aside. "Right, we're good to go now," he said, and it seemed like he was saying a lot of things that confused me. "Reagan, this is Dominic, Courtney's *husband*, but everyone calls him State. State, this is Reagan."

"My girlfriend," Crispin announced.

I bit my bottom lip to keep from giggling.

"Good choice, boy," State said down at his son, and then he looked back up at me. "Nice'ta meet'ya, Reagan."

"Yes, um, you too." I nodded.

Courtney stepped up to my side and placed her hand on my arm. "Don't worry, Ree, my man has that effect on a lot of people. It's a burden I must carry, but at least I do it knowing I have his ring on my finger."

I nodded and kept doing it like I understood how lucky she was.

"Woman, I'm here, and where are you?" State boomed.

Courtney sighed. "The downside of having a biker husband. He's bossy as hell."

"Woman," State growled low, and I kind of swooned over it.

Courtney rolled her eyes, but did it smiling, and then she made her way over to State, got to her tiptoes and kissed him.

Whoa. It wasn't just a touch of lips. It was a full-blown kiss.

"Gross," Crispin cried.

"Jesus," Patty mumbled. "That's my cue to get drinks. Ree, what would you like?"

Shaking out of my daze, I replied, "Anything, thank you."

"You driving?"

"No," I answered.

"Wine it is then."

"Thanks." I smiled.

I happened to glance back at State to see Crispin had moved away and was talking with Calvin, so State had his wife curled under his free arm. "So, you Carter's woman?"

"No," I replied with a smile. Though I wouldn't mind being, I couldn't afford to let my heart and brain take me there. State's eyes shifted behind me. His lips twitched, so I glanced over my shoulder to see Casper lowering his hands.

I narrowed my eyes. "What were you doing?"

"Nothing." He grinned sheepishly at me.

"Ree, how about you come into the kitchen with me while I check dinner," Beth suggested, as she reached out and hit Casper around the back of his head.

"Sure, I'd love to." Even though I really, really didn't. I never knew what I was going to say, and it scared me to be alone around

Beth. Still, if Carter could take a call from my dad and have them in his life, I could try and do the same without worrying about how they would take me.

"Caitlyn, Crispin, come help Grammy."

The kids followed without question. At least I would have some type of buffer.

CHAPTER NINETEEN

CARTER

*A*s soon as Reagan was out of sight, I turned back to my family, who had also been watching Reagan walk down the hall. No doubt to make sure she was out of ear range. Immediately I knew I was going to get attacked with questions.

"Does she know you want her?" Calvin asked.

"Man, you gotta get in that," State said, gaining a punch to the gut from my sister.

"He's right. I can see the hard-on you have already," Casper said.

"Dude, quit looking at my junk," I stated, covering it with my hands.

Casper scoffed. "There ain't much there to look at, which is why all the women jump on this Anthony man over you any day."

"You idiots, shut up," Courtney snapped. Her gaze came to me. "Seriously, Carter. I adore that woman for you."

"She's kinda loco, but in a good way," Calvin added. Shaking his head, he grinned and said, "Her rant about it being her parents' fault... fucking funny."

"She'd fit in perfectly with our family," Dad said, appearing from the hall. "Son, don't know how you managed it, but good work on moving in with her."

"Whoa, you live with her now?" State stepped up for a fist bump, which I returned. "How'd you meet?"

"The school thing I had to do, she's a teacher." I then asked Courtney, "Do you think she knows I—"

"Want her," Calvin said.

"Like her," Dad said.

"Loooove her," Casper sang. Everyone stared at me. "Holy shit. You do. You love her."

My heart and pulse rocketed off into orbit, yet a soft smile grew on my mouth. Hearing someone else say it, that I loved her, was what I needed to confirm my feelings were in fact strong enough to be called love. She was everything to me. I couldn't imagine a life without her in it. That shit was terrifying because, again, it was so soon. But when a guy knows, he knows.

I flicked my eyes to everyone's shocked expression. "How do you know and why would it be so damn shocking to you all?"

"Man, let's face it, you're a tag and throw away kinda guy, until now, until her," State said.

I shrugged. "Reagan's different."

Again, they all looked shocked.

I sighed. "Look, I had a thing for her in high school, but I was too worried about what people would think."

"Because she's not your usual skanky type since she has curves?" Courtney asked with a glare.

"Unfortunately, yes," I admitted.

"Douche," Calvin coughed.

"I know, and I regret it, but then when I saw her at the school, and before I knew exactly who she was, I was already smitten. Since then, I can't stop thinking about her."

State nodded. "It's how love starts. I didn't just want to bang your sister—"

"Dude!" I cried.

"What? I'm saying I *didn't* just want to bang her. I wanted to know everything there was about her, and that's when I knew I loved her."

"Aw," Courtney cooed, and reached up to kiss State's jaw.

"I loved your mom after one glance," Dad said.

"So why are you all shocked I've fallen for Reagan?"

"It'll pass, but you can't be surprised when you've never brought anyone home before *and* never looked at anyone like you do her."

Courtney cleared her throat. "To answer your earlier question, no, I don't think she knows. There's a possibility of her having the barest of ideas, but foolishly thinks you're so far out of her league she won't let herself think about what could happen between you two."

"I'm not out of her league," I said with a hard edge to my voice.

"Oh, we know." Courtney smiled. "But from what you've said, she has no idea she was on your radar back then. You were popular, and she wasn't. You're now this big football star and she's a teacher. She won't understand how you could have feelings for her."

Having my sister's honesty felt like a weight had been placed onto my shoulders. They dropped, and my gut tightened. I hated that Reagan could possibly think that. I nodded. "You're probably right. She did catch my friends saying shit back in school about bigger girls. I didn't stop it from happening and laughed along with them."

"Douche," Calvin coughed again.

"I know," I ground out.

"You'll need to prove you're not that douche," State said. "Though, I think she's gettin' it. Then you'll need to show her she's worth it. Take your time so you don't scare her off."

"Start with little things," Dad added. "A kiss on the cheek."

I nodded. I could do this, I had already started with the little things.

"Touch her arm or leg if you're sitting close," Courtney said.

"Show her she's beautiful to you," Casper suggested. "Take her out on a date but pretend it's not a date. She keeps referring to you as her friend so be her friend first, then make a move to be more."

Everyone looked at him.

"What? I can have good ideas," he exclaimed. When we didn't look away he rolled his eyes and said, "Whatever, I'm going to see how dinner's coming along, and I might just flirt with Re—"

Reaching out, I gripped his tee. "Take it back."

He laughed and patted my arm. "Fine, fine. I take it back." I released him, and he started toward the hall. "Doesn't mean I have to keep my hands to myself." He started to run when I made a grab for him again.

Dad gripped the back of my tee, and he stumbled forward, so I did, and then State was there helping us both.

"Cool it, brother. Casp's only teasing, wantin' to see your reaction. And you gave him one. We all know this shit you feel is serious."

"Casper may be an idiot sometimes, but he had a good idea about Reagan," Calvin said. "Take it slow, but be sure to show some interest in her."

"Got it." Jesus, I must be in love if I was taking advice and listening to my family. Another smile lit my face as my body warmed all over. There was no way I could deny how I felt, and I was okay with that.

"I'm happy for you, son." Dad slapped me on the back and moved around me to head to the kitchen.

"So am I. She's a keeper. Looking forward to seeing what she does next." Calvin grinned. "And if you fuck up, I'll move in."

I shoved him. "Christ, are you serious?"

"Sure. I'm half in love with her already."

"Fuck off, she's mine."

His grin widened. "Good to hear."

"Mom," Crispin called as we all sat down at the table. He was across from my spot, glaring for some reason. Though it could be because I was sitting next to Reagan.

"Yes?" Courtney glanced at him from where she sat beside him. State was on the other side of him, across from Reagan, I wasn't sure I liked it. She seemed to like his looks a little too much. Thankfully, Caitlyn had most of State's attention as she sat on the other side of her dad. Mom and Dad were at the end of the ten-seater table, and to my chagrin, Casper sat on the other side of Reagan. Then again, he was a better option than Calvin, who'd admitted he was already half in love with her. He was sitting next to me.

"Can I move in with Reagan too?"

Everyone paused.

Never in Crispin's life had I wanted to yell no at him, until then.

To stop myself, I thinned my lips and curled my tongue to the roof of my mouth.

State started chuckling, Calvin and Casper followed. I cast a look at Reagan, who blushed beside me. Courtney finally answered, "Maybe when you're older."

Crispin shook his head and sighed. "Fine."

State ruffled Crispin's hair. "That's my boy."

Mom cleared her throat. "Ree, Patty was telling me you teach."

"Yes." She nodded, placing her fork on her plate. "High school English."

"Her students love her," I put in. "Even when she threatens to throw up on them."

Everyone laughed.

Reagan's cheeks turned even redder. "That was one time. Seriously, one time and you just had to overhear."

"What happened?" Casper asked.

Reagan sighed. "I have a squeamish stomach, and my kids know it. A student, Wesley, was blowing his nose and then kept looking at it. When I asked him not to he taunted me by doing it again, so I told him I was going to vomit on him."

Again, everyone laughed, even Crispin and Caitlyn. Though I was sure Caitlyn was just laughing because we all were.

"I happened to be at the door because Tom, the principal, asked me to talk to a few classes." I nudged her shoulder with my own. "Should I tell them what you said when I asked you to have lunch?"

Her eyes widened, her hand landed on my thigh under the table, and she squeezed hard. My cock jerked in response. "If you do I'll... do something really bad."

"We have to know now," State said.

"Yeah, come on, Reagan. Let him spill it." Courtney smiled.

I shook my head. "Maybe I shouldn't. There are kids present."

Casper slapped the table laughing. "It was that bad?"

I nodded.

"No," Reagan blurted and shook her head. "It was nothing. Really. Besides, from memory, you were dragged away by Elena anyway."

Shit.

"Elena? Why does that name ring a bell?" Calvin asked.

"She was Carter's girlfriend," Dad said, and when I sent him an evil stare, he shrugged. "What? I have a good memory."

"Oh, you have a good memory, do you?" Mom said. "Then maybe you can remember to take out the trash." Dad sighed and ran a hand over his face. Served him right for outing who Elena was.

Courtney gasped. "Elena Roup. That Elena?"

"Yes," Reagan replied before I could completely put my hand over her mouth. She laughed and grabbed my arm, pulling it back down.

"Oh my God, she was a total bi—" she glanced down to Crispin. "Ah, witch," she ended. "You have to work with her?"

"Every day, and she used to make my high school days hell," Reagan explained. I knew they didn't like each other, but I didn't know Elena was a bitch to Reagan back in the day. Christ, I felt like an even bigger dick for not knowing and being able to stop it. Courtney gave me a look. Yeah, I got it. That would probably be another reason why Reagan wouldn't be quick to fall in love with me since I dated the she-bitch from hell.

"Anyway," I said loudly, trying to change the unpleasant subject, "I think since Mom was upset about not helping me move and going to Ree's parents' house first, we should all have a barbecue, not this one, but the next Tuesday at Reagan's. With both sides of the families there. I'll be at an away game this coming weekend, so that'll give me a week to get things ready." It'd be the perfect opportunity for our parents to get to know one another. It could make Reagan more at ease if she saw no matter what happened, with her parents there, my folks would still adore her.

Mom clapped. "That sounds wonderful."

Dad grinned. "Perfect idea."

"We'd love to come, wouldn't we, State?" Courtney turned to her husband.

He grinned down at her then over to us, his lips twitched. "Fuck yeah."

"Language," Mom called.

"I'm in," Casper said.

"Me too." Calvin nodded, and then went back to shoveling more food into his mouth.

A hand crept on to my thigh again. All my blood rushed to my head, both ends. All I could think was thank God the hand was from Reagan's side, or I'd be worried about my brother's sanity. When her finger dug into my flesh, I winced.

She leaned in while the others were talking about what they could bring. Okay, so my brothers were telling Mom and Courtney what they'd like, but I ignored it all when Reagan's breast brushed against my arm. My mind blanked for a second. All I could think was *boob, boob, boob against my arm, and it feels nice.*

Her lips brushed my ear, and I nearly groaned aloud. "I'm so going to kill you when we get in the car."

Pulling back, I studied her. Her cute nose was scrunched up, her beautiful eyes narrowed, and she was clenching her jaw. Yep, she was pissed. I really shouldn't have smiled, but I did. "Why?"

"Having me around your parents was one thing, having my family around them…" She shook her head. "Boom. It's bound to be a disaster."

I placed my arm around her on the back of her chair and gave her a side hug. "Relax, it'll be fine. Trust me."

She grumbled, but I could tell she was giving in. "Fine. But I'm blaming you if it's not."

"Okay." I winked down at her. We sat there and talked for a while longer, and I wasn't sure if she noticed her hand was still on my thigh or my arm still around her, but they were, and I enjoyed that moment with a huge-ass smile on my face.

Yeah, I could definitely get used to having Reagan at my side as more than just a friend.

REAGAN

Oh my God, oh my God… Carter was touching me. His arm was around me and his fingers gently rubbed up and down my side. I wasn't sure if he realized what he was doing, but I was more than aware of it because it was turning me to mush. I sat frozen in my seat. If anyone saw how freaked out I was on the inside, they didn't show it. Thank God. Or maybe *I* wasn't showing it. I mean, no one could see my heart beating a million miles an hour or how my skin tingled from each stroke of his fingers on my side.

What was worse was how I was frozen. My mouth may have moved around with words as people talked to me, but my body was as still as a statue, and my hand remained on Carter's thigh!

I was *touching* Carter.

I wanted to pull it away, but then if I did, he'd notice, and I didn't want to draw attention to me freaking out. While he didn't seem to mind I was touching him, still… I didn't know what to do or think.

He was warm under my hand. I liked that I could touch him without Carter shying away from it. Though my naughty hand wanted to slide up his thigh to see if I got a reaction from him, but it wasn't the time or the place to be doing that.

Instead, I just sat with my internal freak-out happening, wondering why he wasn't pulling away from me.

Oh God, this was more than what friends did.

Friends didn't touch like that.

Brooke would probably ask if I was trying for second base if I happened to lay my hand on her thigh.

My mind was a mess while my body tingled, but I'd sit and suffer through it all because it meant I was touching Carter.

When dinner was done I had a respite from Carter's warm leg holding when he and his brothers got up to clear the table. Something I thought was very sweet. I was also grateful for the distance as my ears had started ringing from the way my heart was going a million miles an hour. It gave me a chance to settle my nerves.

We spent the rest of the night in the living room, where I sat next to Carter on one end of the couch. Though I had a feeling I was maneuvered there by Casper. He did, after all, take my wrist in his hand and guide me over to the couch and gently push my shoulders to sit beside an already seated Carter. I found that strange.

At the end of the night we were saying goodbye at the door, I'd really enjoyed my time with them. They were so welcoming and nice; it was easy to fall into relaxing around them. Especially when they all teased Carter in some way.

"You'll have to come back another night," Beth said with a kiss to my cheek.

"Mom, you'll see her at the barbecue, remember?" Courtney smiled.

"Right, of course."

"Still, I would love to come back another time. Maybe we could get together, just the girls. I'm sure my mom and friend Brooke would love it."

Beth brightened. "Sounds wonderful."

"Girls' night, yeah!" Courtney shouted, and I caught Carter's soft smile at me. Was he pleased I wanted to spend more time with his sister and Mom? It wouldn't be any hardship on my part. They were amazing women.

State stepped up behind Courtney, wrapping his arm across her chest. "Babe, you should come to the compound for party night."

My breath caught. Party night with bikers? Wow. "I'd—"

"No," Carter stated roughly as he came up to my side.

State smirked. "We'd take care of her."

"No," Carter bit out.

"Come on, brother, you—"

"Not happening." Carter glared. He gripped my upper arm and started pulling me toward the front door. "Bye, talk to you Tuesday." Carter waved over his shoulder. I could hear his brothers laughing at him.

I turned back. "Thank you for dinner. It was amazing."

"You're welcome, Reagan." Patty grinned.

"Bye." I waved, and they returned it. As soon as we were in the car, I faced Carter as he pulled the vehicle onto the road. "Why did you answer for me back there? I wouldn't have minded going." I was kind of annoyed he took my choice away from me though.

"Reagan, State's a biker. His friends are all bikers. They're rough, can be mean, and I wouldn't like any harm to come to you."

Oh… well, that was nice, and I found myself content with his answer. Still, it didn't mean I couldn't really go one night. I'd have to talk to Courtney to see how safe it would be and maybe Carter would join us. Honestly, I wouldn't want to go without him.

A new thought popped into my mind and had me tensing. What happened if bikers didn't like football or if they went for another team that wasn't Carter's? It could cause problems. They may want to rough him up a bit. I wouldn't want that to happen, so I couldn't have Carter go, which meant I wouldn't go without him.

"Okay," I said

"Okay?" he queried with a frown. "That was too easy."

I smiled. "It's not really my thing anyway."

"All right…," he drew out, probably unsure of my sudden change. He could guess all he wanted, but I wouldn't tell him it was because I cared about his welfare. That would be just awkward.

CHAPTER TWENTY

REAGAN

*T*his weekend Carter had an away game, which gave me time to ponder. Okay, so I was doing most of my thinking the Monday before he arrived home, since I cleaned, buffed, and tidied the house over the weekend before his parents came over. I'd also gone to the movies, had drinks with Brooke, and made sure my parents could come to the barbecue. I was sure Dad cried a little, but he said it was his allergies again. But no matter what I did, Carter was always in the back of my mind. Ever since having dinner at Carter's parents' place, it seemed like a switch had been flicked on inside him. Even though it had been a month since he was at the school, he had changed.

He was just *more.*

Not only was he sweeter, but there was simply more in his actions.

More touching.

More talking.

More texting.

More calls.

It all played with my emotions to the point they were demanding I just love him already.

Of course I was freaking out every time he touched me, especially when my gut reaction was to jump him. Before he left for LA, he'd come into the kitchen where I was washing the dishes to say goodbye.

He'd sought me out to say goodbye.

But that wasn't all.

It was how he'd said it and what he'd done.

When his hands landed on my waist, I'd tensed as I hadn't been expecting it. I'd had to lock my body tight while the thrilling vibe passed through my entire being just from his touch. Then, *then*, he'd leaned in. His warmth had wrapped around my back and against my neck. Then he'd said, all deep and growly, "See you Monday, but I'll keep in touch."

He'd waited for my response, and I'd found it hard to control myself, so I'd breathed out, "'Kay." Then I'd thought it wasn't enough, so I'd added, "Be, um, safe on the, ah, grass."

"Field." He'd chuckled.

His breath had tickled my neck, and then, again, *then*, he'd touched his lips to my neck and left.

He'd done it like it was a natural thing to do between us.

It *wasn't* natural.

I didn't kiss Brooke's neck.

Just thinking about his lips, my body hummed to life. The first night he was gone, I'd masturbated twice thinking of him. The second night I was even naughtier and started while *he* was on the phone, not that he knew, but his voice was just getting to me. Last night, I'd gone so far as to bring out good old Vance the Vibrator. I nicknamed him Carter while I pictured it was him taking advantage of me. All right, of course Carter could never take advantage of me; I'd offer myself up on a platter for free.

I'd never come so many times and in so many days close together.

To say I was satisfied was an understatement... but I knew as soon as I saw him or heard him, I would be a wanton hussy once more.

Things were getting dangerous because I wasn't sure if I could keep my hands off him and stay just friends.

CARTER

Ted, my agent, picked me up from the airport. I would have just caught a taxi home, but he'd said he needed to talk to me and not over the phone.

"Hey, man." I smiled, opening the passenger side door and throwing my pack into the back.

"Careful," he warned, but it was too late, I'd already tossed it over.

As soon as I sat, did up my seat belt and Ted pulled into the road, I asked, "So what's so important you couldn't say it on the phone?"

"The girl you're dating and living with, is she your girlfriend?"

Unease turned my gut. "Why?"

"She's a teacher, Carter. You can do so much be—"

"You finish that sentence we're going to have problems. She's not my girl yet, but she will be, and I don't give a flying fuck what anyone says or thinks. As long as I can make her happy, that's all I care about."

Silence.

Ted and I had never argued over anything, but for Reagan, I would take him down.

He sighed. "I see."

"Yeah, I think you do now. Was that why you wanted to talk?"

"Well, not the only reason why. The team's next few games will be away. I have a few things lined up for you in between them so you might have to stay in those towns."

"You said the manager was going to get us to play here for a while with only a couple of away games, but now that's changed?"

"Yes, due to damage to our stadium that's only happened in the last few hours."

"Man, I don't want to be traveling—"

"It won't be forever, Carter."

"How many weeks?"

"Three at the most."

"Fuck."

"There are some events you have to attend, some interviews and pictures while you're away. You'll be so busy the time will fly by."

"You know I hate events. I haven't done any for ages."

"I know, but you're ending your career soon. These will be the last ones you'll ever have to do. It's more about going out with a big bang."

"You're killing me, Ted."

All I wanted to do was spend as much time as I could with Reagan, yet I had to go away for three weeks. Where would that leave us? Yes, the phone calls and texts were awesome, but I loved being near her.

Ted cleared his throat. "So?"

Shit. I didn't really have a choice. I wanted to leave the team on good terms. "Fine."

"Are you sure this is what you want to do? Leave the team early? You still have a few good years in you, Carter."

I shook my head. It was something I'd been thinking about more and more. I was ready to hang up my helmet and move on. "It's what I want. We've already won a Super Bowl. If we make it again this year, that'll be my last one."

"That's a month away, and your team will make it."

"Can only hope."

"You'll probably win the postseason award for "Most Valuable Player" again."

Honestly, it wouldn't bother me if I did or not. Winning it once was enough. When I got it again, it was great, but I'd be happy if another team player won that award.

All I could do was shrug at Ted again.

His eyes widened. "You're different. You used to live and breathe football."

I did. But I knew my time was coming to an end, and I was getting more and more okay with that. Especially if I had Reagan on the other end. I just had to make sure of it.

"I've heard you've even loosened the reins on your strict diet."

"Got to learn to live. I've had my fun and enjoyed every moment in the game, but it's time I moved forward with life. Moving forward to me means happiness on a new level. I'll play out the season, but that's it, I mean it, Ted."

He grunted. "I know. Never heard you so serious. It'll be a shame to lose you as a client."

I shoved his shoulder. "Aww, you love me."

He laughed. "No, I love your money."

"You'll find new clients."

"I know. I just had to make sure this was exactly what you wanted. What you chose, and no one else is in your ear forcing you to finish when you don't really want to."

I shook my head. "I want to. It's all me. My choice."

Pulling up out the front of Reagan's, I turned to Ted. "It isn't over just yet."

"No. So you won't mind if I throw in a few more interviews and such before it is over?"

I snorted. "Ted, what you have planned will be enough. You throw in any more, you get no bonus at the end."

"You may still need me after you quit."

"If it comes to it, I'll let you know."

He nodded. "Talk soon, Carter."

"Will do, and thanks for the lift." Reaching over, I grabbed my bag and got out of the car. Leaning back in, I mentioned again, "One more thing. I need you to understand if you ever talk shit about Reagan and even consider telling me I could do better again, I'll make sure your career ends with me."

He rolled his eyes. "I just had to check how important she was to you."

"Very."

"Got it, and not that you care, but I do think she's... changing you for the better. Now enough threatening. Robbie's expecting me for a very late dinner."

"Later."

"Goodbye, Carter."

After I closed the door, he pulled back out on the road and disappeared. I knew all that BS wouldn't have all come from Ted. The manager of the team would have pushed Ted to press me, but I wasn't changing anything.

Turning, I glanced at the house.

I was home.

Home.

Wherever Reagan was would be a home to me. Admittedly, it sounded serious after only a month, but I couldn't stop what I felt for the woman. She'd taken my mind, and if it didn't seem too stalk-erish, I wanted to be by her side all the damn time.

I sounded like a sappy puppy.

Oh well.

I didn't care. I also didn't care my teammates gave me a lot of crap over the weekend every time I looked at my phone, got a text from Reagan, or dodged them to go to another room to talk with her.

They were just jealous.

Okay, the single ones were. The married ones, or if they were involved in a serious relationship, understood.

However, when Dustin blurted Reagan didn't actually know how

I felt, the so-called friends upped their taunting. Still, I took it like the good guy I was. Why? Because I got to come home to Reagan in the end.

Except I would have to leave again by the end of the week.

Shit.

Unlocking the front door, I opened it and stepped in to find Reagan curled up on the couch asleep. The sight sent my heart racing. God, she was stunning. Even in fluffy socks, flannel sleep pants, and a tee.

I placed my bag on the ground just inside the door and made my way over. Leaning over the back of the couch, I gently reached down to shift her hair from her face.

She stirred, blinked, and looked up at me. Her soft smile caused my dick to stir. "Hey, you're home," she whispered.

"I am." I nodded. I'd give anything to kiss her, but I stopped myself.

She stretched, her tee riding up, and my gaze landed on her curves. Again, my dick jerked in my jeans. Reagan sat up. "Good game."

"You watched it?" I asked, walking around to sit on the couch.

"I did." She stood. "Have you eaten?"

Was she offering herself up?

"I had something on the plane. It's getting late. We should probably head to bed." I stood as well. To my shock and absolute pleasure, she took two steps toward me and wrapped her arms around my waist. Not missing out on the chance to have her in my arms, I curled mine around her. After a moment she tensed. I had a feeling she was probably still half asleep and didn't know what she was doing, but I'd still take it.

She pulled back. "Sorry, I, um…." Her cheeks heated. I smiled down at her after she punched me in the arm. "Congrats on winning."

Chuckling, I said, "Thanks. We'll talk more tomorrow. House looks clean. You should have left something for me to do."

She shrugged. "It's okay." She took a step back. "I'm going to, yeah, head to bed. Glad you're home safe."

The step she took away from me, I ate up with my own feet. Leaning in, I kissed her cheek, and said, "It's good to be home." Being that close, I felt her shiver, and smiled. I then took a moment to draw in her scent. Strawberry. The smell of her shampoo I was becoming addicted to, just like the woman.

CHAPTER TWENTY-ONE

REAGAN

I opened the front door to Carter's family. He was already out back starting up the grill. Shifting to the side, I smiled and gestured them in. "Hi everyone." I got a kiss on the cheek and a hug from everyone. Even Crispin pulled me down to kiss my cheek.

"Hi, dollface," Crispin said before he moved past.

State, who was behind his boy, cracked up laughing. State stepped up, leaned in and kissed my cheek. "Hey, babe."

"Hey." I sighed.

"Jesus, State," I heard Carter clip. I shook my head, and next Carter was at my side. With his arm around my waist, he turned me and led me away from State back into the kitchen. "Need help getting everyone's drink, sweetheart."

Right, drinks.

Wait... sweetheart?

What the...?

Beth called from in the fridge. "Ree, you need a bigger refrigerator, honey." She was moving things around trying to get in the trays of items they brought with them.

"Ah, yes, one day I will."

"There's a cooler out back for drinks."

"I've got it," Calvin said, and picked up the beer and juices they also brought.

"Casp, check the grill for me," Carter called as he shifted his mom aside and started moving more things around.

"On it." Casper saluted, then disappeared out onto the deck.

"Who'd like a drink?" I asked, my brain still not quite focused because of Carter's sweet endearment. I needed to push it aside, though, or else I didn't think I'd survive the evening. I heard the front door open.

"I'll get the drinks, darlin'," Patty said with a tap on my shoulder. "You go greet your family."

"Thanks." I smiled and took off. I had to get to them before they saw who was here. "Hi." I ran up to them, stopping them in the doorway.

Dad looked kind of pale. "They're here. Do I look okay? Have they asked about us? What have you told them? Shit... I think I'm going to pee myself."

"Herb." Mom sighed. "Calm down."

He shook his head. "Do you know one of Carter's brothers just got his first role in a movie?"

"Yes, Carter mentioned it." It was Casper. I hadn't known he was trying to be an actor, but I could honestly see him going far with it. He had the looks, and I was sure the skills.

Then Dad added, "And the other is a lawyer? Carter's dad's sperm must be amazing."

My head jerked back. "Tell me you didn't just say that?"

"He said it," Mom muttered.

"Dad, I swear if you mention to Patty anything about his sperm, I won't get you tickets to the Super Bowl."

His eyes widened. "My lips are sealed." He nudged Mom. "She called him Patty." He sniffed.

Dear God, please let me get through this night without thinking of murder.

"Come on, I'll introduce you."

I took Mom's bowl of potato salad in my hands and then led them to the kitchen.

Everyone had disappeared except for Carter, Patty, and Beth. "Beth and Patty, I'd like you to meet my mom, Elaine, and my dad, Herb."

Patty stepped forward with his hand out, and I saw when Dad's hand came up it was shaking. "Great to meet you, Herb." Patty smiled.

"Y-you too." Dad nodded.

"Dad," I whispered, and Dad quickly dropped Patty's hand. He grabbed Mom by the shoulders and shoved her forward. "My wife. Elaine."

"Hi, Elaine."

"Hello," Mom replied, and I thought that would be it. My shoulders started to sag, losing the tension I'd been holding, but then Mom just had to open her mouth again. "It's a real pleasure to meet you both. Your son is amazing. You have a fantastic family actually. The genes in your family must be superb."

I dropped my head back, eyes to the ceiling. Beth and Patty laughed. "Thanks, we're really proud," Beth replied.

I only straightened when Carter came to my side and placed his hands on my shoulders. "Relax."

Out the corner of my mouth, I told him, "It's easy for you to say. My dad was just talking about your dad's sperm at the door."

He chuckled. "Don't worry about it. They'll all like each other."

Why was I worried about them liking each other so much? Honestly, I didn't realize just how much that was true until Carter spoke, but the truth was, our families getting along was important to me. Maybe because I was concerned if they didn't like one another, then I could lose Carter from my life.

I didn't want that to happen.

The thought even churned my stomach.

If Carter disappeared from my life, while it sounded strange, my days would be bleaker.

I enjoyed Carter's company.

I liked talking with him and having him come home as if it were his own.

I was falling in love with Carter.

There, I admitted it to myself. Now, what did I do with that information?

If I shared it with him, would he run?

Then again, he'd been the one to first reach out to me, kiss me, and he called me sweetheart.... Was Brooke actually right? Did Carter like me?

Oh God... oh God! It wasn't the time for an epiphany.

"You okay?" Carter asked in my ear. I shivered.

"Yes!" I cried. Then when everyone turned our way, I laughed nervously. "Yes, I'm going to get the cold dishes for dinner set out soon. I can't wait. Everything looks yummy." *Shut up, Reagan.* Turning to Carter, I rested my hand on his back and said, "Why don't you take Dad and Patty outside and help with the meat." I twisted around, shoved him forward and he stepped past me, I slapped him on the butt. "Good job." I nodded when he looked back over his shoulder. I also threw in two thumbs-up.

"You sure you're okay?" he asked.

"Great. Fine. Wonderful." I smiled, only it wobbled a bit.

"Reagan?"

"Carter." I laughed. "Honestly, I'm fine. You should actually tell your parents your news." He'd told me yesterday he was finishing up at the end of the season. He'd thought about it for a while, but he finally told the team manager. Only, due to his plans to leave, he had to go away for three weeks of events, interviews, and away games. The Super Bowl, though, would be in our town, and he wanted me there with my family, and us all to be with his family in the boxed area.

"What news?" Beth asked.

I blanched for blurting it out. Carter ran a hand over his face. "Come on, let's all head outside and I'll tell you."

After more introductions were made, Carter told his family his plan. They were all happy for him. Only Beth didn't like he'd be away for three weeks. I didn't either, but I wouldn't say anything. Carter had to leave, for himself and for his team.

"It's only three weeks, Mom," Carter said. "I'll be back before you know it."

She glanced from her son to me for some reason. "Yes, I know."

I jumped when Casper came up to my side and flung his arm around my shoulder. "Don't worry, Carter. I'll be sure to pop in to make sure our sister is okay."

Our sister?

Had Carter told Casper he saw me as his sister?

Since I was looking at Casper in confusion, I then peered at Carter and was surprised to see Calvin and State standing with him, but with their hands on his arms. Casper chuckled beside me, and I shifted my gaze his way.

"Ree," Court called. "Don't mind the idiot. Come sit by me."

Nodding, I slipped out from under Casper's arm and headed over to where Courtney was sitting. Crispin and Caitlyn went out into the backyard further to throw the ball around with Dad. I could already see how Dad would make a good granddad. As I sat next to Courtney, I glanced at Mom, Beth, and Patty talking quietly. I shuddered. God only knew what Mom could be saying.

Courtney's laughter brought my attention back to her. "Don't worry about them. I have faith everyone will get along."

"I hope so."

"Because you like Carter living here or because you just *like* my brother?"

My body locked, but I felt my eyes widen while my mouth gaped.

She let out another laugh. "You do."

I snorted. "No. I mean, he's great to have as a housemate, but we're friends."

"Hmm," was all she said. I really hated it when people just hummed and said nothing else. I wanted to shake her and make her tell me what that "hmm" meant, but I had a feeling it was best to leave it alone.

"So, ah, how did you and State meet?"

She smiled. "My friend was dating the president of his MC club. She asked if I wanted to come to one of their parties. I was scared. Very scared. But I did, and that's when I met him."

"Have you been together ever since that night?"

She shook her head. "Oh no. He made me feel things too fast which kind of scared the bejesus out of me. I ran, and it wasn't until he walked into my work to ask me out that I realized I regretted running that night because all I could do was think about him and the what-ifs. I said yes to a date to see how it went."

Grinning, I asked, "How did it go?"

"Terrible. He got arrested for being a suspect in a murder. He didn't do it of course. Some of the cops have it out for his club. Think the MC deals in drugs and all types of illegal stuff, but they don't. I freaked out, ran home to Mom and Dad. They helped me find the best lawyer and the next day when he walked out of jail, we were an item."

"Not an item, baby. You were my woman and I was your man," State said, coming up to us. He picked Courtney up, sat in her spot and placed her on his lap. "How you handlin' everyone gettin' together?"

I smiled. "Better now."

"Saw your expression earlier. It wasn't what you think."

I tilted my head to the side. "What do you mean?"

"State," Courtney warned.

He winked at his wife. "Carter doesn't see you as a sister."

My lips parted. *Oh.* What did I say to that?

"Erm…."

State chuckled.

"Oh, look, someone else has arrived," Courtney pointed to the house. I glanced over my shoulder.

"What the fuck?" I whispered.

Brooke saw me. She bounded up and left the other person behind. "She spotted me down the street. Somehow I mentioned the barbecue, and she wouldn't listen to me when I said she wasn't invited. Apparently, she had to show and see Carter's family because she remembered them so fondly."

"Who's that?" State asked in a rough tone.

All I could do was stare at Elena standing in my house. Well, on my back patio. While she knew where I lived, to show up like this was all levels of not okay. She beamed a pleasant smile at Beth and Patty while making her way over to them. Carter hadn't even noticed her. He was talking to Casper and Calvin at the grill.

"Hi," I heard Brooke reply to State. "I'm Brooke. Reagan's best friend. And that's the spawn of Satan."

"Carter's ex, Elena," Courtney supplied.

"Babe," State called.

I fisted my hands so I wouldn't storm over to Elena and shove one of them down her throat. Did she have no brains at all? Why was she still trying with Carter?

"Babe," State called again. Since no one else answered him, I turned. When he had my eyes, he asked, "She a problem for you?"

"I…." I didn't know. I didn't think Carter would be charmed by her, but a small part of me thought she was perfect in looks to be with him. I hated I felt that way. I loved myself enough to know I wasn't an ugly duckling. But Elena was stunning, plus they had a past.

State went to stand. Courtney said, "Wait. Just wait. Carter will deal with it."

It was then Patty called out to his son, "Carter, ah...." When Carter looked over to him and Patty thumbed toward Elena, Carter spat out his drink.

"Elena, what are you doing here?" he called, and then his eyes sought me out. When he rolled his eyes at me and smiled, my body relaxed. I undug my nails from my palms because he didn't want her here either.

Carter handed his beer over to Casper and started toward Elena. Everyone watched in silence. "What are you doing here?" he asked again.

She smiled. "Brooke was telling me you were having a barbecue, she asked me to come along."

"Lying bitch," Brooke coughed loudly into her fist. Everyone glanced at her. She looked over her shoulder. "Who said that?"

State chuckled, and I saw Casper and Calvin look at one another before they made their way over.

"Sorry, but Brooke shouldn't have said anything. This is just a family event."

Oh, wow. That warmed my belly, melting the ice I'd let form.

When she placed her palm flat against his chest, Brooke's hand landed on my forehead pushing me back. I hadn't realized I'd already started to get up, but I didn't like seeing Elena touch him.

"Thanks," I muttered.

"No worries." Brooke smiled. "Sorry about that. I didn't think she'd have the nerve, but she drove right here. I even tried to tackle her out front, but she's a slippery bitch."

"Will you marry me?" Casper asked.

Brooke looked at him, eyed him up and down, and then shook her head. "No. Thanks though."

"Elena, you should go," we heard; it was louder than our own conversation, so I could tell Carter was becoming irritated.

"Come on, Carter. My place is so much better than here. I'm sure Reagan wouldn't even let you have parties. She's so straight-laced.

You can have all the parties you want at my place. Even invite your friends over."

"And there we have it, ladies and gents," Brooke announced. I nodded.

"What?" State asked.

I shook my head. "I didn't actually think she was serious when she wanted me to offer Carter her place to live instead of here."

"She did?" Calvin laughed. "That'd never happen."

"I'm guessin' her ulterior motive is to sink her claws into one of Carter's friends then. Another reason she'd fight to have Carter live with her," State said.

I nodded. "If she has Carter at her place, she'll have a greater chance of snagging a football player."

"When Carter left for college, I was down the street and overheard Elena talking," Casper said. "She was telling her friends the only reason she was with him was she'd get his money to spend if they stayed together."

"Jesus," State clipped. "I swear there are some real dumb bitches out there. It's like she's the evil, yet pathetically stupid character out of a book."

We all agreed. I glanced back in time to see Elena being led out by Mom and Beth. Her arms were flailing around, which told me she would be ranting and raving.

Carter made it our way, while Patty went to the grill and Dad stepped up with him. Carter stopped just before me. "You all right?"

More warmth spread through my belly and up into my heart. "Yes. We all know what she's like."

He searched my face. Maybe to see if I was faking being okay, but he wouldn't find anything because I was fine. He got rid of her.

"Good." He nodded, and then turned going back to the grill with Casper and Calvin following.

"Aww, he's so cutely obvious," Brooke gushed, taking a seat next to me.

I just stared at her wide-eyed.

She sighed, reached up and patted the top of my head. State and Courtney laughed.

I gulped. Brooke had been right. Carter Anthony did like me.

Eeek!

What did I do with that information?

Act on it?

Ignore it?

Try to pretend I didn't know?

Wait for him to act on it?

Maybe he thought that I thought we were just friends. Should I show him I wouldn't mind more or was it too early?

Oh God, I didn't know how to think or what to do.

If it were anyone else other than Carter, I wouldn't be so freaked out, but this was Carter, and I didn't want anything or anyone, myself included, to stuff up what could be between us.

"You okay there?" Brooke asked, interrupting the conversation she was having with Courtney and State.

"Yep," I replied. But I wasn't because I was finding it hard to breathe. Was I sweating? It felt like I was sweating.

"You sure?" State asked.

"Ree, you don't look so good."

Brooke giggled. I felt another pat on my head. "She's all right. Just *finally* understanding something. She'll come out of it shortly."

CHAPTER TWENTY-TWO

CARTER

Something was wrong with Reagan. Throughout dinner, she wouldn't meet my gaze. If I moved over toward her, she would find an excuse to be somewhere else. After the fifth time that happened, I let out a frustrated growl.

"Don't worry," Brooke said from beside me.

"Sorry?" but just then my phone rang. I held up one finger for Brooke to wait, while I pulled my phone out of my back pocket and then answered, "Hello?"

"I have some bad news," Ted said.

"What?" I drew out.

"Some schedules for interviews and photo shoots have been moved up now Alexander knows you're serious about leaving." Alex would have known for sure if he didn't think himself too good to even talk to his own goddamn team. Instead, he went through our agents to reach out to us. He'd been our manager for all of a year. But I was sure Alex didn't know shit about football.

Unclenching my jaw, I asked, "Moved up to when?"

Ted paused, and whenever he did that, I knew it would be bad. "I've booked you on the last flight tonight to make it to your appointment tomorrow in LA."

"Fuck off," I growled out. "Tonight?"

"Yes. I'm sorry, Carter."

"Shit." I shook my head. "What time?"

"You have to be at the airport in a couple of hours."

Frustrated, I ran a hand through my hair and gripped the back of my neck. "You're killing me, man."

"And I do hate that, but it's not my fault."

"I know." I sighed. "I'll be there."

Ted rattled off the information on where he'd have my ticket waiting, but I wasn't really listening. Instead, I glanced up to see everyone's eyes were on me.

"Do you have that, Carter?"

"Uh, yeah."

He groaned. "Just get in the cab I send there and call me when you get to the airport."

"Thanks," I replied and then ended the call. "Looks like I'll have to head off early. Tonight, in fact."

"Sucks, brother," Casper said.

"Yep." I nodded.

"You just have to think at the end of it all, you'll be a free man," Dad suggested.

I nodded and glanced over to see Reagan standing at the table holding a bowl. She gave me a sad smile.

Mom clapped. "All right. Let's get this place cleaned up so Carter can pack." Could always count on Mom to get the ball rolling. Even though she hated me traveling like I did, she'd support me. People moved about, and I went to go to the table to start clearing, but Brooke grabbed my arm.

"This time away from Reagan will be good," she whispered.

"Why?"

She shrugged, her lips lifting into a smile. "Just make sure to call her and text."

My brows dipped. "I always do."

"Good," she said, then punched me in the arm and walked off.

What in the hell was that about?

I put it to the back of my mind and set to help everyone clean up. The faster we did it, the quicker everyone would leave, and I could spend at least a few minutes alone with Reagan before I left. I needed to know she was okay.

BY THE TIME I KICKED EVERYONE OUT, I HAD ABOUT AN HOUR TO PACK before the taxi showed. I quickly raced through my room and shoved things in my bag, knowing if I forgot anything, Ted would help get it to me. My gut was messing with me. I didn't know if I needed to fart or it was the start of something worse. Maybe if it was worse, I'd get to stay home. The truth was it wasn't anything but me not wanting to walk out the front door.

I'd only just come back and had been hoping to at least get a full week of waking Reagan up in the morning and watching her dazed-self gaze at me like I was her favorite chocolate. I wanted to stay and have coffee with her every morning before I hit the shower and she had to leave for work. I wanted those light brushes of skin I allowed myself and the kisses I gave her on the cheek or neck. Shit, just thinking of the last kiss I gave her on her neck, had my cock paying attention to my thoughts. He liked it when Reagan crossed my mind, even better when I was alone in the shower and I got to jerk off while picturing her under me, over me, beside me... anyway I could take her.

Dad was right. I just had to think of the last game and how my life would settle after it. He'd also promised to keep an eye on Reagan for me while I was away.

"Hey." Reagan's soft voice behind me caused me to squeal like a girl, making her laugh.

"Shit, woman. Never startle a man like that. I could come out swinging."

She snorted. "Or squeal like a girl, then hide under the bed."

I scoffed. "I would never hide unless it was from a clown. They're freaky bastards."

She smiled. "That's true. Do you need a hand with anything?"

"If you could grab my bathroom stuff, that'd be great."

She nodded and left.

I put the remainder of items in my bag and looked around the room to see if I was leaving anything I'd really need. Ted would have to hire me a suit for the events. If I took mine, it'd crease and I sucked at ironing.

Reagan was taking a while. I could hear her rummaging through something before she'd stop and then start again. By the time I made it to the bathroom door and opened it, she'd stopped what she was doing and stood quickly. Swinging around to face me, she held one hand behind her back.

My brows rose and my lips twitched. "What are you doing?" I asked, leaning against the doorframe, crossing my arms over my chest.

She shrugged. "Nothing." Then her nostrils flared. "Erm... you know, I mean, packing." She picked up my bathroom bag from the sink and thrust it out at me.

Straightening, I stood and stepped closer, taking the bag from her hand. "Thanks." I placed it back down on the sink. "Reagan?"

"Yes?"

"What do you have behind your back?"

She laughed nervously. "This feels like a *Pretty Woman* moment. Do you know that movie?"

"Yes." I nodded. "So, it's just dental floss?"

"No." She blanched. "It's, ah, drugs. I was going to snort some of the good stuff up." She nodded to herself, while I threw my head back and laughed heartily.

Jesus. I never expected what was going to come out of her mouth.

Shaking my head while my laughter subsided, I stepped even closer to her. The tips of our toes touched. She stiffened, and her breath caught. She then let it out shakily. Slowly, while smiling down at her wide eyes, I reached around her and gripped her wrist.

She tried to keep her arm behind her, but it wasn't too hard. I managed to get it back to her front and took her hand in both of my hands. I gently pried her hand open and found... a condom inside it.

My eyes widened. "Why do you have this?"

She licked her lips, sniffed and shrugged.

"Reagan," I bit out. If she thought she was going to use it with someone while I was away, I'd tell her she was mistaken. The only person she'd be using it with was me.

I picked up the condom and held it in front of her face. "Why?"

She let out a puff of air. "I found it in your bag."

Shit. I'd forgotten I had some scattered in there. "You took it out for?"

She took a step back, but I curled my free arm around her waist and tugged her forward. Right into me. She gasped. Her hands landed on my chest. I gripped her hip with the condom still in my hand and leaned in so my mouth was right next to her ear. "Why did you take it out?"

I needed to know. I needed her to say if it was for her to use or because she didn't want me to use one while I was away. Not that I would since she wouldn't be with me.

"Because..."

"Yes?"

"I-I didn't want you to use it," she whispered, her mouth close to my chest.

I groaned, leaning in even more and touching my mouth just below her ear. Her pulse beat wildly. "I wouldn't," I admitted against her skin.

Her breath came out in shallow pants. "N-no?"

Slowly, I trailed my lips up to her cheek and then stopped just beside her mouth. I kissed the corner of her lips. "No."

Her hands fisted my tee. "Carter...."

A horn honked from out front.

I closed my eyes, pain shooting through my chest. Christ, I was so close to having her mouth. Finally, her cute-as-fuck attempt at hiding a condom from my bag told me I was in with a good chance she'd accept my kiss willingly.

Another honk.

"Fuck," I muttered. "I have to go." Removing my hand from behind her, I brought it up to tilt her chin up so I could have her eyes. "I don't want to go."

"You don't?" She bit her bottom lip.

I traced my thumb over it, and she let it drop. "No," I said, staring at her lips.

Yet another honk.

"We'll talk," I stated.

"Okay," she whispered, her eyes searching my face.

Leaning in, I kissed her nose. "Soon."

Another fucking honk.

I growled in the back of my throat.

Reagan let out a whoosh of breath and laughed. "I'll go tell him you're coming before you think of murdering him."

I snorted. "Too late, sweetheart." I shook my head. "Okay, go, and I'll fix my bag without any condoms in it."

"You don't—"

"Reagan. I don't want them or need them while I'm away. Do you understand that?"

"Um, I think so."

"That'll do." I smiled and stepped back to let her pass, even though on the inside—and especially my dick—cried at me to not let her go.

With a sigh, I ran a hand over my face and looked down at the floor. For the first time ever, I goddamn hated football.

CHAPTER TWENTY-THREE

REAGAN

"*W*hat are you doing, sweetheart?" Carter asked through the phone a week later.

Sweetheart.

He'd been calling me that all the time since the barbecue.

And I loved hearing it.

"I've just walked through the door. Brooke's coming over, we're going to have a girls' night of drinking and watching The Rock."

He chuckled. "Sounds like fun. Wish I was there."

"You will be in two more weeks."

"Looking forward to it."

He'd been saying that a lot as well, every time I'd tell him how long he had until he was home again.

My nerves kicked in a lot more with him in person, they were even there on the phone, just not as much. He made me feel relaxed when he talked about random things. I still couldn't believe the scene in the bathroom before he'd left. The way his heated eyes looked at my lips told me he wanted to devour them. I would have let him, but it was the worst timing ever.

"How's everything going where you are?" I sat down on the couch.

"Boring. I've done so many interviews and had too many people taking my photo. The only part I still enjoy is being on the field."

"Dustin and North have been sending me photos of you at photo shoots and interviews. You definitely don't look happy."

"They've been sending you photos?"

"Well… yes. I thought you asked them to."

"Hell no I didn't. Sweetheart, if you want photos, I'll send them to you."

"Oh, um, okay. That would be great."

"I'll send some of all the places I go to for games, meetings and any tourist attractions. I'll even send some extra amazing ones."

"Are… are you talking about dick pics?"

Dear God. When he said amazing pictures, my mind jumped right to the image of him pulling down his shorts and… yeah, I wouldn't go there, but it was too late to shove those words back into my mouth.

"I have to go," I blurted.

"Do you want me to, Ree?" he asked in a low tone.

How did I put myself in this position? Oh, right, I spoke before my brain could tell me it was a bad idea.

"What?" I laughed nervously. Then snorted and lastly blew out a raspberry. "I-I, no, I mean, no." I laughed again. Thank God, my front door opened. "Oh, look, it's Brooke. I have to go. Talk soon. Miss you," I bumbled out, then hung up the phone.

Brooke took one look at me and asked, "What did you do now?"

Groaning, I slumped back on the couch with my hand over my face. "Kill me."

"I'm presuming that was Carter. Do you realize you just told him you miss him?"

I sat up. "I did?"

"Yes, in your jumble of fast words out of your mouth. But I heard it at the end."

I threw my hands up. "Oh well. Honestly, that's nothing compared to what I just said to him."

"Shit. What was it?"

I shook my head.

My phone rang. I screamed, saw Carter's number and threw it to the other end of the couch. Brooke reached for it. "No!" I screamed. She dropped the phone cackling to herself.

"Now I know it's really bad." She grinned.

The phone stopped ringing, but my ears still were.

Dick pics, really, Reagan?

"What did you say to him?"

"We were talking about photos, the ones North and Dustin send me. I thought he knew about them, but he didn't."

Her brows shot up. "So why would they send them?"

"I don't know."

"Maybe they know he likes you and wants you to know he's trustworthy."

I shrugged. "Maybe. Anyway, he said he was going to send me something amazing and… I asked if it was going to be a dick pic."

Brooke sucked in a big breath. There must have been some saliva in there too because next, she choked and started coughing. Standing, I walked to her and patted her back.

My phone then chimed in with a message.

We both stared at it on the couch.

"Read it," Brooke said, after clearing her throat.

"Nope." I shook my head.

"Do it or I will."

I knew she would. Even if I took her to the ground, she'd fight tooth and nail to get her way.

"Fine." I went and sat back on the couch and picked up my phone. "What if—"

"Open it," she demanded.

"But maybe—"

"Ree, open the damn thing."

"Okay." I nodded. I unlocked my phone and saw it was a text from Carter. An image text. My eyes grew. "It's an image text from Carter."

"Hoo-wee, let's have a look."

I shook my head. "I can't. I shouldn't have said it in the first place. You know how I blurt stuff out without thinking, it was one of those moments. I don't want to see his penis until it's in the flesh in front of me... well, if that happens."

Brooke snorted. "It's going to happen. From what you told me about before he left, it's so going to happen." She grinned.

My pulse raced at the thought.

I jolted when another text came through.

"Open them already."

"Okay." I nodded, and then pressed on it. It went right into Carter's texts since he was the last person I texted about Wesley doing something silly in class, and when the picture Carter sent popped open, I laughed.

My hand went over my stomach and I laughed some more.

"What?" Brooke asked.

My hand came up. I wanted to read the text before I told her.

Carter: You don't need to be embarrassed. I know you, Ree, you said it by accident. I thought we could start out slow :)

Smiling so wide I was sure my jaw would crack, I looked up at Brooke, then showed her the text. She saw it, grinned, giggled and said, "He's awesome."

"I know." When she passed the phone back, I looked at the picture again. It was of his foot. He sent me a picture of his foot.

He was adorable.

Me: I'm sorry I just blurt out random thoughts.

Carter: I don't care what you say or do, but I do care about you not answering my call because you were embarrassed. You don't need to be with me.

Me: I'll try not to. TRY!

Carter: That's all I can ask for. Now, where's my photo woman?

Giggling to myself, I lifted my free hand, snapped a photo and sent it off.

Carter: Love it. Have a good night.

Me: Thanks!

"Awe, you two are the cutest."

I jumped and spun around, nearly falling off the couch. Brooke was leaning over the back of the couch reading over my shoulder.

"You scared the hell out of me."

She snorted. "I could tell, because you forgot I was even in the room."

"I…" I went to deny it, but she was right, and then I felt bad about it. "I'm sorry."

She scoffed. "Don't worry about it, honey. I'm totally happy for you."

"Really?"

"Hell yes."

"But is it too soon to jump to conclusions? We haven't even—"

Her hand covered my mouth. "Stop," she ordered. "Jump to conclusions. You can because Carter is it for you. Everyone knows how obsessed he is with you. *Everyone.*"

"Maybe that's why Casper called today and asked what my plans were on the weekend. He kept mentioning if I needed or wanted to go anywhere with a man, he could take me. He wouldn't want me to go off with some random guy just for company. He said Carter wouldn't like it a couple of times as well."

Brooke laughed. "They're looking out for you for Carter."

I smiled. "That's sweet."

"It really is."

I stood. "Let's get the night started." I walked from the living room into the kitchen with Brooke following. "Vodka, vodka, or vodka?"

"Damn, it's a hard one. Vodka and orange juice please."

"Done. And while I do that, I want to hear all about you."

"Ah, you know all about me. You know when I lost my virginity, when I got my first period, and when I got a scare from trying nipple clamps with Joe, my old boyfriend."

Rolling my eyes, I said, "Yes. But what's happened recently."

"Nothing." She shook her head and went to the freezer to grab some ice. She came back with the tray and saw me glaring at her. "Seriously, nothing is going on."

I just stared, then after a moment, I said, "So it's fair you know everything and I don't?"

Her head dropped back to look at the ceiling. She straightened. "Dustin has called me a few times and asked me out."

My eyes widened. "And?"

"I said no."

"You said no?"

"Yep."

"Why?"

"If I said yes and we went out a few times and he decided he wasn't all that into me, then I wouldn't be able to see Benjie."

I slid a glass her way. "And you want to see Benjie."

She smiled, and it was all warmth. "I do. He's a great kid and makes me see what I'm missing out on. I need to find a man who wants forever so I can start our own family."

"Wow, that's a big step."

She nodded. "I know. But seeing how things are going for you and Carter, how all he can do is see, breathe, and want you... I want that with someone."

"What about if you find that with a woman?" I asked.

She shrugged. "Then it's a woman and we can look at IVF or adopting."

"But what if Dustin could be that one?"

Her brows dipped. "He isn't. He's a player."

"Players can change for the right woman."

"Then I'm not his right woman or else he would have seen that at the start."

"Brooke—"

"Nope." She grinned. "I'm okay with it, and I like hanging out with Benjie."

"You've spent more time with him?"

"Yeah. Just a couple of times. Dustin asked if I could entertain him a couple of times as he's been busy. I've picked him up for ice cream and taken him to the movies. So much easier having a kid to take than seeing Disney movies on your own and getting strange looks."

"Well, I'm happy if you are."

"I will be."

CHAPTER TWENTY-FOUR

REAGAN

"Hi, I just wanted to congratulate you on another amazing game," I shouted into the phone over the noise in the background on his end. I lay back in bed and got comfortable. It was Carter's second week away, and he'd just finished a game that went into overtime; it was that close.

He must be tired, but I felt the need to call him.

So, I did.

As the days passed, it was getting easier and easier to reach out to him without worrying if I was interrupting something or thinking he wouldn't want to talk to me.

He did, because each time I called or texted, he either answered, texted back right away or got one of his friends to tell me he'd get in touch as soon as he could.

I'd been surprised he answered after the game. I was just going to leave a message telling him congratulations.

"Thanks, sweetheart," he yelled into the phone, just before more cheers erupted. "Sorry," he added loudly.

I laughed. "It's fine. I'll call you later."

"No, wait, I'll go somewhere— Shit, who let them in here?" he called. More roars sounded around him.

That was when I heard a woman's voice purring, "Carter Anthony, it's been too long," right near the phone.

My insides tightened.

"I'm on the phone," Carter clipped.

"I'll let you go," I muttered, but he probably didn't hear me.

"No," he demanded into the phone. But was it to the other woman or me?

"Come on, how about we have a special night like last time?" the woman questioned.

I clenched my teeth together.

"Kelly, I—"

"Don't say no, lover boy. You know how good we were betw—"

I ended the call. I couldn't hear anymore.

A second later, I felt like kicking myself. What I should have done was have Carter hand over the phone to the bimbo Kelly and told her to go find someone else to play with. That Carter and I were working on something together. I was sure of it, and I refused to second guess what I felt and what I was sure Carter felt.

Of course there were going to be times women threw themselves at Carter. He was stunning—absolutely the hottest man I knew. Women would try for him, but I had to trust he could put a stop to it when I wasn't around.

I had to trust.

Trust in him and in us.

I couldn't see Carter falling for Kelly's words and cheating... not that it was cheating when we hadn't even talked about what we were. But I knew there was something between us, that damn woman needed to know also.

Kicking my legs so the sheet flung off me, I let out an annoyed, frustrated grumble. I sat up and slapped the bed.

A few moments earlier.

CARTER

I was pumped. We'd won the game, which meant we'd go to the conference championship game. Whoever won next would play in the Super Bowl against the LA Ligers. Teammates cheered and patted each other around me. I'd just finished speaking with North when I turned and slipped off my jersey and pads, flinging them into my locker, then my phone rang.

Grabbing it, I saw the caller ID and grinned.

"Hey, Ree."

"Hi, I just wanted to congratulate you on another amazing game." Reagan's cheery voice came over the phone. It was a little hard to hear with all the noise around me, so I blocked my other ear.

"Thanks, sweetheart." God, I loved she wanted to reach out to me after the game. And all the times she'd been the first to call or text while I was away. It showed me she was ready for us to move to the next stage.

When my teammate's roared again, I said loudly, "Sorry."

"It's fine. I'll call you later," she shouted, and I could tell she was smiling.

"No, wait, I'll go somewhere—" Fuck. Hockey players had puck bunnies. Football players had the same type of women who slunk around the lockers. Jersey chasers. Without thinking, I said into the phone, "Shit, who let them in here?" When some of the team saw the women enter the room, more roars sounded. They were pumped, and all the single guys would be looking forward to the attention. I was just goddamn annoyed someone let them in.

"Carter Anthony, it's been too long." Kelly, someone I hooked up with a long time ago, sauntered over.

Hell. I hoped Reagan didn't hear her.

"I'm on the phone," I clipped harshly. I wasn't in the mood for her or any other woman, except the one on the phone.

"I'll let you go," Reagan muttered. She probably didn't think I heard, but I did, and my gut clenched.

"No," I demanded into the phone, just as Kelly's hand landed on my chest. I shook my head. "Come on, how about we have a special night like last time?"

Fuck. Reagan would have heard that since Kelly was damn close, and I was trying to fight off her octopus hands from rubbing all over me.

"Kelly, I—"

"Don't say no, lover boy. You know how good we were between the sheets." She pouted.

"Not interested," I told her. "Reagan?" When I received no answer, I pulled the phone away and saw a blank screen.

Shit. Crap. Christ. She'd hung up on me.

God no. She could be thinking the worst.

There was no way in hell I would touch Kelly with a ten-foot pole when I had Reagan waiting at home for me. Reagan with a light laugh, soft heart, with an unfiltered mouth, and with a rockin' body. All for me.

Kelly went to grab for me again. I backed up, pissed about the situation and about Reagan overhearing when she could jump to some messed up conclusion.

"Look, Kelly, that was one time, and it'll never happen again, I have a woman now."

Her brows shot up. "You do?"

"Yeah, and she was just on the fucking phone overhearing what you said."

She winced. At least she felt bad for it.

"Yo, Carter. We heading out?" North asked, walking up to my side. He glanced over at Kelly and ignored her.

"I have to talk to Reagan ASAP."

196

"Why?" North drew out.

"She overheard shit that wasn't anything with Kelly."

"Oh crap."

Yep.

But then my phone rang. Pulling it up, my eyes shot wide when I saw it was Reagan's number flashing across the screen.

I glanced at North. "It's her."

"Well, answer it, brother." He turned and shouted, "Quiet it down, dickheads." Things settled a little more.

Nodding, I pressed the button and put it against my ear. "Reagan, I'd never—"

"Can you put Kelly on the phone please?"

"Reagan, I—"

"Please, Carter. I promise to be nice if that helps?"

"It wouldn't bother me if you weren't. I'd let you do anything, so here she is." I held the phone out to a shocked Kelly. "She wants to talk to you."

My heart was ready to punch out of my chest the way it beat so hard, as if it wanted to hit me for the stupid incident in the first place. I should have shoved Kelly away as soon as I saw her and screamed, "I have a girlfriend." But I didn't, now all I could think about was Reagan wanting to tell Kelly she could have me.

Shit, would she move me out of the house?

Out of her life?

Kelly gulped, and said, "Hello? ... Yes. ... I understand. ... I'm sorry you heard that. I didn't know. ... I just like coming to these things. ... Maybe you're right. I could do better. ... Thank you. Yes... you too. ... I'll put him on now. Bye." A smiling Kelly handed me back the phone. "She sounds wonderful, Carter. I'm glad."

Numbly, I nodded and watched Kelly walk off before North helped me put the phone back to my ear. "Reagan?"

"Hi, everything's fine now."

I opened my mouth, closed it, and opened it again to say, "What did you say to her?"

There was a pause.

She sucked in a breath and said, "I told her that you and I could have something going. That I didn't appreciate hearing what I did when I'm so far away, and then I mentioned she could do so much better than hanging around in locker rooms for guys to hook up with."

That woman.

My woman.

She surprised me all the time.

"You're amazing," I said, my voice suddenly thick with emotion. I wanted to tell her exactly how I felt. I didn't care that even though it had been a little less than two months, I was completely in love with Reagan Wild. But I couldn't say it over the phone.

Jesus, I wished I was home, so I could show her and tell her just how special she was to me.

I heard her giggle. "I try."

"You don't need to try, sweetheart. It's just you."

North stood beside me grinning from ear to ear. I shoved him away and mouthed, "Five." He nodded, and I moved to a quieter corner.

"You didn't mind I called and spoke to her?"

"No way. Jesus, I was scared you'd jump to the wrong conclusions. Having you call back to sort it out was better than winning the game tonight."

She snorted.

"Ree, I mean it. I felt sick when you overheard—"

"We all have a past, Carter."

"We do, thank you for understanding."

"I..."

"Sweetheart?"

She cleared her throat. "I didn't like hearing what she said, but what I wanted most was her to back off from you and understand you're out of... um..."

"Out of what?"

I needed to hear her say it.

"The dating game. I mean, that's if I read what you wanted to talk about before you left right. I could be wrong and getting ahead of myself since we haven't actually talked, but—" She let out a cute little growl. "I didn't like the thought of her being there with you when I wanted to be there for you to, uh, yeah, congratulate you."

"Baby," I muttered into the phone and tried to dampen down my huge-ass smile. "You read the situation right back at home. We haven't talked, but that's where I'd like for us to go. Dating. You willing?"

"Yes," she admitted quietly and kind of breathlessly.

"Damn, I wish I was home about now."

"So do I."

Fuck it. My mind was made up. In a few days, I had a free day of nothing. I had to see her. Hold her and kiss her.

I had to go home, even if it was just for the day.

CHAPTER TWENTY-FIVE

REAGAN

*M*om had conned me into taking a sick day since it was her birthday coming up, and she wanted to have a girls' day that involved facials, nails, and massages. Of course, I was more than happy to help her out, and when I rang Tom and told him the truth, all he mumbled was, "Enjoy. Your dad's covering your classes." It was strange, but I shrugged it off since I was getting the day off. And what made it even better was that at least I knew my students wouldn't be bored.

I was watching some morning show and waiting for Mom to arrive to pick me up. I glanced at the time and noticed she was late, which wasn't like her. Picking up my phone from the coffee table, intending to call her, I got distracted by a text from Carter.

Carter: Morning, sweetheart. Hope you have a good day.

Me: Morning, I should. I'm going to a spa with Mom for her early birthday gift to herself. Hope you're not too busy today.

I waited for a response, but it didn't come. Not even from one of his friends to say he was busy. Since it was morning, they could be in the gym or a meeting together. He'd get back to me when he could. Smiling, I went into my stored numbers and brought up Mom's. As I was just about to hit Call, the front door opened.

"Hey, Mom. I was just about to call you," I said, standing from the couch.

Only it wasn't Mom who came around the corner.

My pulse shot with adrenaline as my heart took off beating wildly.

"You're not my mom," I stated like a weirdo.

He smiled. "No, I'm not." His feet ate up the distance to me.

Overwhelmed, I couldn't contain myself. I squealed and jumped at him. Only he wasn't prepared for it.

We tumbled down, landing on the couch, and with Carter on top, with his hand on my breast. He looked down to his hand and then back up slowly. "Sorry," he said, but didn't remove it.

It was hard, since he was on top of me, but I shrugged, smiling. Giddily happy to see him, to have him so close. I wrapped my arms around his neck. "You've already touched my butt, why not my boob?"

His grin was wicked and bright. "Best day of my life helping you out with your panties."

I laughed. "How can you say that?"

"Because…" He licked his lips, his grip tightening around my breast. He glanced down again, as if lost from the action. "Jesus," he cursed under his breath.

"What?" I asked breathlessly.

"Ree." He closed his eyes and then when he opened them, I saw the desire swirling. "It was the best day because you came into my life *and* I got to touch your butt."

"Really?"

"Yes."

"Carter?"

"Reagan?"

"Do you *like* me?" I raised my brows teasingly.

He chuckled, but then sobered and shook his head. "No."

"No?" I parroted. My heart seemed to stutter and stop beating.

Another shake of his head. "I don't like you. I could never *just* like you. Everything you do and everything you say does things to me. *Great* things. So I don't just like you. I love you."

My breath hitched. Tears welled.

He *loved* me.

Me!

Carter Anthony loved *me*.

Wow.

"Reagan, say something."

"Your hand is still on my boob."

He smirked, and glanced down and then up. "Yes. Is that a problem?"

"No."

"No?"

"No. I was just wondering when the man I love was going to kiss me."

"Christ." He closed his eyes. His forehead came down on mine. "You love me?"

"Yes, ah, I mean, I do, but only if you kiss me before I self-combust."

His eyes came open. Then he pulled back enough so I could see his grin. "I can't have that, now, can I?"

"No. Definitely not."

"Then I'd better kiss you."

"Please." I nodded.

Still grinning, he leaned in and gently touched his lips to mine, before pulling back. I grumbled under my breath, causing Carter to chuckle. "Still okay for this?"

"Yes," I hissed.

"You know what it means though?"

"What?" I asked his mouth.

"You belong to me."

I hummed under my breath in contentment at those words. "But you also know it means *you* belong to me."

"Christ, yes," he got out before he slanted his mouth over mine. I moaned. I couldn't help it or stop it. I'd wished and thought of this moment for so long. I gripped the back of his neck, and his hand tightened around my breast, ripping another moan from within me.

We deepened the kiss, opening for one another. For our first taste of each other, I liked it a lot. His warm, wet mouth tasted of coffee as his tongue tangled with mine.

Yet, I still needed him closer. My legs separated as he moved between them. Our bodies lined up with one another, yet he kept a lot of his weight off me with the hand that wasn't caressing my breast.

When I ran my hands down his back, his muscles twitched under my touch, and his kiss turned demanding. I snuck a hand up his tee, circling my fingers over his smooth, heated skin. I wanted to feel more, see more.

I also needed to…. His hips jutted forward when I gripped his tight butt in both hands, a growled-out groan spilling from his mouth into mine. Another grip, and another thrust into me… into the right spot. I had to tear my mouth from his for breath and to whimper from the pleasure.

Trailing his lips down my cheek, my neck, to my shoulder, he then bit.

"Carter," I breathed, and greedily I slipped a hand into his jeans. Only he froze. His hand left my breast and the massaging I was enjoying stopped. He then grabbed my wrist and pulled my hand free. He brought it to the front of him and kissed my wrist.

"W-what?"

He groaned as if in pain, resting his forehead against mine. "Sweetheart, I didn't come home just for a quick roll in the sheets. I had to see you, kiss you, and make you understand I'm all in for this between us. I want no one but you." He pressed his lips against my cheek and ran his tongue down to my ear. "Besides, once I get inside you, I'll not want to leave, and I have to fly back tonight. I want to take my time, cherish each and every part of you. I don't want a wham-bam-thank-you-ma'am moment. I'd like it to be special, because you are to me."

Holy wow.

He just said that.

My heart frantically tried to beat out of my chest to get to him.

I opened my mouth, snapped it closed and then opened it again. "You flew home just to kiss me?"

Smiling, he sat up on the end of the couch and to my shock, picked me up and planted me on his lap. "Yes. And to make sure you knew I was in love with you."

I sniffed. "That's the sweetest thing anyone's ever done for me."

He kissed my neck. "I'm glad."

Still, I couldn't help but feel a little annoyed. Carter would go after kissing me, leaving me wanting more.

"I know," he said as if reading my mind, cupping my face. "I should have waited until I was back fully, but I couldn't. I acted before I thought and booked a ticket because all I wanted to do was have you in my arms. But now I feel like a dick because now we know where we stand with each other, yet I'm just leaving again at the end."

His words rolled around in my head. Honestly, I couldn't be too annoyed. He'd done it to see me, to make sure I understood he loved me.

Smiling, I shrugged. "What's a week between us when we have so much more time together coming up."

He grinned, kissed my nose and said, "I'm glad you see it like that."

"But…" I ran my hands up his chest. "Does that mean we can't fool around a bit?"

His eyes lit with heat. "No. I don't suppose it does." Then he smirked and slowly drew me closer to have our lips just touch.

Against them he said, "I always wished we'd be here, in this spot, with you up against me. I guess wishes do come true."

"They do," I whispered.

He closed his eyes. Mine followed suit, and we kissed. It was heavy, hot, and so damn amazing.

Who'd have thought I would have the guy I crushed on in high school in my house, in my arms, and kissing me like I was treasured. If anyone would have told me Carter was my future, I would have laughed my ass off, but there it was.

I curled my hands into his hair and slanted my mouth against his more. His hardness pulsed between my thighs as he dragged me closer, so our groins connected. I whimpered. He groaned.

Breathless, I broke the kiss. "I never thought having you would be possible. I didn't think...." I thinned my lips, cursing my running mind and mouth.

"Didn't think what?"

Blushing, I buried my head into his neck. His hand slid around me to cup my butt. He jostled me. "Didn't think what, Ree?"

"That you liked bigger girls like me."

He groaned, but it wasn't in pleasure. His hand threaded through my hair and gently, he tugged. I pulled back so he could have my eyes. "I was a douche. The biggest idiot back in high school. Do you remember when I told you I remembered you?"

"Yes." I'd just been too nervous to ask how.

"Well, I did. I remembered you because wherever you were at school, my eyes somehow sought you out so I could get my fill. I used to look for you because I liked who I was staring at. Your long thick hair, your beautiful smiling eyes, and how you'd laugh loudly when you thought something was funny. You had to let that joy out for everyone to hear."

"You used to look for me?"

He grinned. "Yes. Back then I was stupid to let my dickhead teammates control who I should or shouldn't be involved in. It's how I ended up with someone I didn't really like. But I dreamed of having someone I always wanted. You."

"I... um, wow. I didn't know."

His smile softened. "I know you didn't. I love you just as you are, and I always will."

My heart swelled. "You're too much, Carter Anthony."

"I hope in a good way?"

I nodded. "In a very good way."

He tipped his chin up and touched his mouth to mine. That was all it took, just a touch and I was lost in the sensation of having him kiss me with so much passion it hurt to breathe.

Our mouths slanted the other way, the kiss hot and heavy, so much so, I ground down on him again and again. I couldn't stop. My body was humming with desire.

His hand squeezed my ass, encouraging me to rock against his erection. I responded eagerly. Warm pleasure spread through me as my clit hit him in the perfect way, over and over.

Carter groaned in the back of his throat. It ran into my mouth just before his kisses drifted to my cheek and down to my neck. His grip, one still on my ass and the other on my hip, tightened. He lifted his hips and tugged me down to rock back and forth over him.

"W-we need to stop," he breathed into my neck. I'd never heard him stumble over his words before and couldn't help but smile; it was us being together that caused it. It was the hungered ache we had, craving for one another.

"Not yet," I moaned, leaning in to bite his neck.

"Christ, sweetheart, you'll make me come in my pants."

Hearing that made me want to watch him lose himself. I gripped his shoulders and kissed his lips before sucking on his bottom lip to nibble on it. Our eyes caught, both hooded and filled with heat.

"Carter," I begged.

His eyes flared, his jaw clenched, and suddenly I was flipped to my back on the couch with him hovering over me. "I can't say no to you. Deny you."

My smile was big. He shook his head. Reaching up, I curled my hands around the back of his neck and applied pressure. He was too far away. "This means good things for my future."

He chuckled. Only it died when I slid one hand down to cup his hardness, giving it a squeeze. His nostrils flared. He grabbed my hand while his other kept him up hovering over me and pulled me away. I would have complained since I wanted to touch him, to show him he drove me crazy with so much need. That was until he nestled his erection against me. I gasped when he pushed up and down over me, sucking my bottom lip to bite down on it.

He reached between us, and I felt him adjust himself and when he was back over... my God, it was in the right spot. A spot that had me closing my eyes and arching up.

"Ree," was all Carter said. My eyes sprung open to see him shifting up and down over me, but his eyes were on mine.

My hands glided from his waist up to his neck. "Kiss me," I whispered.

He nodded, leaning down. He slapped a hand on the arm of the couch to keep up the grinding, the rubbing against each other. I'd never dry humped before, groped blindly in the dark, yes. But dry humping no, and if this was how it was, I was all for it.

When his lips crashed into mine, I wrapped a leg over his and lifted my hips more, helping. I moaned his name against his lips and our tongues tangled together again and again.

"Sweetheart?"

"I-I'm close."

He grunted, his lips trailing down to my neck, which he seemed to have a fascination with—not that I minded. He licked and sucked. When he bit down, pulling my skin into his mouth, I lost it.

"Carter!" I cried. He rubbed against me harder and faster. His warm breath coming quicker against my neck while I kept coming and coming with each thrust against me.

"Ree," he groaned low in the back of his throat. "Christ." He got to his hand above me and ground his cock against me. His jaw clenched, his eyes widened a fraction as I ran my hand up and over his chest and pinched his nipples. "Shit," he hissed. "I'm going…." He slammed down on me, his mouth on mine and I took his kiss greedily as he groaned into my mouth and his body shuddered over me.

CHAPTER TWENTY-SIX

CARTER

*M*y brain fizzled. All I knew was I'd just blown a load hard into my jeans, and I wasn't even sure I was breathing. The woman I was probably squishing under me was amazing, surprising, and passionate.

Taking some of my weight from her, I got to my elbows to look down at the woman I loved. She was smiling lazily up at me and reaching up to run her fingers softly through my hair.

A giggle escaped her. "If that's how we are with our clothes on, then we're going to be phenomenal naked."

I blinked, and then threw my head back and laughed. Sitting back, I grabbed her, pulling her up to sit. I kissed her lips, her cheek, her nose, and her neck. "Damn right we will be." I stood from the couch. "For now, I'll have a shower and get cleaned up so I can take you on a date."

Her eyes widened. "Like, a *date*, date?"

Grinning, I nodded. "It should have happened before what happened on the couch, but I couldn't resist you."

She winked playfully. "I guess I am a seductress."

I tapped her nose. "Yes, you are." Leaning back in, because I couldn't get enough, I kissed her again before moving off into the bathroom. I stuck my head back out. "Think about where you want to go to lunch."

"Will do, captain." She saluted, a happy look on her face. Pride filled my chest knowing I'd helped put that look there. I closed the door again and pressed back against it.

Reagan Wild was finally mine.

Shit, my smile grew so big I glanced to the mirror and saw I looked like a madman with how happy I was.

Reagan agreed to be mine. I wasn't sure if she knew what she was in for, but there were no take backs. I could kiss her, touch her, smile with her. Laugh with and at her for her unique antics and just love her as she was.

She was mine.

Jesus, I wanted to sing, and that wasn't a good thing. My voice could make babies cry. Instead, I peeled off my clothes, cringing and then grinning like a fool at the stickiness in my boxers, and got in the shower so I could wash quickly and get back out to spend the day with *my* woman. I was damn lucky to have her family at my back, else I wouldn't have pulled off the surprise. The look on her face was one I'd remember always. It was a mixture of shock and pure joy.

I hated that I had to fly back tonight, but I was still glad I chose to see her.

Best damned day of my life.

Even better than winning any game or award.

A knock sounded on the door. "Carter," Reagan called out.

I shut off the shower and stepped out, wrapping a towel around my waist. I went to the door and opened it. Her eyes heated as they ran over my body.

"No taking advantage of me, woman." I grinned.

She snorted. "I do have some restraint."

"Uh-huh, sure you do. Which is why your eyes are eating me up right now." I laughed when her eyes snapped up to mine and narrowed. I smirked. "Did you need something other than me?"

She blushed. "Oh, um, someone's at the door for you."

"Me?" That was strange.

"Yes, he said he's from the *Western Post*."

I screwed my face up, annoyed. If something was going to put a dampener on the best goddamn day, it was the paparazzi. "Shit."

"What's wrong?"

"He's just a shmuck looking for some type of story. He must have got wind of me flying in and thought there's a story behind it. Sorry, sweetheart. I'll get dressed and get rid of him." I slipped out of the bathroom with a swift kiss on Reagan's cheek before I went into my room and quickly dressed.

Making my way into the living room, I saw Reagan in the kitchen; she was at the stove cooking. I went to the front door and opened it.

"Carter Anthony." Mal, from the *Western Post*, smiled. "Can I get an exclusive on why you rushed home for the day?"

"Mal." I sighed. "You know I like my private life private."

"Who answered the door? Is that the girl from the game? Is she your girlfriend? Are you living here with her?"

Shaking my head, I said, "You'll all find out eventually. For now, I'm asking you to leave."

"Come on, Carter. Give me something, anything."

Crossing my arms over my chest, I narrowed my eyes. "How did you find out I was home?"

His brows raised. "Home? So this is where you're living, and from my digging, you don't own it but a Miss Reagan Wild does." He grinned big. "Thanks, Carter, that's all I needed. Unless you want to pose with your girl for a picture?"

Clenching my jaw, I clipped, "Goodbye, Mal, and if I see you lurking or if Reagan tells me you're still around after I leave, then I'll have to stop you."

"Is that a threat?" he asked gleefully.

"No, Mal. It's a warning." With that, I slammed the door and stalked into the kitchen. "I'm sorry, sweetheart."

She spun around from cooking bacon. Her brows dipped, her mouth forming a thin line. "You're not going already, are you?"

I smiled softly, taking the steps I needed to have her in my arms. "No, Ree. Not until late tonight."

"Phew," she muttered and sagged into me, wrapping one arm around my waist, while the other still held a spatula.

I eyed it. "Should I be worried?"

She laughed. "Not yet at least. But what were you sorry about?"

"The reporter's done some digging. He knows you own this house and now that I live here. He's put two and two together and placed you as my girlfriend."

She bit her bottom lip. Her eyes warmed. "And that's a problem because?"

My brows shot up. "You don't care?"

"Well, no. Should I? I mean I am, your, um, girlfriend, right?"

"Yes. Shit, yes. But being with me could mean being photographed without knowing and without your permission. Being hounded by the paparazzi at any given time. Sometimes it's hell on earth, what they try to get out of you or what they could catch you in."

She shrugged. Leaning up, she kissed my chin and then shifted in my arms to turn the bacon. "Then I'll keep my mouth closed and make sure I don't pick up any hookers for a while."

I snorted out a laugh. Placing my hands on her hips, I aligned my body to her back. "You usually pick up hookers?"

She waved the spatula in the air. "It's just something Brooke and I usually do every Saturday night, but we can refrain for a while. It's bonding, you know. Talking to hookers and sharing them."

Grinning like an idiot, I bent to kiss her neck and felt her shiver. "God, I love you and the things you say."

"What, because I like picking up hookers with my best friend?"

She glanced over her shoulder and mock glared at me. "Don't think you can get in on the act with us. It's girls' time, mister."

"I would never."

"Good." She kissed my cheek and turned her attention to the food. "But honestly, Carter, nothing and no one can put me off being with you. They can take photos and ask questions all they like. It won't change how I feel about you, and it never will."

I had no words. Instead, I wrapped her tightly in my arms and prayed it would stay that way.

SINCE WE ATE BRUNCH REAGAN COOKED, WE ENDED UP HEADING OUT to do some shopping. She said she had to stock up on candy for her class because exams were approaching and she bribed her kids with treats if they got questions correct in prep for the exams.

We walked hand in hand through the shopping center. We'd received a few extra-long glances from people, which was nothing new for me. But then I spotted a guy hiding behind a tall standing potted plant with his camera raised. Mal must have spread the word.

Damn it all.

"Hey, mister."

We stopped and turned to find a boy about five looking up at me. "Hey, kiddo. What's happening?"

The boy's smile all but cracked his jaw. "You Carter, the football guy?"

"I am." I nodded, smiling down at him.

He looked at his silent mom standing just behind him. "See, Ma. I told you it was him." He turned back to me. "I told my ma it was you and she said no. But it is you."

I chuckled. "It is."

"Can you sign something for me. My dad is a huge fan too."

"I sure can. Do you have anything for me to sign?"

He looked to his mom as she searched through her bag. When she came up empty, his shoulders dropped. He glanced back up at me with tears in his eyes. "We don't have anythin'."

Releasing Reagan's hand, I got to my knee in front of him. "What's your name?"

"Josh."

"Well, Josh, this is a shopping center so I'm sure we can find a place to grab some paper and a pen."

"Really?"

"Sure." I smiled. Standing, I glanced at his mom to make sure it was okay. When she nodded, I put out my hand for Josh. He looked at it like it was a new and exciting toy before he slowly put his hand in mine.

And that was another reason I loved playing ball. Besides the rush, I loved seeing the kids get excited when meeting with me. Becoming awestruck and then happy when I took time out for them. I peeked at Reagan as we made our way past her into the first store beside us. She was smiling brightly up at me. Her soft smile and warm eyes showed me she was proud.

I ran my free hand against her arm as Josh and I kept walking, Reagan and Josh's Mom following behind us. Reagan started talking to Josh's Mom. God, she was beautiful.

Josh leaned into me. "Is that your girlfriend?"

Looking down at him, I grinned and nodded. "She sure is."

"Cool."

"Hey, how come you're not at school?"

He screwed up his nose. "I have to see the dentist."

I winced. A dentist to me was like having to visit a torturer, and from the look on Josh's face, he felt the same. Damn, I hated being supportive over something I also disliked. "I know it's a pain to see the dentist, but it's also important to make sure your teeth stay healthy and strong. That's why I still go to them."

He sighed and nodded. "I know."

We stopped at the gaming counter, and I asked for some paper and a pen. The guy behind the counter looked at me weirdly, probably not knowing who I was, but that didn't bother me. He still grabbed them for me and placed them on the counter.

"Josh, what's your dad's name?"

"Dad."

I laughed. "His other name, that your mom calls him."

"Oh, honey-lumkin."

I burst out laughing. Josh's Mom cleared her throat. I glanced to see her blushing. "His name's Ben. And I'm Linda."

"Thanks."

Leaning over the paper, I quickly wrote a short message for both Josh and Ben, then handed it over to Josh. His hand shook taking it, and then he brought it up to his face. "To Ben and Josh. Wishes can come true. I've found mine, and it's good to try and reach for yours. Carter Anthony."

I ruffled his hair. "Great reading, Josh."

Linda grinned proudly. "He's at the top of his class."

I held out my fist, and he knocked his tiny one against mine "Good work, man."

"Thanks."

With a quick goodbye, they left the store, and I walked up to a beaming Reagan. "That was amazing," she said, and wrapped her arms around my waist.

"Love making kids happy."

"I can tell."

I glanced over her shoulder to find we still had company. "Another reporter is following us."

She just grinned up at me. "Then we'd better make it a good show." Threading her hands behind my neck, she pulled my head down and kissed me right there in front of everyone.

Since Reagan wasn't fazed by the extra attention, I pushed it back in my mind and enjoyed the rest of the time out together without caring about being photographed or even when another few reporters came up to us as we were leaving after a late lunch to ask question after question. Which I ignored. Yep, things were fine, great even, until one dickhead appeared and ruined my mood. Though, I should have figured Reagan would find the upper hand and make me fall that much more in love with her.

We'd just made it to her car, being followed by at least five reporters, when a guy called out, "She's not your usual type, Carter. She's fat and just a school teacher."

I started around the back of the car for him when Reagan stepped in front of me. Her hands landed on my chest. I paused and looked down at her. She winked up at me and then moved to stand at my side, facing the reporters. She laughed, then smiled, even threw in an eye roll. "Haven't you heard having something big is better?" People laughed. "I like who I am, *just* the way I am. So does Carter. Please let there be no judging here. It's no good for anyone to be that way. Lastly, I'm not *just* a teacher. I'm an awesome teacher helping shape young minds." Reagan waved to a camera I hadn't seen because I was too busy glancing down at my girlfriend in awe. "Hi, guys. Don't forget to study. Sorry I'm not there today. I had to visit the dentist." I wanted to laugh at her lie, an idea she must have gotten from Josh. She took my hand in hers and dragged me back to the front of the car. I dropped her hand and placed mine on the small of her back, guiding her to the passenger side while reporters yelled more questions around us. All I could do was smile down at Reagan as I opened her door and she got in. I leaned in and kissed her quickly on the lips.

"You're perfect."

She grinned. "Thank you."

CHAPTER TWENTY-SEVEN

REAGAN

"*A*re you sitting down?" Carter asked through the phone. He'd just gotten off his plane, and I was already missing him. Seeing him walk out of the house and knowing I wouldn't see him for a while longer was harder because I knew he was mine.

Thinking he was mine didn't make me so nervous anymore. What helped was the amount of affection Carter showered upon me, which made me believe it so much more.

Carter Anthony was mine.

Openly showing Carter affection was something easily done, and it was also because I couldn't resist. I wanted to show Carter I wanted to touch, kiss, and hug him. I didn't think he minded though. I loved the way his eyes would warm each time I initiated the contact between us.

"Reagan?" he called.

"Sorry." I shook my head. "I'm still half asleep. I'm sitting down now and turning on the TV."

"Quickly, woman."

"I'm going as fast as my sleepy self will let me." I turned to the channel Carter was talking about.

"It's going to start."

"I have it on. What am I watching and why was it urgent I had to get up for it and more importantly, where are you watching it from?"

"The airport and you'll see."

A presenter came on. "Today we have a sweet story for you all about Carter Anthony. You all heard earlier he's leaving the Wolves to begin a coaching career. Many will be sad to see him finishing his career in football, but we can all hope he'll be coaching more talent for our future. Carter was spotted shopping with a Reagan Wild, who is confirmed to be his girlfriend. He stopped to sign an autograph for a child and from this photo, we can all see the caring man and his proud girlfriend as she watches on. But that's not what we're all talking about in the studios. It's the video that I'm sure will go viral of Carter about to defend his girlfriend when someone called her fat. Yes, I know you're all hoping for a fight in the video, but it doesn't happen. Something even better does. Watch it for yourself and hit up the site to tell me what you think." The video of me standing beside Carter and saying what I did started.

I was surprised I actually didn't look how I'd felt in that moment. Scared out of my mind. I looked happy and calm. Content, even after I'd heard something harsh being shouted at me. All I could think about was saving Carter from beating someone's head in, so I had to step in and say my piece. Honestly, I didn't really take it all in at the time, but I could see others in the video, how they smiled and laughed with me.

The presenter came back on. "I know I won't be the only one supporting this new relationship. As far as I'm concerned, Carter Anthony has made the right choice with Reagan Wild. She's inspiring, I'm glad she's out there teaching the children of our city."

Carter chuckled in my ear. "Lucky they don't know about you threatening to throw up on them."

I laughed. "I'm unique in my teaching ways."

"You are, and that makes you more loveable. Only now it won't be just your family, your students, and me loving you. You'll have so many in the country too. Not sure how that makes me feel."

I snorted. "I think you're over exaggerating. Nothing will change."

It was Carter's turn to snort. "You'll see. Now I'll let you get back to sleep. Don't forget to set that other alarm I got you." I grinned. While Carter and I had been down the street, he'd found an alarm that guaranteed to wake the most difficult person. He'd grinned at me, and said, "Just until I get home," before purchasing it.

"It's all set," I told him.

"Good, it should help while I'm away. Then you won't need it when I'm beside you."

Oh, wow.

For some stupid reason, I hadn't thought of Carter sleeping beside me in my room, which could be our room when he got home. I hadn't really thought past the day.

"Ree?"

"Yes?" I whispered into the phone, gripping it tightly.

"Are you okay with me saying that?"

"What?" I pretended I didn't understand him, just so I could hear him say it again.

"Sleeping in your bed when I get home?"

God, yes. But... "Are you sure we aren't moving too fast?"

"Sweetheart, I know where I'm at in the relationship, but I don't want to scare you off. So, if you want to slow things down I can stay in my room until you're ready," he said gently.

"Where are you in the relationship?"

A pause, and then he replied, "I don't want to scare you more. Maybe it's best we leave it until I get home and then talk about it."

"I'm not scared, just worried if we jump into things too fast, then things will... I don't know, fizzle out maybe?"

"I can't predict the future, but I want you to know I'll try and do anything in my power to keep us going."

It was my turn to pause. I was constantly amazed at how open he was with me, and how sweet. To me, it sounded like Carter could already see a future for us beyond dating, and I liked that thought a lot.

"I'll do the same."

"Good. For now, we'll leave it at that and talk more when I get home."

"Okay." I nodded to myself, though I was already picturing waking up to Carter. Only instead of him waking me standing over me beside my bed, he was in it and touching me in ways that made me hot all over.

"Get some sleep so you can mold kids' minds tomorrow." I could hear the smile in his voice.

"I will, and you too, except about the kids' part, but, um… enjoy your day."

He chuckled. "I will." A breath, and then he added, "I love you, Ree."

My heart stopped and then took off flying over the invisible rainbow to happiness. "Love you too. Night."

"Night, sweetheart."

When he hung up, I sank back into the couch and sighed. Then I smiled and did a giddy little dance. Thankfully, no one was around to see it.

"OMGEEEE, MISS. I SAW YOU ON TV, AND I WAS LIKE SO EXCITED I texted everyone I knew, and they were all like wow that is super cool, and it is, like really super cool because you said hi to us. In front of millions. It was the best thing ever!" Penny, another of my students, exclaimed.

Murmurs started up around the room of my favorite class. My

hands came up in front of me. They quieted. "First, Penny, what were you doing up so late? You really need to get at least eight hours of sleep each night to rest your brain for learning."

She rolled her eyes, but did it smiling. "I was working on my math homework."

"That late?" I asked.

Bradly scoffed. "She was up late wanting to be the first to view Conor Maynard's video."

"Shut up, Bradly."

"Who's Conor Maynard?" I asked.

Penny gasped. "Who's Conor Maynard? Miss, are you for real?"

Was that a trick question? Would it lead me into hearing all about Conor Maynard? Probably.

"Yes?"

"He's like the best. A singer and a blogger on YouTube. Totally the best. I love his songs, *all* of them."

"He is really good, Miss," Jenifer added.

"Then I have a feeling that no matter what I say to you, Penny, about your late nights that you won't listen."

She grinned. "Not when it comes to the love of my life."

Dear God.

"Okay then, let's move on."

Wesley's hand shot up.

I wanted to groan, but I refrained. "Yes, Wesley?"

"So you are dating Mr. Anthony?"

"Duh, stupid, it was all over TV," Penny snapped.

Wesley glared. "I don't stay up late, Penny. I get the right amount of sleep because I don't want to be dumb when I'm older."

"You—"

"Class," I shouted. "Enough. No name-calling in here. You both know this." They still acted like they were six and not in their teens. Then again, I still had my moments, but what I hated the most was name-calling. I'd had enough of that myself when I was younger. I wouldn't have it in my classroom.

"Sorry, Miss," Penny said.

"Yeah, sorry," Wesley called.

"Okay, how about I tell you all what happened, and then we can actually get some work done?" They eagerly sat forward in their seats. "I'd been out with Carter shopping, after my dentist appointment, when a reporter said something about me that wasn't very nice. I stopped and told him how I liked myself as I am. Which really everyone should, no matter how you look or act. You should be the first to like who you are. I know it's hard sometimes, but you shouldn't care what others think." I gave them a pointed look, letting that sink in. It was advice my mom had always given me, but she was my mom, and I hadn't listened to her back in the day. I wished I had because I knew it to be true. "People seemed to like what I said, and it was aired on TV. The end."

"And Mr. Anthony?" Wesley pressed.

Shaking my head, I said, "Mr. Anthony and I would like our private—"

"They're so dating. It's all over the Internet, and you could totally tell he's like 100 percent in love with her by the way he was looking at her. I'll show you the video later," Penny exclaimed.

Wesley nodded.

A knock sounded on the door, then it opened and... crap, Elena poked her head in. "Sorry, Miss Wild, but may I have a quick word?"

My brows shot up. She managed to say that without glaring or a snarl in her voice. I suddenly felt wary. Didn't all murderers become pleasant before striking?

"Of course," I said, and made my way to the door. Before I closed it, I added to the class, "How about you all pretend to study and then watch the video?"

"Yes, Miss," was called out. I knew I wouldn't have their attention until their curiosity was dulled.

Closing the door, I stepped to the side to face Elena. Her eyes narrowed for a second before she shook her head. "Look, I know you played me. You have one up on me for once, but did you have to make me look like such a fool?"

My head jerked back. "What are you talking about?"

"Saying you and Carter were just friends. Lying to me so I looked like an idiot."

Sighing, I said, "The world doesn't revolve around you, Elena. At the time we spoke, Carter and I were just friends. I honestly didn't think anything would happen. I mean how could I when you were the one who drilled into my mind no one like him could see something in someone like me."

She actually winced. "I know I'm a bitch. You just need to ignore it. I said those things because I always saw the way Carter looked at you."

I gasped. "What?"

She rolled her eyes. "He never thought I noticed and I know he used to listen to his friends too much, but I'm glad he did, else he wouldn't have dated me. But it didn't mean I was blind to the fact that if you walked into a room, his eyes were on you. It pissed me off. Still does. But I know when I'm beaten. I just wished you'd said something earlier."

"I... um.... You've shocked me. I don't know what to say." And I didn't. Elena wasn't as stupid as I thought. She knew what she was doing all along. She was only with Carter and wanted him recently because she was jealous of me.

Mind blown.

Never would have expected that.

"I'm sorry."

She shrugged. "Yeah, well, whatever. Just take care of him."

I smiled softly. "I will."

She huffed and then walked off.

My phone in my pocket vibrated. I took it out.

Brooke: WTF, you didn't tell me you'd been on TV. Stinky Steve just showed me.

Me: I tried to call you. I assumed you must have seen that by

now, but you didn't answer. Where were you when I was in crisis mode? I have so much to tell you.

Brooke: I was at home.

Me: LIAR!!!

Hearing heels clicking on the floor, I looked up to see Brooke coming down the hall. My hands went to my hips and I narrowed my eyes at her. "Where were you?"

She snorted. "That look may work on your students, but I've known you too long, it does nothing for me."

Damn.

"Fine. At least tell me where you were last night?"

She waved her phone at me. "You rang at 1:00 a.m. It was the middle of the night and I was in bed. My phone was on silent."

I crossed my arms over my chest. "I rang your house phone too."

She tensed, then sighed. "Fine. I was doing a favor for Dustin while he was away and his ex was out of town. I was at his place minding Benjie."

"Why didn't you just tell me?"

She threw her hands up in the air. "I don't know. He confuses me. I confuse myself, and sleeping in his bed which smells like him confused me even more." She shook her head. "I won't date him and I know you want me to give him a chance."

Fisting my hand, I reached out and punched her in the shoulder. "If you tell me not to say anything or hound you about dating him, I won't. You just have to tell me."

She groaned. "I know. I'm just being silly."

"Yes, you are."

"Okay, no need to agree so fast. We'll talk more about it later, but for now, tell me what's happened with Carter before your kids start lighting things on fire."

"That was one time, and I was..." She raised her brows. "Okay, two, but I was there both times and we were reenacting—"

"Yes, yes. I know the story, but spill about Carter, woman."

I smiled. "We're dating."

She groaned and thumped her forehead. "I know that. It's all over everywhere, but I want the best friend details. Have you slept with him? Is he a good kisser? What size is his cock?"

"Shush," I hissed and looked around the empty hall. "No, yes, and I'm not saying, but I will tell you there was some dry humping going on, and it was amazing."

She grinned, rubbing her hands together. "Really?"

"Oh yes."

"Yay!" Her hand went up in the air just as my classroom door opened and Jenifer poked her head out.

"Miss, Penny's going to gut Bradly because he's talking trash about Conor Maynard."

Shaking my head, I said, "I'm coming." Looking back to Brooke, I said, "I'll talk to you soon."

She grabbed me in a quick hug. "I'm so happy for you."

"Thank you," I whispered back before I went back in and had to break up a fight.

CHAPTER TWENTY-EIGHT

REAGAN

*C*arter was coming home. I stood at the terminal waiting with Brooke, who had Benjie with her and she was right; he was an amazing kid. She'd been minding him again while Emily, Dustin's ex, was out of town on business once again. At first, I thought it was strange how a mother could leave her child with a complete stranger, until Brooke told me she'd met with Emily and took all her credentials with her, so she knew Brooke wasn't a criminal. Carter's mom had also called Emily since she'd known her from back in the day and praised Brooke to her. Which I thought was sweet.

Beth had got to know Brooke over the time Carter was gone. We'd had even spent one day talking, drinking tea and then in the evening drinking tequila. I was floored by the amount Beth could drink and hadn't realized how funny she was until that night.

When Patty had come to pick her up, I was standing at the front door yelling my goodbyes, as Beth turned and raced back up to me for a hug.

"Thank you," she'd whispered.

"What for?"

"For making Carter happy."

My heart had warmed. "Then you're welcome."

Of course, Mom had also been touched, and when she'd heard our exchange, she burst into tears. Dad arrived just after they'd left, Mom still crying. He took one look and hung his head, grinning. Mom had always been an emotional drunk.

Around us, the noise grew, so I knew the team had arrived.

Carter had arrived.

He was home.

People filed off the plane. I searched and searched, ignoring the camera trained on me. I didn't care if I looked crazed. I was eager to see him, to hold him and kiss him. The phone calls hadn't been enough, not since I'd had the chance to taste Carter. He was like my favorite candy, and I was addicted.

When I saw him through the crowd, he was already looking at me and grinning brightly. I let out an excited squeak and dodged through the people. He watched me coming and braced. I leaped into his arms and wrapped mine around his neck, his went around my waist, and I was lifted off the floor.

"Carter," I breathed into his neck. A sudden swirl of raw emotions clogged my throat.

"Sweetheart," he murmured against my neck. He placed me back on my feet, a hand of his threading through my loose hair and he tugged my head back a little to capture my gaze.

"Happy tears?" he asked, worry causing his brows to dip.

I nodded. "Very happy tears."

His smile was back. "Good." Then he kissed me. I heard a few catcalls, but I ignored everything except the feeling of Carter's lips on mine. The warm kiss soon turned heated when I opened my mouth under his tongue trailing over my lips. I wrapped him up tighter in my embrace, still, it wasn't enough.

Someone cleared their throat, and then I heard, "Benjie."

"Daddy!" was yelled.

Carter pecked my lips once more and then straightened, beaming his grin down at me. "Glad to be home."

"So am I."

I glanced beside us to see Dustin as he bent low and swooped his son up into his arms for a warm hug before planting him back on his feet.

"How's my boy?" Dustin asked.

"Awesome. Miss Brooke took me to the library yesterday after school. I got so many comics it's not funny. We can read them when you're not playing."

"Sounds great, kiddo." He ruffled Benjie's hair and then hooked an arm around his shoulders, bringing him close to his side. Dustin looked up at Brooke standing beside us. She was smiling softly down at Benjie. "Thanks again, Brooke."

She shrugged. "Not a problem."

"Dustin, Dustin, who's your lady friend?" was called by a reporter behind the roped off area.

"Benjie, are you proud of your dad getting the last score that won the game?" another yelled.

"Of course," Benjie cheered.

Dustin shifted. He grabbed Brooke's arm and tugged her to his side. She stumbled and righted herself, her hands landing on his chest and stomach. "This here is my girlfriend."

My eyes widened. Carter cursed low. Brooke's eyes narrowed, and I couldn't help but notice Benjie's look of hope that crossed his features before Brooke straightened and smacked Dustin in the back of the head.

She laughed humorlessly, and told them, "He means a girl who is a friend. The trickster."

I leaned into Carter and whispered, "She's going to kill him for that."

He chuckled. "Think she'll wait until after the Super Bowl?"

"Hmm, I'm not sure." The angry vibes coming from Brooke's body told me Dustin would be in a body bag by the end of the day.

"Let's get out of here," Carter said.

It was probably a good idea to start the bloodbath in private.

We made our way out of the terminal, picked up the luggage, and went to the cars in silence. Well, except for Benjie firing off question after question to his dad. I was glad to see that the paparazzi didn't follow us to the cars.

When I kept glancing around, Carter chuckled. "Apparently, there was a tip-off some big singer was landing shortly."

Dustin snorted. "You got Ted on it then?"

"Sure did."

"Hey, Ree, can you give me a lift home?" Brooke asked. She threw the keys to Dustin and then diverted off to my car instead of Dustin's, which she'd driven in for him with Benjie.

"But, Miss Brooke, you said we could build a fortress later." Benjie ran up to her and wrapped his arms around her waist, looking at her with a pout on his face.

She winked down at him, running a hand through his messy hair. A look of adoration, one I'd never seen on her face, showed. "I promise our next time together we'll do it."

"Brooke—"

She shot her gaze up to Dustin, her eyes narrowed. He sighed. Brooke turned to me. "Is it okay?"

I glanced from Benjie, whose shoulders drooped as he slunk his way back to his dad, to a frowning Dustin and then back to Brooke. "Please," she mouthed.

"Sure. Not a problem."

"Kiddo, can you jump in the car while I have a quick word with Brooke?"

"Sure." Benjie smiled and took the keys from his dad, skipping to the car and jumping into it.

"Ree, let's get in ours," Carter said as I watched Dustin walk toward Brooke. She crossed her arms over her chest and scowled at him.

"But—"

Carter smirked. "Sweetheart, come on."

Rolling my eyes, I said, "Fine." I then called to Brooke, "If you need help maiming him, just call."

She smiled over her shoulder and nodded.

Carter loaded his bag onto the back seat and then we both climbed in. Of course, I got to my knees and stared out the back window where Dustin stopped in front of Brooke with his hands up in front of himself. Ready to block an attack, which was wise.

Carter chuckled. "Reagan, sit back around."

"Nope, this is live action fun. Besides, she'd do the same for me. Keeping an eye open, in case I need to get involved. Just wish I could hear them."

Carter rolled his eyes, then ran his gaze over me. "I could think of better things to do while we wait for Dustin to grovel."

Smiling, I kept one hand on the headrest and moved the other to Carter's thigh and leaned his way. "What were you thinking?"

"Hmm." He licked his lips, his eyes running from my eyes down to my lips. Then he grinned. "Eye spy?"

I giggled. "Sure." I went to move back, but he caught me with a hand on the back of my neck.

"Not so fast." He tugged me close and touched his mouth to mine. I nipped at his mouth. His opened for me and just when things were getting good, something bumped into the car. I pulled away and looked out the back window.

"Oh my God," I whispered. Dustin had Brooke pressed against the back of the car with his arms tightly wrapped around her waist. I saw hers were on his arms and it looked like she was trying to push him back for a moment until they changed and gripped.

I got low in my seat to see Dustin kissing Brooke.

"They're kissing," I said gleefully.

"Finally," Carter said.

But then Brooke must have come out of her daze. She pushed him back, said something, and stomped to the passenger side door, on Carter's side. Carter chuckled as I quickly shifted around to face the front, just as Brooke opened it. She got in with a huff and slammed it closed.

"Can you believe that idiot?" she snarled. "Carter, do me a favor and run over him as you back out."

He snorted. "Not sure the team would be happy with me."

"But we'd be happy, and Ree will make you even happier if you helped her BFF out. Won't you, Ree?"

I bit my bottom lip, only I couldn't contain my grin. "I'd make him happy even if he ran Dustin over or not."

"Some friend you are," Brooke grumbled. "Damn, he's moved." And he had, to Brooke's window where he bent to look in at Brooke with a huge satisfied smile on his face. She gave him the finger. He winked.

"Talk soon, darlin'," he called through the window.

"Can we go already?" Brooke snapped.

Carter started the car, and Dustin moved off around to his car and climbed in.

As Carter pulled out of the park, I turned to Brooke and asked, "You okay?"

Her eyes stayed looking out the window, and she shrugged.

"Brooke?"

She glanced at me. "Do you think Benjie saw that?"

Out the corner of my eyes, I saw Carter shake his head. "I glanced in Dustin's car. He had his head down probably on some device or something."

She relaxed a little. "Good. He's already going on and on about how great his dad is. I think he wants me to date him."

I reached over and rested my hand on Carter's thigh. He threaded his fingers through mine. I nodded to Brooke. "He seemed very happy when Dustin introduced you to the reporters as his girlfriend."

She groaned. "I don't want to disappoint him when it doesn't happen."

"Even after that kiss?"

Her nose screwed up. "You saw that?"

I laughed. "It was a bit hard not to when our car rocked from the impact."

She blushed. "The prick."

"Why? Because he did it or because you liked it?"

Her eyes flared. She glanced at Carter, but his attention was on the road. "Carter won't say anything to him."

Brooke scoffed. "I doubt that, men gossip more than what we do."

"This is true, but if you don't want me to say anything, I won't. I want you to be able to speak freely in front of me because Ree's your friend."

Sweet molasses. He was amazing. When I squeezed his hand, he looked my way and smiled.

Brooke sighed. "It's fine. Ree and I can talk later. Turn left here to head to my place, please."

"Do you want me to come in for a while? I can catch a taxi home so Carter can take the car," I offered.

"No way. Your man just got home. I'm sure you have catching up to do."

"Brooke, Carter and I can catch up later."

"True. I'm home now so she won't be getting rid of me," Carter put in.

Brooke shook her head. "I'm good. Honestly, I'm fine. There's nothing really to talk about."

I narrowed my eyes. "Brooke."

She threw her hands up in the air. "Fine. You really want to know where my head is at? I'm confused. Totally confused. I don't know if I want to punch him in the face or kiss the idiot."

"Dustin often brings that feeling about in a lot of people. I've felt it many times," Carter commented. We both stared at him and then laughed.

It was just what Brooke needed. She relaxed more into her seat. "Turn to the right. My house is on the left. Number 210."

"What are you going to do about him?"

She gave me a tight smile and another shrug. "Not sure yet. But we'll talk more about it soon. Promise."

"Okay." I reached back and held out my hand. She took mine giving it a squeeze. "If he's too much of an idiot, you let me know. Even if he's a friend of Carter's, I'll beat him up."

"Thanks."

Carter pulled up to the curb, and Brooke got out with a final goodbye. When Carter pulled back out onto the road, I asked him, "Do you think they'd be good together?"

"Yes." He glanced at me, then back to the road. "Dustin's been through a lot with the divorce, then women only using him for his money or status. None of them liked the fact he has a kid. Brooke's already in love with Benjie. That woke Dustin up and he sees she's different from all the others. She doesn't want his money, doesn't care who he is to the public. She'd be good for him. I think if she gave him a chance, he would be for her too."

"Might be some tough times ahead for them though. Brooke's stubborn."

Carter snorted. "Dustin will win her over in the end. Once he sets his mind on something, nothing will stop him."

"As long as he's not just wanting her because she's already good with Benjie."

"Believe me, he's not."

"What's that mean?"

Carter groaned. "Guys talk. North, Dustin, and I are close. We share things." He quickly added, "Though I don't overshare anything, but let me just say that Dustin thinks Brooke is hot. He was thinking about asking her out after I'd moved in, but he was worried because of his history with women."

"I guess we'll see how things go."

"Yes, and if he does mess things up, I'll help you beat him up."

"Aww, that's sweet, wanting to commit assault with me."

He chuckled, picked up my hand and kissed the back of it. "Anything for you."

CHAPTER TWENTY-NINE

REAGAN

"*G*et them, baby. Kill them!" I screamed over the railing to Carter. My pulse raced under my skin. Adrenaline pumped through me at seeing Carter in all his football glory. He was a beast on the field.

"Reagan, maybe while reporters are around, a death threat isn't good for you to shout to your boyfriend," Beth suggested with a warm smile. She sat in the front row with Patty on one side. My seat was on the other side of her, but I wasn't sitting; I was standing near the fence. Dad, in his seat, was next to me, leaving Mom on the end of the row. Behind us in the other family seats were Brooke, Benjie, and the rest of Carter's family.

"Nothing's wrong with a little threatening, Beth." Mom grinned down the line at Carter's mom. Over the weeks since the barbecue, they had become fast friends. It was good to see how well both our families got along.

We were at the Super Bowl, Carter's last game with his team. It had been just a few days since Carter arrived home. Over those days, we'd still had our normal routines, only his training went later than normal due to the championship game being so close. In fact, we hardly saw each other. Besides a few kisses, hugs, and snuggles on the couch, which involved groping, we hadn't moved forward to home base yet. Carter had decided to stay in his room, so he wouldn't wake me when he got in late. Though I was sure it also had something to do with my fear of us moving too fast. We were going to reevaluate the sleeping arrangements after the Super Bowl was over, something I suggested we do. He'd told me he didn't want a quick romp between the sheets, only to rush off in the morning. While I could understand it, even though I didn't like it, I knew one thing was for sure. Carter Anthony was moving into my bedroom tonight.

I grinned to myself, probably looking a little crazed, but I couldn't ignore the thrill drumming inside of me about the idea.

Of course, he could be too tired to do anything. Regardless, I wanted to feel him next to me. It'd been hard knowing he was only a room away from me. If I wasn't a deep sleeper, and so busy marking assignments with school exams coming up, I would have waited up for Carter each night or at least snuck into his room to sleep beside him.

Then again, he was right about one thing. If we had slept beside one another, then we wouldn't have been able to keep our hands off each other.

Still, I wanted to try having him in my bed that night.

Even if they won or lost.

The game was close already with the other team ahead by two points. Only it wasn't even halftime. It was still anyone's game.

Come on, babe.

"Ree," Calvin called. "Come sit down before you jump the fence and play the game for them."

I heard State chuckle, even over the noise of the other people screaming and cheering. "We'll grab her before she has the chance."

"We hope," Casper said with humor in his voice.

My hands came up to my neck, and I gasped. Carter got the ball. He dodged to the left, barely missing a tackle. He kept running, his teammates making a clear path, but then an asshole came out of nowhere and took him to the ground, hard.

"Grab her," Patty yelled. I had one leg over when I was seized from behind and brought back into a chest.

"Is he okay? Is he all right?" I asked over and over.

"He's fine, honey. Look, he's getting up," Dad said. He was right behind me; it was his fast hands that had grabbed me. Cheering sounded around us. My heart slowly crept down from my throat and slipped back into my chest. I breathed in relief to see Carter was walking about.

"Thank fuck he's finishing up. Not sure Ree would be able to handle it," State said. People agreed with him.

Dad's hands on my shoulders gave a gentle shake. "You okay?"

I nodded, finally able to relax as the game went on, and since Carter was still out playing, he couldn't be too hurt from the tackle.

"Still can't believe I'm here in the family box," Dad commented with wonderment clear in his voice. "Guess this means I can forgive you for telling us late that you two were dating."

I snorted. It had been literally the day after things were finalized between Carter and me. One day and he made it sound like I'd kept our relationship from him for years. Truth be told, I'd been greedy, I had wanted the day just for us before Carter had to leave. Without Dad crying. Hence the one-day delay.

Thankfully, they hadn't seen the video clip of us together. If that had been the case, Dad would have been even more annoyed with me.

Since I hadn't called my parents to tell them I was coming over, I knocked on the front door. I didn't want to walk in on anything. Mom opened it, took one look at me, and yelled, "Herb." She grabbed my arm and dragged me in.

Dad came running in from the kitchen. "What? What is it?" he asked frantically.

"Reagan's here and something's wrong," Mom announced. She ushered me over to the couch and sat me down, taking one spot next to me. Dad stalked over and sat on my other side, studying me.

"What's wrong, Ree?" Dad asked. "Is it Carter? Is he okay?" his voice wavered a little.

"He's fine."

His eyes narrowed. "Did he upset you?"

"No." I smiled.

"Do you have an STD?" Mom asked, both Dad and I swung our shocked gazes her way. Her hands came up. "What? It could happen. She's had a dry spell. She could have hired a prostitute and then—"

"Mom. Stop. Just stop."

"Jesus, Elaine. Where does your mind go? I'm blaming all those cop and doctor shows you watch."

She rolled her eyes. "Then what is it? I know when something's happening with my baby girl. You don't just pop in without calling first. Is it about yesterday with Carter? Something that happened at school? Did Tom fire you? I'll let your dad beat him up if he did. Or is it a gambling problem? Are you on the run from your bookie?"

I shook my head. "I don't gamble, Tom didn't fire me, nothing happened at school. Well, except... actually, don't worry about it. And yes, it has got something to do with Carter—"

"Are you pregnant?" Dad asked, hope filling his voice.

"No!" Sheesh. My parents were crazy. If anyone had to question my sanity, then all they had to do was look at my parents, and they'd understand where I got my outbursts. "If you just let me talk—"

"But something is wrong, right?" Mom asked.

"Actually, nothing is wrong. I'm not even sure where you got that from."

Mom huffed. "Your smile was a little crazy, I thought you were about to crack."

I snorted. "Okay, so here it is. Carter and I are dating."

They blinked, looked at each other and blinked again. Dad's eyes teared. Mom sniffed.

"Are you two okay?" I asked.

"Yep," Dad choked out, wiping his nose with the back of his hand.

"Of course." Mom cleared her throat. "I knew he'd step up."

Dad nodded. "You did, Elaine. You called it."

"What are you talking about?"

Mom took my hand in hers. "The day you brought him here, I watched him. I'm good at just knowing things about people—"

"Tell that to Mr. Milton when you accused him of taking your carrots from your garden. You'd always said he was a shady character, but it ended up being the rabbits."

She huffed. "He was still shady."

"Mom. He moved to get away from you watching him all the time."

"I was keeping an eye on him for the community. Anyway..." She waved her hand in the air flippantly. "As I was saying, I watched Carter that day and could already see the feelings he had for you. Every time you talked or laughed his eyes shone."

I raised my brows. "Are you serious?"

"Yes. That's why I asked him to move in here. I knew you'd overreact then offer up your place, and I knew he would accept."

"You two played me? Your own daughter?"

Mom smiled. Dad grinned, and said, "We'd do it again if we saw the possibility of something great for you. Don't worry. I've already warned him that if he hurts you, I'd hurt him."

"You did?" I gushed. "Did it pain you to do it?"

He nodded. "It really did."

"So... he worked his charm and finally admitted his feelings yesterday?" Mom asked. I nodded. "I'm so glad he called us to help him out."

"Meaning how you got me the day off so he could come home to see me."

"Yes." Her smile widened.

"Are you saying this happened yesterday and you didn't think to call us to inform us he was your boyfriend?"

My eyes narrowed. "I'm here now telling you."

Dad stood and threw his hands in the air. "I could have had at least *eleven more hours of torturing Tom about this.*" He glared down at me. "*You should have called last night.*"

I rolled my eyes. "*Yeah sure, of course my life revolves around yours and Tom's stupid mind games of bragging.*"

"*Glad you see it my way. I'm going to call. I'll let you know when I can forgive you for your tardiness.*" *He started to walk off when he abruptly turned and came back to me, pulling me up and into a hug.* "*Good job on snagging Carter Anthony.*"

"Hey," Brooke said from beside me, pulling me from my thoughts. I glanced to see Dad was now sitting beside Patty while Mom and Beth talked quietly. Benjie was playing with Crispin and Caitlyn.

"I'm so glad you could come tonight," I told Brooke.

"Couldn't miss the entertainment. I think I've lost count of the times your dad has side hugged Carter's whole family."

I laughed. "Probably way too many and he's moved into the uncomfortable stage."

"True." She grinned.

I bumped her hip with mine. "Dustin still annoying you?" I questioned.

She bit her bottom lip to hide her smile, but I knew Brooke too well. She was enjoying Dustin making an effort for her.

She nodded. "Guess who was at Nana Bev's when I went to dinner Friday night?"

My jaw dropped, my eyes widening. "No," I gasped.

"Yes." She nodded. "Apparently, he got her number off my phone when I left it at his house 'accidentally'. Since I always talk about her, he rang her up and they had a good old chat."

My hand fluttered up to my neck. I choked back my giggle, and asked, "What happened?"

"Of course he charmed Nana. When I got there, she gave me a lecture about being silly and not giving Dustin a chance. Which got my back up." She shrugged. "Still, I couldn't keep up my aggression when the idiot's around for a long time. I ended up enjoying the night. When I left, Dustin walked me out and...."

"What?"

"The bastard kissed me again. My brain shuts down when he does that. He begged me, actually got down on his knees and begged me for a chance."

"Are you going to give him one?"

She smiled. "Yes. Just one. But we're not going to tell Benjie anything until we know if we're okay with dating each other."

I couldn't help it. I grabbed her in a hug. "I hope things work out," I whispered.

"I hope so as well, but we'll see."

CHAPTER THIRTY

REAGAN

*A*fter entering the house, I went straight into the living room. It was late, very late after the celebrations. Carter must have been exhausted, but as I turned to see him walk in after locking the front door, I noticed he was a little jazzed. Winning the Super Bowl could do that to a person.

"Are you happy?" I asked with a smile.

He came right up to me, his smirk changing into a big grin. When his warm hands landed on my waist, I placed mine on his shoulders. He replied, "More than happy."

"Do you think you'll regret giving it up?"

He shook his head. "No. I've wanted to for a while, for my body's sake."

"As long as you're sure."

His smile softened. "I'm very sure. So, are you?"

I laughed. "Am I what? Sure you should leave?"

He flicked my ear gently. "No. Are you happy?"

"I'm not the one who won a Super Bowl. Still, it was all very exciting and nerve-wracking."

"State told me you nearly jumped the fence."

"I nearly ate my heart as well. I was so scared you weren't going to get up," I admitted.

"I'm strong, sweetheart. No one could keep me down when I know I've got you to come home to."

My body flushed pleasantly. "Carter?"

"Hmm?" He leaned in to kiss my neck.

"The living arrangements," I said.

Straightening, his brows dipped. "Yeah? What about them?"

"Well, it's after the Super Bowl." He chuckled. I went on, "I was wondering if things could change?"

"Change how?" he asked apprehensively. I had to grin, wondering if his mind led him to the thought of me kicking him out. That would never happen. Never. If he tried to leave, I'd just have to tie him to my bed rails.

Oh, that could be an idea. Then I could explore his body without him distracting me with his hands and mouth. I'd love to roam freely over his body, tasting every inch of him.

"Sweetheart, where did your mind go to make you blush like that?"

"Um... let's set a pin in that and get back to it later maybe."

He laughed. "Okay, so what were you saying about our living arrangements?"

Slowly, I slid my hands down from his shoulders to his chest. I watched my hands run over his sculpted muscles and got lost in the sensation of his hard body.

"Ree, I swear to God if you don't—"

"Would you want to sleep in my room from now on?"

His body stilled, even with his mouth half open from interrupting him. Gradually, his expression changed. His eyes widened, and a smile crept onto his lips.

"You want me in your bed?"

I nodded, gazing at his chest. "Yes."

"Look at me, sweetheart." I pulled my gaze up. "Are you sure this is what you want? What about your fears of moving too fast?"

Were we moving too fast?

I wasn't sure.

But I was willing to take the risk, I couldn't let Carter sleep in his own room any longer when we were under the same roof.

"If it's moving too fast then so be it. All I know is that I'd like to sleep beside the man I love and wake up next to him."

"Yeah?" he said gruffly.

"Yes."

"I'd love that, sweetheart. So goddamn much."

"So… tonight?"

"Hell yeah. Tonight, and then every night."

"I like the sound of that." I rolled my eyes to the left and then back again, biting my bottom lip before saying quietly, "Are you tired? Would you like to sleep now?"

"I could go to bed." His eyes darkened. "But I'm not ready to sleep."

My lips twitched. "Do you want to read?"

He snorted. "No."

"Watch a movie?"

He smirked. "No."

Grinning, I said, "I just can't think of anything else to do."

"Then I'll have to show you." He picked me up with his hand under my butt. I gasped, and wrapped my legs around his waist, my arms moving around his neck. He started down the hall before his lips landed on mine.

We fell through the bedroom door, kissing as if our lives depended on it. Carter released his grip, and I slid down his body while his hands ran all over me. Caressing my ass, my hips and back. He then touched my stomach and breasts, where he gave them both a good strong grip. I tangled my hands in his hair, loving the feel through my fingers.

We came up for air. It was unfair how we had to catch our

breaths. I could easily kiss Carter all day and night. His mouth was amazing. Hot, tasty, and something I very much liked. Just like the rest of him was.

"Clothes," I muttered against his jaw before licking and biting there.

"Hmm?"

"There's too many," I complained. He chuckled against my collarbone and then straightened to drag his shirt over his head.

My mind blanked. Yes, I'd seen him half-naked before, and each time I enjoyed the view, but that time I knew, *knew* I was going to get to touch it, explore it, and taste it.

All mine.

Leaning in, I kissed his chest and glided my tongue across and down to his nipple. There I swirled my tongue around and gently took a nip, causing him to shudder.

"Ree," he growled low in his throat. His hands took hold of the bottom of my tee and tugged. After another kiss to his other nipple, I stood and threw my arms up in the air. He pulled the material free from my body. I quickly unhooked my bra and dragged it down my arms, throwing it to the floor.

I heard his quick hiss of breath. I glanced up to see his eyes hooded and heated, eyeing my chest. He met my gaze. "You're beautiful."

Carter bent as if tranced, and kissed the top of my left breast, then the right. He kissed his way along the curve of each breast again and again. His hot breath and soft lips were driving me insane, and he hadn't even gone near my nipples. He cupped my left and then sucked my right nub into his mouth, curling his tongue around and around it.

"Carter," I moaned. I clung to his back, his shoulders and then into his hair. His other hand on my waist dragged me forward. My back arched, presenting my breast to him more. Wetness soaked my panties, and a deep quake started inside of me. Pleasure I'd never felt before made me whimper.

I wanted more.

I wanted Carter inside me.

But after I'd had the chance to taste him.

I let my fingers drift to the belt of his jeans, tugging at it, trying to unbuckle it. Only I had to slow down my eager fingers to stop fumbling with it and actually progress to undoing it. Once that happened, I smiled happily. After undoing his button, I then slid his zipper down.

I slipped my hand in, under his boxers, and took hold of his erection. Carter sucked in a breath against my nipple and then he bit down hard enough pain shot through me, but it quickly changed to pleasure.

I dragged my hand up and down his length. On each slide, he groaned around his mouthful. With my free hand, I ghosted my fingers through his hair and then gently pulled his mouth free so I could claim his lips with my own. He pushed his jeans down his legs, giving me more access. Carter then thrust his cock into my palm over and over.

His fingers went to the button and zipper on my slacks, and he made quick work on undoing them. My body trembled when he slid his hand under my pants and panties to grip my ass tightly.

Carter took his lips from me, pressing his forehead against mine. "Sweetheart. Jesus, you have to stop or I'm going to make a fool out of myself and come."

"But—"

His chuckle interrupted me. I wanted to see him lose control. "I'd like to at least be inside you when it happens."

Liking that idea more, I released my hold and ran my hands around to grip his sweet ass and tugged him close. My pants skimmed over my skin as he pushed them down.

"Ree." Carter groaned, eyeing my naked body. I kicked the rest of the clothes off, along with my heels. "You're stunning. So damn beautiful."

Heat hit my cheeks from his compliments. I wasn't used to

hearing something like them. "You're pretty handsome yourself."

He smirked, only it slowly dropped. "I have condoms, always use them. But need you to know there hasn't been anyone in a long time, so other than the fact this may go quick, I've been tested. I'm clean."

I glanced down his gorgeous body, and whispered, "I'm on the pill, and I've been tested too. I'm all in the clear."

Meeting his gaze, I saw his cheeks start to color. "Would you... can I... I'd like—"

I covered his mouth with my hand, giggling. "Usually it's me not knowing what or how to say something." I smiled, guessing what he was trying to say and added, "I'd like you to be the first inside me uncovered. I want to feel all of you, Carter Anthony."

He kissed my hand. His eyes darkened as he dragged it away and held it down at his side. "Christ, I'd love that."

"But first...."

"What?" he asked.

Releasing his hand and delicious butt, I dropped to my knees in front of him and took hold of his erection in my hand. I kissed the tip of him.

"Ree," he said through clenched teeth. He shuffled enough to be free of the jeans, and then I sucked him into my mouth, and he groaned. He closed his eyes and dropped his head back, God, I loved that reaction. It was like he was too lost in what I was doing, so instead, he just felt and enjoyed without thinking. My wet mouth glided up and down his thick length. It had been so long since I'd been with anyone, I didn't realize I missed it so much. More importantly, it was with someone I loved, which was so much more. My heart thumped fast, my core tightened, and I knew I was soaked. Ready for him.

I lost his cock when Carter bent and hooked me under the arms, picking me up, cradling me close with his arms under my ass, supporting me. I wrapped myself around him. His jaw clenched, his nostrils flaring again and again.

He clipped low, "I need to calm down a bit."

My brows dipped, and I ran a hand over the side of his face. "Do you want to stop?"

"God, no."

"So…?"

He smiled. "It's my turn to taste." With that, I gasped as he threw me down on the bed. I bounced a little, ignoring the fact Carter could see all my bits wobble because he'd told me enough times he liked me as I was. Even though I had accepted myself and liked who I was and how I looked, those words from someone else, someone important, were empowering.

Carter took hold of my ankles and spread my legs. He made a noise in the back of this throat as he climbed on the bed between my legs, running his hands up to massage the edges of my hips. I was bare and open, Carter could see everything.

His eyes flashed. He slid a finger over my lower lips and then inside me. I arched, panting. Carter hummed under his breath. "So wet for me." His voice was thick with desire.

"Carter," I moaned when a second finger joined the first.

"So goddamn stunning, and all mine."

It felt like my body was glowing from his words of claim.

Carter removed his fingers, slid both hands under my bottom and dipped his head in. His gaze crashed into mine. I caught his wicked smile before he kissed my clit.

"Oh, God." I was so turned on I felt dizzy with it. The way Carter licked, sucked and drank me into his mouth rippled my body with pleasant tremors throughout.

"Carter, please," I begged, wanting, needing him inside me.

I glanced down. His eyes met mine as he kissed his way up my body. Our mouths connected, our tongues swirled. I tasted myself on him, and heck if I didn't love it. I wrapped my arms around his neck and hooked my legs over his.

With his hands on the bed, he supported himself over me. "Hell, you look amazing under me." He kissed my shoulder and then rubbed his shaft against my wetness. I hummed under my breath, eager to have him inside me.

I placed my hand against his cheek and ran my thumb over his bottom lip. "Carter, make love to me."

His eyes closed tightly before he opened them and reached between us. "Lift a little, sweetheart." I did, and in a swift thrust, he pressed all the way in. I gasped and gripped his shoulders. "Christ," he groaned. "Ree, so hot, so tight. I-I'm not going to last."

"Neither am I." And I wasn't, not with the way he rocked leisurely in and out of me. How his slick, warm skin dragged over my breasts. "So good," I murmured. Lifting my head, I pressed my lips to his shoulder, then licked and finally bit.

"Reagan," he groaned.

My lower belly tightened and swirled. "Close," I warned.

He upped his thrust into a crazed frenzy, pumping in and out of me faster and faster. My back arched, I gripped his shoulders and pulled him closer. Kissing his jaw, his cheek and then his lips. I used my heels to dig into the bed, driving him deeper inside of me.

"Yes," I cried, just before my orgasm overtook me. My inner walls clenched around him and he grunted out a deep growl.

Carter took both my hands up above my head, his lava gaze running down over me and stopped where we were joined together. "So good. Christ." His grip was almost painful, it felt deliciously perfect. Carter leaned in, then touched his mouth to mine before he jerked inside me. A groan slipped from his mouth into mine as he swelled and thrust his hips forward on one last stroke before coming.

Even after orgasming, he slowly moved in and out. He angled back, releasing my hands and gliding one down over my shoulder, breast, then stomach. "You undo me, in all the right ways."

Exhausted and sated, I smiled up at him, rubbing his sides up and down. "I'm looking forward to our future."

He grinned. "So am I."

EPILOGUE

EIGHT MONTHS LATER

CARTER

"I'm going to be sick," I complained, rubbing my stomach. I groaned and sat back in the seat behind me. Thankfully, it'd been there, or I would have fallen on my ass.

Dad laughed. He came up and clasped me on the shoulder, applying pressure in a reassuring way. "You'll be fine."

"How can you say that? I'm a nervous wreck. I should have gone to the bathroom and then maybe had something to eat. I haven't *eaten*, Dad, which says it all."

He laughed again.

The door opened, and I saw Tom peek around the curtain. "It's just a student."

Then I heard Wesley's cry, "She's coming. She's coming." I stood and went to the edge to see him take his place in the front row of the gym. Reagan thought she was joining the after-lunch assembly because Tom wanted to talk about the school dance. She was wrong. I was there with my family and hers to ask her to marry me. That was if I didn't throw my guts up and clear the room out because it stank.

"You ready?" Tom asked around the curtain on stage.

I jumped like a little girl, forgetting he was standing there. Sweat formed on my brow and hands. "Yes," I squeaked. Clearing my throat, I nodded. "Yes," I said again, only manlier.

The door to the gymnasium opened. I heard the *click-clack* of her heels, the ones I'd picked out that morning for when she asked me to grab her some shoes since she was running late. *Again.*

Though, I did enjoy the way I woke her, with my head between her legs. She loved it too, then refused to leave the bed without returning the favor.

The room quieted.

Damn it, someone had to talk or at least make a noise. Assemblies were usually loud with the students talking and stuffing around.

I caught sight of Reagan standing near the door, searching the room with her brows dipping in suspicion. I waved my arms about like a mad-man to Brooke standing below the stage. She glanced up and I mouthed, "Do something."

Brooke nodded and then went over to Reagan. Thank God she caught her attention before Reagan's gaze ran too close to the back of the room where some of my former-teammates and our family members were. Brooke took hold of Reagan's hand and pulled her along to the other side. I shoved Tom out onto the stage.

He stumbled forward. A look of shock and then annoyance crossed his features, but in my defense, I panicked and needed to get him out there to get things started.

He cleared his throat into the mic and then tapped it. "Well, it looks like my lecture about silence has been listened to. Good work, students." He clapped, and I saw Reagan relax a little. *Smart thinking, Tom.*

As he rattled on and on about the dance, my nerves settled down more. Why? Because I got to watch Reagan standing there, smiling, pulling faces to some of the students and whispering to Brooke. I grinned, knowing I was making the best and most important decision I had ever made in my whole life.

Reagan Wild was made for me.

She was supposed to be my wife.

And I couldn't wait to make it happen.

We'd been inseparable since football ended for me. I'd moved into her room the night after the Super Bowl and never left. I couldn't imagine my life without going to sleep and waking up next to Reagan each morning before I left for my coaching job at the local college. I enjoyed my new job, glad it was close to where we lived—though one day we'd need a bigger house once Reagan and I started a family, another part of life I was very much looking forward to. I loved the woman I was about to ask to marry me.

Only...

"Carter, slow your breathing down," Dad whispered.

I took a deep breath, nodding. Doubt crept into my mind. What happened if Reagan hated the idea of me proposing to her here in the school? I rationalized it was where we'd first reconnected. Where our paths crossed. When I fell in love with her a little after she asked Brooke to pick her underwear from her butt.

Hell, would she even want to marry me?

Screw those thoughts.

Yes. Yes, she would. Why? Because she loved me and showed it each and every day, like I did with her. In each look, touch, and word. We were a match, and no one could say different.

"And the award for funniest teacher goes to... Reagan Wild," Tom announced into the microphone. I caught Reagan's look of surprise before Brooke pushed her toward the stage steps. She climbed them and made her way over to Tom who was holding a trophy.

Her happiness shone in her eyes and grin. She took the trophy from Tom and looked down at it. Her brows dipped. Her head tilted to the side.

"Huh?" she said. She glanced up at Tom. "Why is it a golf award with your name on it?"

I walked onto the stage with Dad giving me an encouraging pat on the back. I stopped just behind Reagan. Tom took the award back with a bit of a struggle since Reagan wasn't letting it go. People laughed.

I got to one knee behind her, and Tom told her, "Look behind you."

She relented her grip and slowly turned. Spotting me, her hands flew to cover her mouth, but I heard her gasp. Tears filled her eyes.

"Reagan Wild, even as a teenager you captivated me. Fate made sure we reentered each other's lives, and I couldn't be more grateful for it. Never have I loved anyone as much as I love you. I'd be honored if you would become my wife, so we can spend the rest of our days together."

Silence.

Shit. Nothing but silence as she blinked down at me, tears falling with each blink.

Tom got close to her. "This is where you answer him."

She was statue still, and for a moment I was worried... until she sucked in a ragged breath and whispered, "Are you sure?"

People laughed once again.

I grinned up at her. "Positive."

She nodded, then nodded again, and before I could brace, she flung herself at me. I went to my back on the stage, chuckling. Cheers and screams erupted around us, but I only had eyes for the woman smiling brightly down at me.

"I love you, Carter Anthony."

"I love you, Reagan Wild, soon-to-be Anthony."

Then, right there in front of everyone, she kissed me.

"Keep it clean, kids," we heard Tom mutter.

Breaking the kiss, I smiled softly up at my fiancée and reached for her hand to slip the ring on her finger. This was us. Two people who fumbled their way through it all but came out loving each other in the end.

"You're mine forever now," she whispered.

"And I wouldn't want it any other way."

SNEAK PEEK: MAKING CHANGES

A STANDALONE ROM-COM

CHAPTER ONE

While I sat in the restaurant waiting for my husband, I couldn't help but glance around at the couples eating together and wonder if they were truly happy. From the way they shared smiles and sweet looks, they certainly seemed content. My shoulders slumped. I wanted to projectile vomit all over them because it had me pondering, yet again, on where had I gone wrong? How had I become the doormat in my relationship?

I had instantly fallen for Robert in my final year at college. I had been in the library sitting in the corner at a desk on my own. A group of idiots across from me were calling me fat and ugly, among other things.

I'd ignored it to start off with, thinking they were only trying to be cool with each other. But after some time, I'd had enough.

Lifting my gaze, I'd glared across at them and asked, "Do you want to suck my little toe?"

Silence followed. One scoffed and said, "Why in the fuck would we want to?"

Shrugging, I placed my pen down and said, "Well, I just thought unless you want to suck each other off, which would be about the size of my little toe, it's the only action you guys will get from the opposite sex because you're nothing but fucking pricks."

"You need to—" The guy didn't get to finish because Robert showed up out of nowhere and took them down another notch or two. Once they'd left, he'd sat with me and asked if I was okay. My heart melted right there and then.

Back then, I was accustomed to being invisible, the girl who wore thick glasses, loose clothing, no makeup, and I didn't care about any of it. If people tried to crap in my cheerios, I told them where to go.

Six years later, I figured out somewhere along the way, I had lost myself, and it pissed me off.

Over time, he'd shaped me into a different woman. One who wore stupid frilly dresses like his grandma used to wear—which got me thinking he may have had a thing for geriatrics—to please him, who did as she was told—eye roll—and who thought herself useless. It was hard not to believe those things after hearing them every day.

Was I strong enough to change?

To be who I wanted to be?

I wasn't sure.

Though as time went on, I was closer and closer to breaking free. To standing on my own two feet and learning once again to appreciate the person I used to be before Robert.

However, the move to do so, to leave him, was terrifying.

Why was love, lust, or even like such a miserable aspect of life? It may not be the case for most people, yet for me it was. I should have known my love life was going to suck donkey's balls right from the start.

In my teens I had crushes, but those crushes tore my heart out of my chest, spat on it, and threw it to the ground. Not that I cared. They probably couldn't handle all my sass. Though their brush-offs could have been why I fell for Robert immediately and did as he advised so willingly. Then again, he was a different person to start with. Caring and sweet, he'd taken me places. Wined and dined, only he never sixty-nined me. Which was a disappointment as I'd heard how amazing it was.

I jumped when the chair beside me was pulled out. Robert smiled down at me before he sat, but his eyes were hard and filled with contempt. "Randal will be here soon." His new business associate, or at least that was what Robert hoped. My husband had told me to meet him at the restaurant for a Friday lunch meeting because he wanted to show Randal he was a family man. Apparently that meant he was a man who could be trusted with money and was a man to trust with any legal affairs Randal may ever have. "I asked you to dress nicely, Makenzie." He glared at my dark blue summer dress. I cut off my snort. I thought I had dressed nicely. Once he had even said he liked it. As I went to comment, the dick continued, "You do know people have designed undergarments that help suck some of the fat in? Maybe you should invest in a few."

A blush heated my cheeks. I flicked my eyes down to my hands in my lap and clenched my jaw. It was something I seemed to be doing a lot lately, which annoyed me, made me feel weaker when I never used to be. What I would have preferred to do was throw my water in his face, kick him in the shin, and stab him in the eye with my fork, then sit back to watch him bleed, before storming from the place.

Still, I was grateful I had my imagination; it was only my backbone I had lost.

As my mind caused him harm, the weak me sat there and said nothing. So what if I had put on a few pounds? Did he have to be an ass and point it out? And hell, I was happy with the way I looked.

"Too late to do something about it now. Suck it in," he hissed and then turned in his seat and boomed, "Randal, good to see you."

"Fuckhead." I froze. The word was coughed out through a manly voice behind me, startling me. I itched to turn around, to see where and who it came from, but didn't, and if Robert had heard it, he gave no indication. Instead, he turned back to face me with a bright, fake smile on his face.

"Randal Muller, this is my wife, Makenzie." Robert gestured with his hand in my direction. Looking up, my eyes landed on a god. He was absolutely breathtaking. With his wide frame, I could have sworn he once would have been on the football team back in the day. He was tall, slim, but firm. His eyes were light, like the ocean on a clear, calm day. He ran a hand through his blond hair before smiling down at me.

"Great to meet you, Makenzie. Robert has told me many wonderful things about you."

I just bet he has. I winced and knew he had caught it, if his raised brows were anything to go on. I smiled politely, fiddled with my fork, and said, "Robert certainly has a way with words." That could cut me to the bone.

Robert's hand slid across the table and grabbed mine. Anyone would think it was an affectionate touch. It wasn't. His hold tightened on mine. I bit my bottom lip and smiled so I didn't cringe from the pain.

Robert wasn't one to hurt a person. He hated pain in fact, and later he would be very apologetic, saying it was my fault and in the end, he would be so convincing I would somehow believe him. Never once had he beaten me, hit me, or hurt me more than a hard squeeze or pinch.

Instead, he used words to cut me down.

Robert chuckled and said, "Only with you, sweetheart."

Turning my gaze to him, I made sure my eyes held adoration as I replied, "Of course, pumpkin." I had a translation for each pet name I'd used for Robert. Pumpkin was prick.

As soon as Randal sat down, Robert got down to business. At least he tried. Randal cleared his throat, picked up his menu, and suggested, "I'm sure Makenzie doesn't want to hear all about work. Why don't we order?"

Robert laughed. "Of course." My husband turned to me. "Sweetheart, do you want your usual, a salad?"

I pulled my hands from the table and clenched them so tightly my fingernails bit into my palms. What I wanted was a nice, big, juicy steak. "Sounds great." I smiled, refraining from throat punching him.

It seemed the silent me was more violent than what I actually was.

"Tell me, Makenzie, do you work?" Randal asked.

Sitting straighter, I replied, "I don't at the moment, but I would love to get back out into the workforce. I have a degree in business—"

Robert chuckled and ran his hand down my arm. "Sweetheart, don't be silly, you don't need to work."

"Oh, I know I don't need to, but—"

"Honey, that's enough. We'll talk about it later. Randal doesn't want to hear about it."

He asked, you ass.

"Of course." Clearing my throat, I moved my gaze back to Randal and asked. "Do you like to play golf, Mr. Muller?" It was a question Robert had said I could ask. Stick to topics Robert was passionate about so he could talk about himself.

Honestly, he may as well have gotten on his knees under the table and given Randal a blow job.

"Randal, please, and I do actually. Do you?"

"No, I—"

"Makenzie isn't really into sports"—he leaned into Randal—"if you couldn't tell." After a quick laugh, he then talked about golf. My gaze darted between the two men, fascinated by their interaction. Robert was oblivious to Randal's quick sneer and his bored expression. My stomach dipped in nervous excitement. It wasn't just me who was thinking my husband was a dick.

Robert was always, always like that. Yes, a dick, but oblivious to those around him, pretty idiotic when trying to woo a client. He was always Robert this, Robert that. Robert, Robert, Robert.

God, why couldn't I find it in myself to stand up and stalk from the restaurant?

My head dipped down, no longer feeling the thrill of not being the only one to recognize my husband for what he truly was. My chin almost touched my chest as my eyes stared at my lap. And even though my body had stilled, my mind kept going, kept flashing past comments made by Robert.

You're so pathetic, Makenzie.

You're too fat.

I can't breathe when you're on top of me during sex. You need to lose weight.

You went out like that? Jesus, I hope no one saw you, Makenzie.

Why can't you be more like Danny's wife? She's good at everything.

I have to picture someone else while I'm having sex with you. How do you think that makes me feel?

You always look like a slob these days.

I saw Heather today. She's so smart, got her head screwed on that one, and she looked hot.

We have nothing in common.

You don't want to have sex with me. It's like I'm living with a roommate instead of a wife.

Sure we have sex, but we need to be friends also and do things with each other. Only it was things he wanted to do, never what I wanted.

Honestly, no matter what I did, how I changed, I was never going to be the one who would satisfy Robert in any way.

In his eyes, I was never going to be good enough. I was useless, ugly, fat, stupid, and unworthy.

God, I was sick of feeling that way. I needed to get out before his words seeped into my blood, like they had already in my mind. I knew once they caught the hint that there was a gaping passage straight to my heart and body via my blood, I knew it would be over.

I'd lose myself completely.

"Makenzie?" Robert's irritated voice broke through. "What are you doing?"

Blinking, I realized I was standing. I glanced at Randal and then the waiter. When had he arrived?

I had an epiphany, damn it, and I was going to roll with it. Even if my body felt like revolting as it trembled, and my mind screamed at me to sit back down because I wouldn't find anyone better.

Licking my suddenly dry lips, I said, "Sorry, but I'm not feeling well."

"Oh," Robert cried. He stood next to me and took my hand. When I pulled free, he raised his brows in question. Though, he went on, "Sweetheart, why didn't you say something? Maybe you should head home?"

Studying him, I noticed his clenched jaw and narrowed eyes. He thought I was being a fool for interrupting his talk about himself. A snort left me. I covered my mouth and nose with my hand.

Six years.

Four years of marriage.

Two somewhat happy years and then two years of hell.

I had been so stupid. So, so stupid. Robert had hated my job, my dad, my sister, my friends, and even my car. Now I had none of them. Silly me had given it all up because a handsome man had paid attention to the geek in college. Regret threatened to overwhelm me and drag me to my knees. I regretted everything I ever did for him.

But no more.

"Yes, I think you may be right." While I'm there, I'll be packing and leaving, starting fresh. The thought of it actually brought a smile to my face. My hands still shook, but something inside of me bloomed. Looking to Randal, I offered, "It was a pleasure meeting you, Randal. Sorry to have to leave." And don't let Robert bite down on your nob too much.

Randal stood from the table and held out his hand. I quickly shook it. He smiled. "The pleasure was all mine. Hopefully we'll see each other again."

"Yes." I nodded with a small smile. Then I made a slurping sound because my mind was still back on Robert sucking him off. The poor guy. I wanted to reach over and pat Randal on the back, wishing him luck. Still, I refrained and thought I should pat myself on the back because I did tend to do and say silly crap all the time. Robert hated it. I'd learned to accept my uniqueness.

Robert's jaw clenched. "I'll see you at home, sweetheart."

No, actually you won't. I wanted to throw my head back and cackle like a madwoman. Robert leaned in as if he were going to kiss my cheek, until he pulled back and chuckled. "I better not. Can't afford to get sick."

Picking up my purse, I quickly excused myself. As I took the steps away from Robert, my hands shook even more. Was I really going to do it? Yes, I had to. I was tired of being walked over, tired of being the one in the wrong, because apparently, it always turned out to be my fault in the end.

Just like my leaving.

I knew Robert would lay on the guilt trip, pleading for me to understand what we had was perfect and not to leave. He'd insist I would just have to change a few things and everything would be back to the way things were when we had first got together.

Yet the things he would ask to change would be more of myself, and I wasn't willing to let go of myself anymore.

Unless… maybe it was me? All in my head?

Shit. No, it wasn't.

Shaking my head as I stepped out front into a warm afternoon, I had to believe I was making the right choice. It wasn't me imagining things.

Placing my bag strap over my shoulder, I searched through it while the valet waited for my ticket.

"Excuse me?"

As soon as my fingers landed on it, I lifted my head and held it out to the valet, only he wasn't looking at me, but over my shoulder. Following his gaze, I jumped when I found a handsome man standing there.

"Sorry?" I asked, looking left and then right, just to check he was, in fact, talking to me. Had I done something on my way out? I clenched my free hand to make sure I wasn't holding anything, in case I had stolen a fork in my haste. I wasn't. The ticket slipped from my fingers. I glanced back at the valet to see him give me a nod, and then he left me alone with the stranger.

"Hi," the smooth voice said behind me, and again my body jolted when I felt his hand at my elbow. When I turned, I stepped back out of his reach. His hands came up and a soft smile tipped his lips up a little. "Sorry, didn't mean to scare you."

Robert didn't like me talking to men. I flicked my eyes over his shoulder and then back.

Huh, screw Robert, he wasn't there.

"It's okay. I'm, ah, I'm gay," he blurted, and I watched his cheeks heat before his palm thumped his forehead.

A laugh escaped me from his outburst. My palm came up to cover my mouth. I found myself thinking how it was a pity the man before me liked penis.

He removed his hand and smiled down at me. God, he was tall. My head came up to his chest. He wore a designer suit and, as I glanced down, he had on shiny shoes. I supposed most gay men dressed really well, or was that something someone made up? I wasn't sure, but the man before me certainly seemed to take pride in his looks. Even his dark brown hair was gelled to perfection.

"Did I do something?" I asked.

"No. Not at all. In fact, I couldn't help but overhear—"

My eyes widened, and I interrupted, "Were you the one to call my husband a fuckhead?"

His brows dipped, guilt flashing across his features, and then he ran a hand over the back of his neck. "He was being a fuckhead at the time. But that's not why I stopped you. I heard you may be looking for work."

My head jerked back in shock. "And you followed me to offer me a job?" I guessed.

"Well, yes. Sort of. Actually, it's my brother who's looking for an assistant."

Leaning in, I whispered, "Why would you ask me?"

Did he pity me?

"The truth, my brother goes through a lot of assistants and when I heard you had a business degree, I thought you may have more brain

ACKNOWLEDGMENTS

To the readers who read my work no matter what I write, thank you so much for your support. For your trust in my writing. I'm glad you like and understand my humour because I love writing stories where I can gain a smile, even a laugh, from readers. The world can be very trying a lot of the times, I wanted to help share even a little light to get a person through their struggles... I hope, in one way or another, this story has done that for you!

Becky, at Hot Tree Editing, thank you always for being such an amazing editor.

Amanda and Lindsey, thank you both for all your help with Fumbled Love x

Wander, for getting the perfect photo for the character Carter.

Letita, I'm so glad to have gained you as my cover designer, your work is amazing.

ALSO BY LILA ROSE

Romantic Comedies

Making Changes

Making Sense

Hawks MC: Ballarat Charter

Holding Out

Climbing Out

Finding Out (novella)

Black out

No Way Out

Coming Out (novella)

Hawks MC: Caroline Springs Charter

The Secret's Out

Hiding Out

Down and Out

Living Without

Walkout (novella)

Hear Me Out

Break Out (novella)

Fallout

Standalones related to the Hawks MC

Out of the Blue (Lan, Easton, and Parker's story)

Trinity Love series

Left to Chance

Love of Liberty (novella)

Paranormal

In the Dark

Death (with Justine Littleton)

3 1333 04782 1713

CPSIA information can be obtained
at www.ICGtesting.com
Printed in the USA
LVHW011217030319
609304LV00015B/752